Reserves

by

H. G. Hedger

Cover Art by *Lea Schizas*

The Wild Rose Press, Inc.
PO Box 708
Adams Basin, NY 14410-0708
Visit us at www.thewildrosepress.com

Publishing History
First Edition, 2025
Trade Paperback ISBN 978-1-5092-6238-0
Digital ISBN 978-1-5092-6239-7

Published in the United States of America

Dedication

To My Family
(My Everything)

Chapter 1

Black Gold

When Graceland Walker was seven, she summoned black gold from the earth.

Her handsome, open-faced father dropped to his knees, his slate-blue eyes flashing with adoration. "This wouldn't have been possible without you. You are my muse." And Grace believed him.

With her help, her father, the petroleum geologist, had accomplished something extraordinary. She didn't know what this meant then, but the electricity in the atmosphere was palpable. Grace vibrated with exhilaration. She almost hadn't been part of the discovery. Her father took her to the drill site only because her mother and sister were quarantining at home due to chicken pox.

"Let me tell you a secret," her father said, rubbing a smear of oil between his fingers. "This incredible substance contains the remnants of sea animals and plants that died millions of years ago." His gaze intensified. "Oil makes our world run. It is the earth's lifeblood."

A hot wind blew through his neatly cut blond hair. "What a team we are!" He scooped her up amidst a swell of recognition, cheering, and hard hat-throwing and settled her on his shoulders.

Workers, petroleum engineers, and drillers surrounded her father. They pumped Michael Walker's hand, her knobby knees often bumping into their chests. They congratulated him, thanked him, patted him on the back, touched his shoulders, and grabbed his arm as if some of what he had might rub off on them.

"We should call you Midas Mike." A short man in a lightweight suit sidled next to him. "You have that special touch."

Her father's body stiffened.

"Not once have your seismic surveys been off, and not once have your core drills failed to produce. Your track record is beyond impressive. Our company wants to bring you in-house."

From Grace's vantage point, the man was a skittish rabbit in linen, tufts of white hair springing from his ears and his nose twitching.

"Think about it, Mike. We'd like you to come work for Caligula, one of the world's largest oil and gas companies–complete with a healthy paycheck, bonuses dependent on oil production, and a corner office in our corporate headquarters. Consider our proposition and get back to us." The suit handed him a folded piece of paper.

As her father opened the wafer-thin parchment, a slight tremor shook his hands. The current traveled upward, through his arms and shoulders, and into her body, where she absorbed it all.

After the suit left, her hands cupped his capsized face. His grin was upside down. "Gracie, our lives are about to change forever."

What was to come, she couldn't imagine, but she trusted him implicitly. Perched there, high on his solid shoulders, she felt invincible. From this dizzying height, she saw beyond the drilling rig into an endless Oklahoma sun-drenched sky that widened and stretched before her. It was so intense that the buffalo grass seemed to catch on fire.

Chapter 2

An Irrevocable Alteration
Twenty-three years later

"Chic Dark? In the context of a funeral, what does that even mean?" Grace wrestled with the zipper of her newly arrived extra-large Fit-and-Flare dress delivered overnight. The garment looked trendier, sleeker, and more flattering on the website's model.

"Here, let me help." Her mother's tiny hands pressed into her back with surprising force as she gathered swaths of fabric together while steadily yanking the zipper upward.

Grace took a deep breath. Trying to squeeze herself into something that wasn't quite right was a familiar sensation.

"You look fine, just fine." Her mother's smile was thin. She wiped the tears in her oldest daughter's eyes. "Oh, Gracie, I'm sorry. I know this has been hard on you. You did all you could, and I'm sure your father appreciated you dropping everything to come and care for him."

"We were supposed to have more time together, Mom."

Some people lived beyond the projected six months of hospice care. But Michael Walker had not been one of them. And though Grace hadn't resided in the same town as her father since she left for college, she was overwhelmed by the loss. Grace wanted to fling herself on her mother's bed, pull the familiar quilt over her, and wish the next few hours away. Avoiding what was to come, however, was impossible. Besides, any sudden movement would surely split the fabric that was barely holding her together.

On the floor, her daughters—aged four, six, and eight—intently colored pictures to slip into their grandfather's casket. Their chic tulle dresses, explicitly selected for the occasion by their step-grandmother, fanned about them–moody, dark shades of grief.

In an instant, everything had changed. Grace was on a path, a planned trajectory propelling her life through space and time, oblivious to how precarious this was. All it took was an unforeseen event obliterating everything in its wake. When her stepmother, Brandi, called to say Grace's father's cancer was back and he was in hospice, Grace knew what she had to do.

"I am a nurse," she petitioned Andrew, her husband of eight years. "I won't let him be cared for by strangers in his final months. My thirty-two-year-old stepmother," —the word stepmother coiled in her throat— "has arranged for round-the-clock care so her dying husband will not inconvenience her life."

As always, Andrew understood. "You're a terrific nurse educator but haven't been a bedside nurse since Ally was a year old. Will you be okay?"

Grace ignored the sudden doubt, accompanied by an invisible fist in her stomach. Andrew was right; she hadn't done direct patient care in a long time, but this was her father. Her skills had not disappeared; they were simply dormant. She nodded, determined to project confidence she did not feel.

"Of course, you need to be there," Andrew said. "You'll have to take the girls, though. The start-up for my pharmacy is too intensive. There's no way I can be a full-time parent and get this going."

"My mom's semester just finished. She should be able to watch them when I'm with Dad," Grace responded.

Granted a family leave of absence from the hospital, Grace packed up her three daughters with their final weeks of school assignments and flew from Birmingham, Michigan, to Tulsa, Oklahoma, to care for her father as he disengaged from life.

The trip was a chance to make up for lost time, to pour her all into their relationship, and to show her father that she held nothing against him for walking out on their nuclear family when she was eight years old. He was on wife and household number four, but what did that matter? Where were the others now that he needed them the most? Where were the ones who greedily sucked his time and attention over the years, claiming they were his chosen priority, his newest iteration of a family?

Grace immersed herself in his care. She fed him, changed the dressings on his surgical wounds, regulated the flow of the oxygen tank to keep his saturation above 92%, and adjusted his position in bed for maximum comfort and to avoid bedsores.

As she tenderly washed his frail feet, she saw herself as a nine-year-old flower girl, dancing with him at his second wedding. With her stockinged toes firmly planted on his shiny shoes, he transported her effortlessly across the dance floor, spinning and turning, making it impossible to see where they were going or from where they had come.

Surely, he would finally see that she had been loyal and faithful to him. She was the one upon whom he could count. She was the one who fit perfectly on his shoulders. She was his muse.

Chapter 3

One Last Day

"Come on, Dad. We're busting you out of this joint, even if it's just to the backyard. The morning is perfect."

"I don't know if I have the strength, Gracie. Maybe after lunch?"

"You do better in the mornings. Leave the driving to me." Grace slipped his oxygen tank into the cylinder holder on the back of the wheelchair. The air softly whistled into his nostrils through a transparent tube. "Let me help you sit on the side of the bed. Perfect. Put your arms around my neck, and I'll pivot you onto the wheelchair. There you go. That wasn't too bad, was it?"

Her father smiled weakly. She smoothed the chemotherapy-thinned hair back from his forehead and grabbed a throw from the chair. "A blanket for your knees and off we go."

Grace wheeled her father through the floor-to-ceiling glass doors onto the expansive terrace. Like the interior, Brandi's modern taste filled the outdoor space, making Grace feel like she was in a Hollywood star's home. A sleek waterfall-fed pool, an outdoor gourmet kitchen, a stone fireplace, and several distinct lounging areas dotted the terrain. She parked her father beneath a cabana with a view. Depending on where he turned his head, it was possible to see his estate or, in the distance, the city skyline.

"Funny how life works out," he said. Recently, her father's thoughts were scattered and nonsensical–because of cancer that had spread to his brain. But he spoke clearly and sounded more robust than he had in days. She leaned in to hear.

"What's funny, Dad?"

"How I ended up here—in this concrete art exhibit—in this position, with my fourth wife. I've done many things wrong, but one thing I did get right was you, your sister, and your mom."

Four shapely women spilled out of the pool house. One of them was her stepmother, but from this distance, it was difficult to tell which one she was. Her father observed the activity with detached interest.

He continued talking, his breath short from the exertion. "When I was a kid, my family was poor and dysfunctional, but that didn't matter to me. Growing up along the banks of the Mississippi River, I found solace in the steadiness of nature. Every day before and after school, during the weekends and summer, I explored. The fossils told me her story. The river belied her current state. I'd take what I found to school: a rock, a water sample, a bug, or a leaf from a plant I didn't recognize, and my teachers helped me understand. Before I graduated high school, she hooked me. My first love was the earth. That's why I wanted to be a geologist. I wanted to know what made this planet run. I wanted to understand the processes that shaped her. Yet I failed this planet like the first woman I loved. I lost sight of what mattered."

Grace looked at her father and waited. This was the

most he had shared with her. His story brought to her on a warm yet persistent Oklahoma wind. He shivered beneath his silk pajamas. She wrapped the blanket around his shoulders.

He was immersed in the past. "Around the corner was always something shiny and new. Crushing student loan debt led me to become a petroleum geologist. I convinced myself I would do it ethically. I was so good at reading the signs that I usually only needed one core drill to make the tap.

"After my second marriage, the strain intensified. Everyone around me asked for more. The company pressured me to expand my expertise from drilling to fracking. I held firm for a long time. Then, as material demands increased, I cracked, promising to do this with consideration and use the least amount of toxic material to expand the shale. I told myself that I would be as responsible as possible. What a joke. The irony, my first-born daughter, is that my oncologist strongly believes my exposure to benzene, methanol, hydrochloric acid, and other contaminants in the fracking fluid contributed to my cancer. Of course, the doctor can't definitively say this. But I know my truth: I violently force-fed the earth this venom to extract her resources, and she, in turn, gave everything back to me."

Across the distance, as if she had just noticed their presence, Grace's stepmother, dressed in an exorbitantly priced designer swimsuit in baby blue, strolled toward them. Grace was aware of what type of suit she wore and how much it cost because her younger sister Dallas had pointed this out five days ago when she popped in during her lunch break.

As Brandi approached her father stopped talking. The incredibly put-together woman, who looked like she had stepped out of the Sports Illustrated swimsuit edition, grazed his forehead with a kiss so light she did not transfer one spot of lipstick.

"Hello, dear. It's good to see you out enjoying the day. Can I have anything brought to you?"

Her father, ever the charmer, mustered a smile. "A pitcher of lemon water might be nice."

Brandi nodded. "I'll let the kitchen know." Her perfectly manicured hand skimmed the fleece draping his shoulder. "I will leave you two alone. A few of my friends came to visit."

Brandi glided toward the oversized lounge chairs on the other side of the pool, where the three other scantily clad women stretched and preened.

He waited until she was out of hearing distance before he spoke. "When I go, the scorpions will come tumbling out of the woodshed."

Grace turned to him, shocked.

"It's fine, Grace. I'm not under any illusions about what I mean to them. But I need to ask you something. What I tell you is important."

He had her attention.

"You, Dallas, and your mother will get some cash. It's not much compared to the others. But it's enough. You'll be fine. I don't doubt that. You are resourceful. And I don't want others gunning for you, making your lives miserable, tangling up your days with needless lawsuits."

"Okay, Dad, no worries."

"There's more." He reached out his bony hand and grasped hers with an intensity counterintuitive to his condition. His fingers were cold, his nail beds pale purple.

"Listen, Grace. I've been working on something. A way to make things right with the earth while helping humanity. I'm leaving this to you because I trust you. It won't make sense initially, but I'm confident you'll figure things out and decide what to do. I need you to recall some of the conversations we had when you were in nursing school. Remember my visits when I had a connecting flight through Detroit? How we would grab something to eat and talk? You'd tell me about your studies and clinical rounds."

"I remember, Dad." Grace didn't tell him how she saw through these "visits." As though she was a line item on his to-do list. 'I haven't seen my oldest daughter in a year. Tell the secretary to schedule my next flight through Detroit.' Check. Still, Grace was grateful for any scrap of time he offered her, and she had skipped classes and even a clinical once, feigning a gastrointestinal issue, just to spend an hour with him.

"Good. I found our exchanges about implantable medical devices particularly fascinating. Think back to those conversations. You'll find useful information in them. Get your mother's input also. She's one smart cookie." His blue eyes pierced as he released the grasp on her hand. "Promise me you won't shove my legacy in a closet and forget."

"I promise, Dad."

"Good." He drank some of the recently delivered lemon water. "I'm tired. It's time to get me back to bed."

After lunch, his verbal rambling increased. Nothing he said was logical, yet Grace listened and tended to him. He refused dinner and closed his eyes with a long sigh. He did not open the azure windows to his world again, and less than twenty-four hours later, with Grace by his side, Michael Walker drew his last breath.

Chapter 4

Mortuary Rites

Once Grace left her father's home, she would have no reason to return. "Did Dad leave anything for me?" she asked her stepmother.

"What do you mean?" Brandi regarded Grace suspiciously.

"I don't know. Did Dad specifically ask you to give me anything? A letter? A book? A paperweight?"

"Everything in this house is mine." Brandi's silk-covered hips swished as her bejeweled fingers pointed at her. "Don't get any big ideas."

Grace put her hands in the air and backed away.

The moment her father's body was carried out of his hospice room, with Grace trailing behind, into the waiting hearse, Brandi's cleaning crew pounced. When Grace returned to retrieve her purse, the area was scrubbed, devoid of evidence he had ever been there. How could the imprint of a man who had been her stepmother's husband for a year be erased with such precision and finality?

Brandi's intent stare implied that Grace was the vulture and the one not to be trusted. "I think it's best you leave."

Maybe her dad hadn't been lucid. Delirium and confusion often accompanied the dying, or perhaps the pressure of the cancer pressing on his brain had taken him on a fantastical flight of delusion.

****

Grace picked a loose thread on her fit-and-flare dress. Even after the divorce, even after Dallas and Grace set up separate households, their mother had not moved. These walls held the texture of their childhood. As Grace was about to ask her mother about her father's deathbed appeal, the front door opened. The tell-tale creaking of the hinges was audible in the back bedroom.

"Anyone home?" Dallas called.

Grace's three daughters flung their crayons aside and flew down the bungalow's narrow hallway, nearly knocking the petite woman over. "Auntie Dallas!" they cried.

"It's been wonderful having my nieces and sister in town for the past two weeks." Dallas giggled at their exuberance and gathered them in a hug. "Even though it took the death of your grandpa to get you here, I wish you could stay forever."

"But we can't, Auntie Dallas." Ally, the oldest, broke away from the embrace first and smoothed the cascading tulle ruffles of her dress. "Our house is in Michigan."

"I know, my bunny." Dallas kissed her head. "I miss you guys, that's all. Here, let me redo your sash. You'll make a statement if we crisscross it in the front."

"Me next!" cried Ora, Grace's youngest.

"Can you do mine, too?" Grace's middle child, Amanda, was used to being last.

As Dallas worked her magic on the girls' shiny sashes, she spoke. "Brandi texted. The car will be here in five minutes. This has turned into quite the event. Invitations to a funeral with a dress code attached— now that's a first. Speaking of dresses, my sister, with your natural hourglass figure, you are rocking that mail-order dress like it's the sexiest thing there is."

Grace laughed incredulously. "That's exactly the look I was going for at my father's funeral." She hugged her diminutive sister. As always, a surge of protectiveness passed through Grace. Fingers crossed, Dallas just finished her first go around with the fertility drug Clomid, and she was already two weeks late. Grace was grateful the pregnancy had happened quickly and that her sister didn't have to go down the infertility rabbit hole. Her finances and constitution were fragile.

"And why can't we drive separate vehicles?" Dallas continued as she brushed her non-existent stomach, smoothing a seatbelt wrinkle out of her size 2, fashionable yet economical, black sheath. "I want to be able to leave if needed. I can never predict when a wave of nausea will hit, and I'd hate to ruin the funeral of the century by vomiting all over the after-service spread."

Grace started to reply that she wouldn't mind having a monkey wrench thrown into her stepmother's send-off party. But she didn't want to appear uncharitable. "This is over the top. Dad would be embarrassed. How can Brandi pretend to know what his wishes were? They were only married a year."

"And we've been his daughters for thirty years." Dallas picked up the thread, her voice on the edge of an adolescent whine. "She gets to plan everything. It's not fair. Why won't she allow us to be part of the service, to have a say? Who does she think she is?"

"Oh, my children," the first Mrs. Walker, Mary,

responded, with tempered reason honed over a lifetime. "She is the stunning, sophisticated trophy wife he never had in me. Internment is a ritualized response to the physical cessation of life and is as old as humankind. Brandi's prerogative is to orchestrate whatever send-off she deems appropriate. We will comply."

Grace and Dallas regarded each other, their eyes wide with amusement. "Thank you, Margaret Mead." Grace affectionately hugged her tiny mother, who also happened to be an anthropology professor at the University of Tulsa. The observations their mother offered her daughters as they grew, especially after their father walked out on them, were insightful and, often, downright hilarious.

"Let's just hope she doesn't copy the mortuary rites of the Old and New Kingdom's Egyptian royals."

Grace and Dallas exchanged quizzical glances. "Anticipating the dead's needs in the afterlife was important to them. So, they processed the remains accordingly. The tombs contained extra painted stone heads. That way, if the deceased's natural head fell off because of decay, they would have a readily available 'spare.' What if Brandi stashed a few extra heads in your father's casket, just in case?"

The three of them started giggling. They survived this way because laughter mitigated the pain of loss, the deeply guarded personal hotspots that each carried inside.

"Whoever heard of a country club funeral?" Grace said, pulling her dark hair back in a loose knot.

"Burial rituals evolve, but I agree this is somewhat unorthodox," her mother replied.

"Exclusive membership entitles Brandi to anything

she wants." Dallas pulled open the heavy drape, drawn to protect the bungalow's interior from an unrelenting sun.

The window-mounted air conditioner hummed. Mary sank into a worn sofa. The long, exhausted springs barely registered her presence. "We have to be considerate. Brandi is grieving, too."

Grace's firstborn, Allysa, climbed next to her grandmother. Amanda followed her older sister. They snuggled into her side, like bookends.

"Mommy, up." Grace helped her youngest daughter, Ora, climb her body as though she were a piece of playground equipment. She gathered skinny limbs into her arms and settled Ora on the soft curve of her hip, just where the dress began to flare. She could feel the pull of the zipper stretching to its limit.

When Brandi finalized the memorial arrangements, Andrew booked a flight, even though the date conflicted with the last day of his high school's twenty-year reunion. It also meant he had to find someone to oversee the pharmacy in his absence. Grace wanted to grab her phone to check the status of Andrew's flight. He promised he'd be there for her and the girls.

An overwhelming feeling of exhaustion and loss settled into her bones. Grace missed the familiar comfort of Andrew's arms. When was the last time they slept entangled? Lately, despite sleeping in the same bed, their backs were to each other, never quite touching. When was the last time they'd gone out, just the two of them? Surely, their last date hadn't been on their seventh wedding anniversary when they laughed, over a bottle of wine, at the concept of a seven-year itch. Their eighth anniversary had come and gone with cards and promises that they'd plan a getaway when life calmed down. Grace searched for a recent memory of them sharing a moment of intimacy. She came up empty. Caught up in the daily navigation of their busy lives, they lost sight of the big picture. This was a reset moment.

Grace gently slid Ora, her golden-haired, wild child who resembled her father and grandfather, off her side onto the couch and checked her phone–no missed calls, no new texts or voice messages from Andrew. But that would make sense; his phone was off or in airplane mode. His flight, delayed by storms over the metro Detroit area, was due to land in ten minutes. She wished he'd arrived in time for the ride to the country club to help corral the girls. Still, if he got a taxi directly to the venue, he'd arrive in time for the service.

"Okay, gang, show time, and what a show it promises to be." Dallas waved like a game-show hostess, an arm toward the large picture window. Two stretch Hummer limousines stood before the modest brick bungalow.

Like sunlit minnows flashing in a shallow pond, Grace's daughters forgot their mother's instructions to be on their best behavior and raced toward the sleek vehicles. Their voices shrieked with delight. Grace surveyed her mother and sister and shrugged. Who could blame them? The limos were something they had only seen on television. As the girls started to clamber aboard, an impeccably dressed chauffeur stepped in front of them. He smiled graciously and swooped his arm, pointing to the limo behind them. "Mrs. Walker has arranged for a childminder. The children are to ride in the second limo. But don't worry. Miss Penny will be present throughout the ceremony and reception to attend to their every need."

In other words, Grace thought, her stomach cartwheeling, Brandi hired a babysitter to ensure that her children, her father's only grandchildren, did not get in the way or do anything to mess up the orchestrated production—third-class citizens.

The chauffeurs, masters of their craft, were courteous but did not yield. They had their directives and operated on the current Mrs. Walker's wishes. Her estate, after all, was footing the bill. Grace watched helplessly as the attendant ushered her children into the temporary au pair, Miss Penny's vehicle, their yelps of joy turning to confusion. How swiftly tides change. At the same time, the chauffeur firmly and expertly guided Grace into the front limo with her sister, mother, and waiting stepmother. When Grace realized what was happening, she frantically tried to change limos. She needed to be with her daughters, but everything appeared non-negotiable and happened faster than a hunter's bullet finding its mark.

As Grace registered the frightened looks on her children's faces—*This new experience would be fun if you, Mommy, were by our side. And who are these strangers? You told us never to get into a car with someone we don't know.* Grace tried to rationalize. *It's only a ride to the country club. I can't make a scene. This is the day to pay homage to my father. I can't be the person who wrecks his funeral.* Grace wasn't even fully seated when she ascertained there weren't any seat belts in the limos, let alone booster seats. Her youngest two were both under forty pounds and needed them.

Grace had anticipated her stepmother's lack of

foresight about the children's needs and had Ora's car seat and Amanda's booster seat on the sloped curve of her mother's lawn. Too late–they were in motion. The day was falling apart. Grace registered Brandi's cool, amused demeanor as the limousines accelerated into traffic. Ally, Amanda, and Ora pressed their faces into the tinted glass. As the distance between the vehicles grew, the outlines of her three children faded into negative space.

Grace shot Andrew a text. —*Help! Get here ASAP. Evil stepmother's staff has kidnapped our children.*—

Chapter 5

The Wind Beneath My Wings

If the funeral hadn't involved the father of her two children and a man she once loved, the first Mrs. Walker would have observed the ceremonial rite with detached amusement. Her job, after all, was to study and catalog different aspects of human behavior. She was fascinated by what the fourth Mrs. Walker had orchestrated for her dead husband's liturgy.

Every detail was excessive, from the color-coordinated dress code to the extravagantly decorated viewing room. An admixture of scent rose from the multi-tiered floral arrangements and the combination of colognes and perfumes of guests. Assaulted by the competing smells, Mary was grateful she took an antihistamine before she left home. The first row of high-back, draped chairs was reserved and roped off with white silk. The chamber orchestra played a curated program of what Mary assumed were modern songs, for she was familiar with very few. Once everyone was seated–including the second Mrs. Walker (number three had not bothered to show)--the music ensemble crescendoed into a bold yet melancholic rendition of Bette Midler's song, "The Wind Beneath My Wings."

They marched in single file, a procession of high-ranking business executives and attorneys with exclusive suites in the downtown high-rise building. Next came the elite country club members, men Michael Walker played golf and drank with. They filled the reserved front row, the place usually designated for those closest to the deceased, for family.

Then, in a hushed intake of breath, she appeared, the epitome of 'Chic Dark.' Brandi Walker, a funeral bride, was draped on the arm of the CEO of one of the world's most dominant oil and gas companies, where her deceased husband once worked. All eyes were on her, the fourth Mrs. Walker.

She moved with deliberation, a sleek silhouette in an elegant form-fitting mini dress. Intricate hand-stitched lace hugged her grieving body. Brandi did not acknowledge anyone as she passed. Her eyes were straight ahead, focused on the still corpse of her husband lying in wait in his precision-tailored, Italian designer suit. Brandi's high heels, crafted from pieces of interlocking leather, sported thin, sharp-pointed heels. As she walked by, the precise tap tap of Brandi's stilettos were Ball-Peen-Hammers firing in Mary's head.

After the ceremony, Brandi announced that a *Celebration of Life After Party,* would take place in the adjoining ballroom. The doors flung open. The moment the last attendee poured into the opulent gallery, the doors to Michael Walker's lifeless body were firmly closed.

****

The afterlife party was in full swing, complete with a band playing requests and a large screen that flashed images of her father (the majority of which included Brandi). True to the chauffeur's word, the childminder,

Miss Penny, attended to her daughters' every need. The girls were having a terrific time in a corner, watching something on an iPad, engaged and laughing. Grace was grateful they were content, for she was still reeling from the embarrassment of riches.

Absorbed with memories of her father, Grace did not hear the officiant who asked Michael Walker's children to rise when he called their names. When poked on both sides by her mother and Dallas, she shot up so quickly that, to her horror, the zipper of her fit and flare separated. Even though she stood still, the expanse slowly widened, incrementally exposing her Spanx firm control bodysuit, something meant to keep parts of her hidden.

The kindly lady who maintained the country club's bathroom had tsk, tsked under her breath, "You poor dear, losing your father and now this." She withdrew from who knows where a needle and thread. "I'll get you stitched up in no time, deary. But you'll have to find someone to rip the threads out when you want to disrobe." She winked, her eyes sparkling.

****

"Brandi tells me you were a big help in his final days." A contralto voice oscillated behind her. When she turned, the Oil and Gas Company CEO stood, looking directly into her eyes–Mr. Renny Richeza. Though a slight smile played on his tanning bed face, his eyes were cold, alerting Grace. She doubted Brandi had told him this. Her stepmother had seen Grace's presence as an unnecessary imposition. She already had the around-the-clock care arranged, and Grace, inserting herself into the mix, had tossed her stepmother's meticulously laid plans asunder.

"I am sorry for your loss," he continued. Not a hair was out of place on this man, not a wrinkle on his vicuna wool suit, not an ounce of compassion on his face.

"Thank you," she murmured and started to leave.

He raised a hand—an open palm directly in front of her, one used to being obeyed. "Your dad was working on a project for us. I'm curious," —his fake smile widened, showing more of his precise teeth— "Did he mention anything to you?"

Maybe her father had been thinking clearly. Perhaps he was planning on leaving her something after all. She needed to know more. No way was she going to share this with the CEO of a company that coerced her dad into doing things he wasn't comfortable with, acts that might have cost him his life.

"Dad was too weak to work on anything those final days. And most of the time, he wasn't coherent. He didn't mention anything about a project he was working on for Caligula."

Mr. Richeza nodded, his lips pulled thin. "If you come across any papers that might be business-related or remember anything, let me know." He handed her a business card. "The company will generously reward you for returning our property."

Grace dropped the card into her purse and walked away. She was beyond anxious. The CEO's inquiry set her on edge. She wasn't used to being interrogated and was sure Mr. Richeza hadn't believed her. She needed to talk to her husband. He would help put everything in perspective. He'd calm her down and tell her she imagined intrigue and subterfuge where none existed. What was taking Andrew so long? His plane landed

25

over ninety minutes ago. Why couldn't she reach him? Why wasn't he responding to her texts or calls? Had he been in a horrible wreck on the way to the airport? Had he been hit by a car while hailing a cab? Were the authorities knocking on the door of their home in Birmingham at this very moment?

Okay, calm down, be logical, Grace told herself as she examined her phone's history. Since coming to Tulsa, they'd texted less than usual, which was understandable; both were incredibly busy. During their years together, text threads were conversations. Sometimes, they lasted days. Recently, his messages were questions–*where did you put my dress shoes*–or direct responses to her questions–*I haven't heard back from the insurance company*, nothing more–no inquisitive probing, gentle prompting, or easy innuendo. He had also missed some of their nightly video chats before the girls went to bed. The whys weren't important. Grace, too, was swamped. She was, after all, taking care of her father while helping him get his affairs in order and overseeing the girls' final school assignments. If she were in college, Grace would be panicking, reading the impending signs. She had been through countless breakups before she met Andrew. Eight years of marriage and three daughters had to count for something. There must be a logical explanation.

Her head pounded with tension. The culmination of events over the past few weeks and the escalated "celebration of life" noise made it impossible to keep everything in perspective. Grace eased open the door to her father's viewing room and slipped in. Her once larger-than-life father, diminished by death, was lying on a bed of velvet.

Bent over him were her mother and sister. Grace joined them.

Chapter 6

Points of Light

Mary's daughters stood side by side in front of their father's casket, holding hands for comfort as they had done as children. Graceland and Dallas were so different. Night and day, autumn and spring. Both were beautiful in contrasting ways. Dallas was slim with shoulder-length blonde hair that was always stylishly cut. Her pale skin, light blue eyes, and diminutive stature lent her a look of fleeting fragility. She was softness and light, able to slip in and out of a room without detection—her mother's height with her father's coloration.

Grace was the opposite, encompassing her father's stature and her mother's features. At five feet eleven inches, Grace was a good ten inches taller than her sister. When Grace walked into a room, people noticed. Statuesque, with long legs, high cheekbones, honey-kissed skin, a dark brown mane, and cinnamon eyes, she exuded strength and confidence. Grace's vulnerability came from within.

When Mary took a drugstore pregnancy test, she and Michael were on vacation, visiting Elvis Presley's former home, Graceland, in Tennessee.

"Graceland if it's a girl and Landon or Elvis if we have a boy." Her husband beamed. For all of his education, his rural roots found surprising and unconventional ways to manifest. Mary did not argue; they had been trying to have a baby for years, and she was overjoyed. Four weeks after Grace was born, Mary found herself pregnant again. They conceived while attending a conference in Dallas; hence, whether male or female, a name was already in place before their subsequent progeny drew their first breath.

They were born the same year, nine months apart. Grace automatically assumed the role of the older sister, the protector. Mary was curious: from where did that imperative arise? Yes, Grace was taller and more full-bodied, but this went beyond physical stature and birth timing. Even when they were directly vying for their father's attention, something they both valued above all, Grace deferred to Dallas. When Grace started kindergarten, Dallas wailed at being left behind, so Grace refused to go. She listened to the adult's logic of why her sister should wait but remained undeterred. "I'll help Dallas. I won't let her fall behind," she promised. And she had done just that. Whenever Dallas needed guidance on any subject, Grace helped her–even after it became evident Dallas needed no one's assistance.

The muscles of Mary's heart tightened, not from disease but from unadulterated love, an abiding ache from knowing she couldn't protect them. Mary alone was never enough for her daughters and cannot be now.

The same overwhelming knowledge filled her when she came home from the hospital thirty years ago with a four-pound bundle in her arms. Dallas was born five weeks early. Her lungs, however, hadn't received the memo. She wailed when placed in her car seat and continued crying the entire way home.

Mary stood amid the chaos, holding a newborn in her arms. She'd only been gone thirty hours, but everything had fallen apart. Since Michael was preparing for an important presentation, he only did the essentials: feed Grace and change her diapers. He was fast asleep with noise-canceling headphones on. His next freelance job and their family's finances depended on him being well-rested.

Dallas ceased crying when Mary held or nursed her, but furiously started again the moment she left her mother's arms. When Mary tried to slide the sleeping infant onto her mattress, Dallas immediately began screaming. Mary was anxious that the shrill keening would disturb Grace, who had slept through the night since she was a month old.

Mary scooped up the wailing Dallas, praying she wouldn't end up with two screeching infants, and peered into Grace's crib, jammed between Dallas's bassinet and the wall. Grace was awake. Her dark eyes were wide and watchful, taking everything in.

"Oh, thank you, sweet one." Mary crooned while opening the flap to her nursing gown. "Thank you for being a patient big sister and such a good baby."

Through the night, Mary tried to put Dallas down, to no avail. And in that fugue new mothers often experience, a place that extends beyond mental and physical exhaustion into a realm of disconnected reality, Mary moved. Detached and stumbling toward the cribs in the dark, she asked the universe for assistance. *Please, let Dallas sleep. Let us find a few hours of reprieve.* And miraculously, it happened.

As dawn broke, her heart thumping against full and

leaking breasts, Mary raced from her bed to the cradles. Dallas' berth was empty. But there, in the next crib, curled together as if they were one, slept two infants.

In a sleep-deprived stupor, Mary slid Dallas next to Grace.

The literature warned of an increased risk of sudden infant death syndrome if two babies slept in the same space. Countless cautionary tales told of how one child wiggled out of their swaddle, blocked the other's airway, or rolled over onto their sibling, causing unintentional harm. Mary understood all this. On the other hand, she also studied child-rearing traditions in different cultures. The practice of children sleeping together arose out of necessity. Dallas would not stop screaming at night unless she was in her mother's arms or nestled beside Grace. Mary was merely listening to what her daughters told her long before they could speak. Even when they were older, she often found them curled together in slumber, the hues of their hair blending, wavy chestnut cradling straight strands of flax.

Mary was grateful; her daughters had become her friends. Though genetically distinct, everyday experiences bound them in the way childhood does, and as they both turned from the open casket, they looked to their mother as they had throughout their years growing up.

"What are we going to do?" Grace asked.

Somehow, her daughters expected her to have the answers. In Grace's eyes was a chasm of loss. What will we do now that half of our foundation is gone?

Early in life, Dallas learned the art of compartmentalization. This coping mechanism served her well. While she tucked losses into a tidy nook, Grace's emotions were all over the place, an unfurled parachute caught between the earth and the trees.

Desperation and loss were seeded in her oldest daughter's eyes. Grace had the same look when her father walked out on them. Her eight-year-old had fought for all she was worth, for what she believed in and wanted. She threw her arms around Michael's trousered leg and clung for dear life as he moved toward the door, suitcase in hand. She screamed at the top of her lungs for him not to go, begging him to stay, for them to be a family.

He stopped and extricated her from his body and yelled above her screams until she stopped, startled by the force of his voice. "Don't make such a scene, Grace! No one likes a hysterical woman!" She stood stunned. Her father had never yelled at her before. He continued, his voice more tempered. "Get yourself under control. You'll never get anyone to love you if you don't."

Michael's words and Grace's sobs reverberated through the darkened hallway. Dallas burrowed into Mary like a wounded marsupial. Tears still coursed down Grace's face as she fought for control and watched her father put his house key on the entryway table and walk out the door.

Mary took her daughters' free hands in her own. "We will do what we did the first time he left us, what your father would want us to do. Get on with our lives. Dallas, you'll carry your baby to term and raise your son or daughter with Bryce. Gracie, you'll take your lovely daughters back to their father in Michigan. We'll live long, productive lives, visiting each other, spending holidays, and taking vacations whenever possible." She pulled them to her in a gathered hug.

Grace's shoulder bag began to vibrate. "Oh, thank goodness," relief washed grief from her face. She reached into her purse, smiling. "It's Andrew! I'll catch up with you guys in a bit." Her step was lighter as she moved to the back of the vestibule. Her father's customized bronze coffin with gold hardware glistened and refracted the overhead chandeliers, sending points of light into the atmosphere.

Chapter 7

The Ten-Minute Lunch
Nine Years Before

"Is this seat taken?"

Startled, Grace glanced up abruptly, causing the study notes in her lap to fall to the floor. A cafeteria tray holding a tightly wrapped tortilla, a bottle of water, and a single red apple slid before the empty chair beside her.

"I only have a few minutes of my lunch break left." She stammered, looking at the tall, golden-haired man before her.

"That's all right." He bent, helping her gather the loose papers. His hair's precise, sharp-edged cut rested above his collar. The cursive stitching on his lab coat under the University of Michigan logo read: Dr. Andrew Holden. "I don't have much time myself." He sat, long legs stretching out, and regarded her with a relaxed, white smile that said this is your lucky day—you won the lottery. And Grace felt she had. The color rose up her neck.

A week ago, Grace suffered through another breakup. Why couldn't she get this relationship stuff right? This time, at least, he'd broken up with her in person. On her way to her nine a.m. class, he stopped Grace outside her apartment, grabbing her wrist. "It's not working out."

He was an auto mechanic she met four weeks ago when her roommate's car broke down. He usually was at work by eight. Wait, was that a hickey on the left side of his neck? Once again, Grace was blindsided, though she should have seen this coming. He hadn't made an effort to get together in over five days. What could she say? She had learned men weren't concerned with her needs or what she wanted from a relationship. They called the shots. Men didn't respond to crying women either, and once they made up their minds, discussing ways to move forward was fruitless.

And even if she wanted to dissuade him, she didn't have time. Her class was starting.

She always found the most unsuitable men. Or maybe they found her. They were guys who materialized out of the landscape, asking her out, surprising her that they were interested. Yet if she had given herself a minute before responding to their enthusiasm, she would have found out besides the fact she wasn't physically attracted to them, they shared nothing in common. Despite this, she would tell herself to give him a try. Maybe you'll grow to love something about him. Perhaps the relationship will work this time. On a deeper level, Grace understood. She set her sights so low because no decent man could see anything in her to love. She offered no good man a reason to stay.

After her breakup with the mechanic, she promised herself no more dating. *Only nine months until I graduate with my Bachelor of Science in Nursing. It's time to decide what field I want to enter and what I want in a relationship.* Though a name sewn onto a uniform wasn't new for her, Jack, the auto mechanic, had shirts sporting this feature; the title Doctor had to count for something.

"Are you a pediatrician?" Grace was trying to place the man before her. Parts of him were familiar. Maybe she'd seen him in passing while doing her clinical on the children's unit, or perhaps during another rotation.

"Nice try."

"Orthopedics?"

Her always reliable attention to detail helped her excel in nursing school. Assessing and addressing the patient's needs and the family's concerns had become a well-honed skill on which she prided herself. But her perception was failing her. She needed the pieces to come together. Here was a handsome, friendly man challenging her to remember him.

Before her lunch break, she called an attending physician about increasing the oxygen her charge was receiving. Though the seven-year-old had an O2 saturation level within normal limits, the little boy's thin chest was heaving with each inhalation. He was using accessory muscles to do what was essential for life: to breathe. After assessing the child, the doctor agreed. He walked by Grace on his way out of the room. Her head was bent over the computer on wheels, charting the child's latest vitals.

"Good call, Nurse Walker." She glanced up, but he was already at the nurse's station, his back to her, putting in new orders. Was this the man with whom she had recently spoken? The voice didn't sound the same, but she hadn't paid attention to tone or cadence. How awkward.

Thinking about her patient's diagnosis, she tried

one more time. "You're an oncologist?"

Dr. Andrew Holden shook his head as he toyed with the water bottle.

As Grace stared into his cool blue eyes, flickers of amusement danced like sunlight skimming across an arctic lake.

She wanted to come across as attentive and intelligent. She felt like a rare butterfly had landed on her hand and she worried. If she moved unexpectedly, it might fly away. But in the end, Grace was at a loss. She shrugged with deprecating embarrassment. "I give up."

He uncapped his bottled water and swallowed, his eyes never leaving hers. "I have my doctorate in pharmacy. Last week, you picked up a replacement dose of amiodarone. But I'd seen you previously. You've gotten medications from the inpatient pharmacy before."

"You noticed. Me?" The surprise in her voice was difficult to conceal. The heat was high in her cheeks. Why did her body give her away?

"It would be impossible not to. There aren't many top model student nurses around."

When their ten-minute lunch encounter ended, Grace entered her phone number into Dr. Andrew Holden's cell. Forgotten was the vow she made–not to date until after graduation.

That night, she called her mom, uncontainable excitement rising. Everything would be different. This time, she was going to dinner with a pharmacist.

Chapter 8

A Man, Just Like Her Father

Dallas kissed her mother's cheek. "I think I'll go check on those delicious nieces of mine and eat while I'm not feeling sick." Dallas slid through the door, returning to the afterlife party. Mary paused, watching Grace talk animatedly with her husband.

"The app said storms delayed your flight." Grace's voice was forgiving. "Oh, you missed it?"

There is a theory that women end up marrying men who are like their fathers. How a girl is treated by him as she grows shapes her view of men. She learns what to expect. Because of this critical relationship, women learn to love that kind of man. He becomes her standard.

In high school, Grace never dated. Dallas, on the other hand, always had a boyfriend. She flitted from one to the next, a honey bee searching. Only in her final year of community college, when she met Bryce, who was getting a degree in construction management, did she stop looking. Mary worried that Dallas would break up with him as she had done with every man since her father. But Bryce was different. He didn't cling or get upset when Dallas wasn't emotionally available. He was steady, attentive, and devoted. Bryce was nothing like Michael Walker. They had been married for six years and were expecting their first child.

Then there was Grace. In college, she lurched from one bad relationship to the next. Even with the most disparate of them, Grace struggled to make it work, striving for approval while ignoring warning signs. She hung in long after the expiration date until she found out they were cheating, became threatening, or texted— *We are over.*— The act of wanting something so badly, in this case, acceptance and love, rendered her oblivious to the true nature of the men who pursued her. They were the kind of men who had written across their chests in invisible tattoos: self-absorbed, mean-spirited, unfaithful. They were men other women spotted a mile away, women who spun around and ran when they saw them coming.

So, Mary was dubious when Grace announced she had a new boyfriend in her senior year of nursing school. A clinical pharmacist she met at the hospital had asked her out. But after eight years and three daughters, the relationship endured, defying the odds. Mary tracked her oldest daughter as she walked about the room, in and out of shadow, her cell phone pressed to her ear.

Grace stopped moving. Her voice, which was excited and breathy became silent. A ripcord tension ran from the clenched phone in Grace's hand through her taut shoulders. Goosebumps rose along Mary's arms as the trembling cell slipped from Grace's grasp. Her daughter's tears started to fall, but not for her deceased father. Mary had witnessed this enough over the years to know what was happening.

She rushed toward her daughter, who slid down the wall and tucked around herself as if she could disappear inside her body. Revealing himself had taken time. But ultimately, Grace married a man who was just like her father.

Chapter 9

The Home Field Advantage
Nine Years Earlier

Their relationship progressed quickly. Six weeks in, Grace still could not believe her luck.

She was on her stomach, studying, stretched on the bed in his condo. Andrew sat beside her, reading. He put the Applied Pharmacology journal down.

Grace, already in tune with his cues, glanced over her shoulder and smiled. "Pondering a new medical application, or maybe the article's peer review has flaws?" She enjoyed debating with him intellectually. She loved that he valued her insights.

He took off his glasses and folded them on the nightstand with an almost imperceptible sigh. *Oh no, here it comes*. Grace flipped over and sat facing him, her body stiff, bracing itself. *I knew this was too good to be true*. She tried to quiet the roaring in her head. This was it. Today was the day when this affable golden man would tell her the relationship was a mistake. Will she please pack her overnight bag and get out of his life?

"About Saturday's football game."

What was he talking about? Grace forced herself to listen, to breathe in through her nose and exhale slowly out through her mouth, a technique she used countless times with anxious patients. She nodded, afraid to speak.

"As you know, the Ohio State, Michigan game is a big deal. My family has this long-standing tradition. Every year, we go with the Anderson family. We tailgate, catch the game, and have dinner at the Gandy Dancer afterward. Even before they had children, mother and father were best friends with Mr. and Mrs. Anderson. Our families are close. I can't get out of going this year." He stroked her ankle and leaned forward to brush his lips against hers.

"I know we were planning on attending the game together. I'll have to think of another way to make this up to you."

Grace relaxed. He wasn't kicking her to the curb. This was only a football game with family and friends– a tradition. Then came the realization. "Your family doesn't know about me, do they?"

He shrugged and put his palms upward as if seeking an apology. "I was going to tell them at the game. I will tell them, I mean. The thing is the Andersons' daughter, Sabrina. We've known each other since we were in diapers. Starting in kindergarten, we went to Cranbrook schools together. In middle school, we started dating. Everyone assumed we would end up together, you know, getting married."

"Wait, you had a girlfriend when you asked me out?" Grace leaped off the bed, jamming her notes into her book bag. Her worst fears had materialized. This was equivalent to a breakup, only he was putting her in a position where she had no choice but to leave. She may be desperate, but she had standards: no two-timers, no married men.

"Grace, stop!" He had never raised his voice before. "Listen." The intonation softened. "Please." He pulled her onto his lap and wrapped his arms around her. Grace struggled for a moment, then stopped. The least she could do was to hear him out.

"We tried the long-distance thing in college. It didn't work. So we broke up, saying if we were meant to be, the fates would bring us back together." He brushed the hair off her nape and planted a feathery kiss. "Sabrina got a job offer in Detroit. She's moving back to the area. Saturday will be my first time seeing her in over a year. I owe her an explanation in person. I will tell her and my family. Grace, you came out of nowhere, a long-legged midnight horse I never saw coming. You surprised me." Another kiss, more fervent this time, against her skin. He inhaled, taking her in. Her body responded. "I want to be with you. I am choosing you, Graceland Walker."

****

They came in droves, bees to a hallowed hive, some journeying over hundreds of miles.

"Too bad McDreamy can't join us." Josie, Grace's apartment mate, jostled by her side in the sea of maize and blue pulsing toward the Big House. The crisp November Saturday was merely a backdrop to the charged atmosphere. As far as the eye could see, streets teemed with bodies, lively tailgate parties filled yards and parking lots of business. Fans shouted and laughed. Loud music blared; grills hissed and popped. The game was an all-encompassing, surrealistic experience–much more than a three-hour athletic contest.

Grace's hand reflexively reached back, feeling the outline of her cell in her pocket. "Andrew's coming tonight when he finishes his family obligations." She smiled at Josie, unable to contain her excitement. Grace couldn't wait. He'd rather be with her. Andrew made that abundantly clear. Since they couldn't go to the game together, she planned a private affair: an intimate tailgate party on a U of M blanket, a robust sporting event followed by an elaborate post-game flashlight-lit meal. She spent the morning scrambling, cleaning, cooking, and finishing her homework to be ready when he came.

Standing sardined in the rowdy student section, Josie passed Grace a flask. The raucous spectators, vocal, confident, and sure, owned their stadium—a mass of noise and intimidation nearly as crucial as the team. Her mother had explained the phenomenon to Grace when she was touring the Ann Arbor campus as a prospective student.

She pointed to the stadium. "If you come here, you must go to one game." Grace tilted her head inquisitively, interested in hearing her mother's quirky insights. "I went to a few football games with your father while working on my Ph.D. at Oklahoma University. A familiar stadium, predictable routines and tailored locker rooms are not the only advantage the home team has over their rivals. Avid fans become an additional factor in the outcome of the game. Their frenzied support and intimidation of the competitors subconsciously influences referees."

Grace grinned. "You taught us to be good sports, to respect our opponents, and that a victory would be hollow if the playing field weren't even. Are you suggesting I join a browbeating, coercive crowd?"

Her mother shook her head, laughing, "Oh, my

straight and steady daughter. The experience is unlike any other. Even if you only go to one game, cut loose, paint your face, cheer, be part of something out of control and huge." And Grace had done that. At the start of her first year, she purchased season tickets in the student section, figuring she would sell them if she didn't like going. After that first game, she was hooked.

Michigan scored first. The crowd roared, and the marching band played the fight song, sending decibel shockwaves into a clear autumn sky. Amidst the undulating wave of gold and azure frenzy, Grace saw him.

She hadn't been looking for Andrew. This feat would have been virtually impossible in the largest stadium in the Western Hemisphere, with a crowd of nearly 105,000 people. Grace hadn't even thought to ask in what section his family and the Andersons were sitting. But there he was, close to the 40-yard line, his familiar form highlighted by the slanting afternoon sun. Next to him was a woman she assumed was Sabrina, for she flung her arms around his neck, and kissed him. Not a short, we just scored a touchdown celebratory kind of peck, but a longer, deeper draw. Grace watched. Andrew did not pull away. Score one for the home team.

Chapter 10

The Talisman

Grace's head reeled after spending the morning with her father's attorney and harem of ex-wives. His estate went to Brandi, their father's fourth wife. And most of his financial holdings were split equally among wives two, three, and four. Grace, Dallas, and Mary each received seventy-five thousand dollars. As promised, the amount was not enough to cause the remaining wives to be bothered going after them. He didn't want his first family tied up in lawsuits, which were already percolating. The claws were out. Attorneys were readying to file motions, and everyone was hurling barbed insults and threats like darts.

The escalation of entitlement was about to rupture in full force when Michael Walker's attorney slid a book-sized box to Grace. He leaned over and whispered in her ear, "Your dad asked me to hand this to you personally."

His legacy. Grace's fingers trembled as she swept the package off the table, out of sight.

"Hey, what's that?" Brandi's attorney trained his carrion eyes on Grace. "I want full disclosure as to the contents of his assets. We have to know what's in the box. It might be an expensive piece of jewelry he meant for his wife."

Everyone in the room stopped squabbling and stared. Her father's attorney nodded once. Grace opened the box. On top of a layer of crushed velvet was a stone.

But not a diamond or a rare gem. She pulled the rough sandstone out, holding the rock aloft, hoping no one would ask to see the case, for under the lining was a small key.

Her father's attorney beamed at her, looking pleased as if she had passed an important exam. He explained to the assemblage, "This stone has sentimental value. Michael Walker wanted his daughter Grace to have the memento because she was with him on the dig, which changed his life. This sandstone was the talisman that told him about the oil reserves deep below. And if any of you feel left out, I have a box of rocks in my office with the dates and locals of his other successful drills."

The audience regarded him dumbfounded, and the fighting started again. Grace grabbed Dallas' hand. They slipped out of the office unnoticed.

Chapter 11

The 'A' Team

"Let me in! Come on, Grace, what has gotten into you?" Andrew muscled his way into her bedroom.

She tried pushing him out, but he wouldn't budge.

"You were making out with her!" Tears spilled onto her polyester game-day jersey. She hated the way her voice sounded—whining and needy. Her father's words returned to her—no one likes a hysterical woman.

"You were spying on me?" Beneath the bill of his U of M ball cap, icy blue eyes fixed her with enraged intensity, pinning her like an insect on a specimen board.

Now, she was the bad guy who invaded *his* privacy. How had this encounter deteriorated so quickly?

"I wasn't looking for you. You never told me where your tickets were. I saw you after the first touchdown." What was the point of telling him she couldn't turn away once she spotted them? She saw the way his arm easily looped around Sabrina's shoulder, the way they leaned into each other for a kiss after every extended drive, after every touchdown. And the Wolverines had shown no mercy.

Grace pressed a clenched fist into his chest. "Are

you leaving me for her?"

Andrew locked his arms around her.

"Come on, give me a break. I didn't expect Sabrina to kiss me like that. I couldn't humiliate her. We have a history together.'

Grace wanted to tell him that, even from a distance, she saw how he held Sabrina when kissing her. He had not pulled away.

Instead, she kissed him as she had never done before, putting all her hopes, fears, and untapped desires into a long, soul-screaming kiss. *I want you to remember how good we are together.*

Amidst the abandoned, ruinous tailgate party, Grace and Andrew worked through their emotions. Grace ultimately understood that he didn't want to hurt or embarrass Sabrina in front of her family and his parents. A man attuned to his partner was something that had been lacking in her previous relationships. Grace needed a man like Andrew.

Four weeks later, when he learned that Grace's pregnancy test was positive, he found the strength to tell Sabrina and his family, and they moved on as a team, never looking back.

****

Before Grace started to show, shortly after the three months of morning sickness waned, Andrew pressed his mouth against her abdomen and whispered as they lay tangled in early morning bedsheets. "Hello, baby Holden. Your mom and I haven't talked about your legacy yet, but I hope that if you are a boy, you'll carry the family name into the future. You'll be Andrew William Holden the Sixth. I know that's a mouthful, and they are big shoes to fill, but with your heritage, I have no doubt you will meet the challenge."

The pride in his voice was undeniable. It bore the hope that this child, his son, would carry on the family name. When he explained the long-standing tradition on their second date, his face was earnest. "My legal name is Andrew William Holden the Fifth." Grace smiled and nodded, thinking, how cute, how very upper crust. At the time, his moniker didn't matter. She never imagined they would date beyond a few weeks, let alone have a baby together. Her fingers, gently twisting through his sandy hair, stopped.

He regarded her. "I know this seems old-fashioned, and I pride myself on being a modern man. But I'd never hear the end of it if we chose another name. Even though my parents are making life difficult for us, this gesture would show them that you are trying to be part of the family. Doing this would mean a lot."

The pressure to produce an heir? Family lineage? Ancestor worship? Grace didn't have a reference. Having parents from humble beginnings with no historical heritage, who was she to interject her views? Grace would gladly yield if this were so important to her soon-to-be husband. Even as she reached this decision, her stomach lurched, and reflexively, she put her hands there, an act of protection.

"What if it's a girl?"

Andrew turned from her abdomen and put his hands behind his head. "Then we'll give her a name starting with an A. How about that, Grace? All our children will be part of the 'A' team."

The 'A' team. The club sounded exclusive and fun. And despite producing their offspring, she would never be an official member. Grace held this to herself. What was the point? Her horizon stretched, full of promise. Next week, they were flying to Vegas for their wedding. Dallas and her mother were meeting them there.

Andrew's parents and Grace's dad would not be coming. All three had prior engagements and could not rearrange their lives on such short notice.

Chapter 12

The Edge of Balance

Grace fastened her seat belt and slid off her pumps as her sister accelerated out of the parking structure. Dallas was buzzing from the chaos caused by the reading of their dad's will. She thrived on drama. "Oh, sister, I loved the rock spectacle. If you had pulled out a diamond necklace, those women would have clawed your eyes out. Man, that whole ordeal was vicious."

"Polished sandstone wasn't the only thing in the box." Grace pulled out the key, with the bank name and deposit box number embossed on the back.

"Well, I'll be damned. Our old man wasn't entirely off his rocker when he forced you to make him a deathbed promise."

"The jury's still out on that. Will you go to the bank with me?"

Dallas shook her head. "Not interested. If you need my help or anything, just yell. But I'm manufacturing a baby. I'll leave saving the world to you."

Her sister's right hand momentarily left the steering wheel and brushed her midsection. Even though Dallas wasn't visibly pregnant, the touch was an affirmation, a mantra, a prayer. Grace recognized the altered state of awareness brought on by pregnancy, the abiding sense of connectedness. Grace understood what

Dallas was experiencing and felt closer to her sister than she had since she left for college.

Dallas shifted the jeep into fourth gear. "Compared to what Brandi's getting, our shares are a spit in the bucket. But it's enough to make a down payment on a house."

"Or a piece of land where I can build." Grace had to construct a life to protect her daughters. A rock-solid, impervious existence where she never let anyone else in. If she provided a stable home and remained focused on her daughters, life would move on. Never again would someone have the power to pulverize the ground upon which they stood. Until the terms of her father's last will were read aloud, she wasn't sure what this future looked like.

Andrew was pressuring her to move back to Michigan. Even though they were divorcing, he said he wanted to be part of their lives. But he meant he wanted to be part of their lives only if it was convenient for him. His daughters were not his primary focus anymore. Over time, they would work out a custody agreement. Grace would never deny her children access to their father. But her children's needs came first. And having a support system in Oklahoma was best for her daughters.

Dallas slammed on the brakes at a red light, then, as an afterthought, put her turn signal on. "Here's the deal. Mom's watching the girls. You're coming back to the complex with me and going for a swim, then we'll get a pedicure and lunch."

"Not happening." Grace didn't mean to sound so clipped.

"Ms. Grouchy–No Fun Zone Sister. What

happened? Did marriage do this to you, or did someone wake up on the wrong side of the bed?"

"Haha," Grace's voice softened, and she smiled. Hearing the phrase, 'Someone woke up on the wrong side of the bed,' when being grumpy or cantankerous was what their mother used to say to them. Though outraged when they were young, Grace and Dallas thought it comical now.

"No, I got a ten on my bed dismount this morning, ask the girls. It's just that I don't have a change of clothes, let alone a swimsuit."

"Come on, Gracie," Dallas whined, using her little girl voice, which ensured she got her way. "We haven't had any alone sister time in forever. Besides, I had Mom pack you a bag."

****

Grace ignored the swimwear and went straight for the biker's shorts and a loose cotton top. Shedding the morning's formal attire was freeing. She moved before the window-mounted air conditioning unit and lifted her T-shirt until the fabric caught the cool air and billowed.

"Y'all set?" Dallas, wearing a floral cover-up, a neon-pink bikini, and sandals, appraised herself, turning side to side in a full-length mirror. "I don't think anyone can tell I'm pregnant yet. What do you think?" She opened the refrigerator door, grabbed two water bottles, and eyed her sister. "Where's your suit?"

"I'm not up to this yet."

"You go swimming at the Y once a week, if not more. You're up for it."

"I go when hardly anyone else is around and swim laps. I don't feel like being on display."

Dallas nodded. "Just come out to the pool for a while. It will help get your mind off Dad." She handed a container to Grace and muttered, "And that jerk."

He's only the father of my children, someone I spent the last eight years married to. But she could only say, "He's not a jerk," a reflexive response. And even as Grace said this, she heard the lack of conviction behind her words.

Dallas stopped her stride down the dark, chilled hall and linked Grace's arm through hers. "Honestly, Grace, I cannot believe you're defending the creep. Any man who attends his twenty-year reunion and doesn't dare to tell his wife in person that he's leaving her for his high school sweetie on the same day his wife is burying her father is a first-class JERK in my book."

"Come on, Dallas, you know my marriage wasn't like that."

"I don't know anything, Grace. You stopped talking to me and sharing anything after you married Andrew. Doesn't that tell you something?"

Grace shifted her bag, weary of explaining the complexities of her marriage, a union she believed to be correct at the time but only partially understood.

****

"Eleven in the morning, and this place looks like an all-inclusive resort for the young and restless." Grace sat on baked concrete, on the edge of balance, dangling her feet in the chlorinated water while Dallas stretched in a lounge chair.

"I know," Dallas replied, generously applying suntan lotion over lean, pale limbs. "This is a terrific place for singles. You should check to see if they have any units available. We'd be neighbors. I'll introduce you to some of the eligible bachelors."

"Not dating. Ever again."

Dallas grunted. "Right."

"As if this place needs three little girls running around, doing cannon balls in the deep end, splashing sunbathing beauties, and interrupting intense mating rituals. No, thank you. I'm going to find some land and build."

Dallas peered over the top of her sunglasses. "You're kidding, right? You can't be serious."

The sun beat down relentlessly on her neck and shoulders. Grace scrounged through her bag and pulled out her oldest daughter, Ally's, baseball cap. She scrutinized the interplay of bodies in and around the pool, grateful she didn't put on her suit.

"Solid" was what her father called her growing up. "Honey, you take after my side of the family. You're big-boned, statuesque." The Walker women, at least her mother and sister, had 'petite frames.' Grace remembered walking into the shared bedroom one day and finding her sister and two friends flat on the floor, their shirts up, measuring how far their hip bones stuck out from their bellies.

"Anything less than your thumbnail shows you're overweight," one of the girls quipped. "And you can't press!" Grace never met this criterion. "She's the smart one," the ladies at church used to say. "She'll make an excellent mother and wife."

"Not swimming?" A masculine voice broke Grace's reverie. In front of her stood a deeply tanned man with a dad bod, a rather snug speedo, and a lopsided grin.

He looked familiar, the way people do when you

see them out of context. Then she remembered he was a respiratory therapist at Hightop Hospital, where she'd recently become a quality control nurse. She struggled to remember his name.

"It's Peter," he said, as if reading her mind.

"Hi, Peter. I didn't recognize you with clothes on." He indulged her and smirked at the tired joke hospital employees repeated and had heard countless times when they ran into a co-worker outside the hospital. Seeing someone out of their scrubs or hospital-required uniform in everyday garb was disorienting.

"A man has to strut his stuff occasionally. But what about you? Why so formal?" He grabbed her bag and started to rummage through the contents. "There has to be a suit in here, somewhere?"

"Hey, cut that out." Grace recovered her belongings, ensuring the lock box key was still in the bottom, and placed the sack in her lap. "I just don't feel like getting naked with the masses." Other than wearing a swimsuit when no one else was around to do laps at the Y, Grace hadn't strutted her stuff in public since the birth of Ally.

"I would introduce you, but it's obvious you already know each other." Dallas winked at Grace as if to say, *see what I mean?* Eligible singles live here.

Grace stared at her sister long and hard–*not interested.* "How long have you guys known each other?" she inquired.

"I met Peter before I met Bryce. Ten years ago, I rented a studio unit here when I was single. We met in the exercise room. Does that sound right, Peter?"

"Something like that."

Dallas turned over on the lounge chair, unknotting

the top of her suit.

"Want some lotion?" Peter was already pouring a measured amount of sunblock into his hand.

"Sure," came the muted response. "Some offers a gal can't refuse."

"Speaking of offers..." Peter started with Dallas' shoulders, his hands moving in easy, practiced circles. "How about you two join us tonight at Rumors?" He glanced at Grace. "Lots of people from work and the complex are going. I know you've only been at the hospital for a little while. What do you say? I'll introduce you around."

"Thanks for the offer, but I'll take a raincheck. My girls are a handful. I don't want to overwhelm Mom."

"Come on, Grace." Dallas lifted her head and smiled thinly at her sister. "It's a terrific crowd. We eat, talk, and dance. I'm heading over once Bryce gets home from work. Mom wouldn't mind watching the girls a little longer so we can go out and celebrate. You need to cut loose once in a while."

Peter stopped, put more cream into his hands, and began working on Dallas' legs. "What are you two celebrating?"

What are we celebrating, Grace wondered–*the dissolution of my marriage or the money gained through the death of our father?* Peter tended to her sister, appearing comfortable and relaxed. So did Dallas. Her sister was right. They had stopped sharing anything beyond the superficial when Grace married Andrew.

I don't know my sister anymore. But now that I'm living in Tulsa, that can change. Not tonight, though, not at a crowded, too-loud bar with people she did not know.

In the intense heat of the day, Grace felt overwhelmed. Dumped again–an unavoidable thread that wound through her life–first as a child by her father, repeatedly through college, and now by her husband. An uncertain future with three dependent children stretched before her. Andrew was forging a redefined life with his childhood love. She had to honor her father's dying wish, whatever that might be. Not to mention that the man rubbing down her sister wasn't her husband. Grace gathered her belongings and stood. "Hey, Dallas, I have a splitting headache. Do you have any ibuprofen?"

"Check my bedside drawer." Dallas softly moaned as Peter applied pressure to her thighs. "You know the key code to get in."

****

It must be in here somewhere. Grace forgot to turn on the overhead light, and with the blackout shades drawn to keep the midday heat at bay, the bedroom was dark. Scrambling with her right hand, she felt one bottle, then another, and pulled them out. She turned on the bedside light: ibuprofen 200mg tablets, her headache's savior.

The other bottle read: Clomid, 50 mg. Take one pill by mouth once a day for five days–Dallas' fertility medication. She peered into the container and counted. Five. Dallas and Bryce had tried for years to conceive, and everyone assumed that the first round of treatment had been a success. What was going on? Did Dallas get pregnant without the pills? If so, conceiving without treatment would have been a cause for celebration, not deception. Grace grasped for a reasonable explanation.

Maybe Dallas took the first round successfully, and this prescription was a backup. So many questions, all clamoring for answers.

The overhead light snapped on. Dallas stood, frozen, her face blanched, looking at her sister Grace, holding the prescription bottle.

"I can explain, please. Give me a chance. Please, don't say anything to Bryce."

Then, from behind Dallas, arms reached around her waist. Bryce ran his hands over her abdomen, his fingers grazing her exposed skin. "Don't tell me what?"

"Bryce! What are you doing home? You work until five." Dallas turned to confront him.

Grace was uncomfortable when Dallas talked to him like this— as if something perfectly normal was a personal affront to her. But she was in no position to judge; every relationship had a dynamic. Grace tucked her sister's fertility medication into her spandex shorts, grateful for her oversized shirt.

"I forgot some blueprints." Bryce, used to his wife's tone, remained unfazed. He walked past Dallas and scooped a folded roll on his drafting table. He glanced back and forth between the sisters' faces and smiled affectionately at them. "What isn't Grace supposed to tell me?"

Dallas's beseeching blue eyes resembled those of their father's. Dallas bit her lower lip, something she had unconsciously done since she was little whenever she was worried. Whatever was going on was not Grace's business. How could she expose something she didn't understand? Grace loved Bryce as a brother, but her instinct to protect her sister was stronger.

"Well, sis, your surprise is out of the bag." Grace

assessed Bryce, his open face expectant and curious. "Sorry, wait a minute. Hanging out with our stepmothers and their attorneys all morning has given me a headache." She opened the over-the-counter pain relief container, popped two tablets into her mouth, and swallowed before she turned back to him. "Dallas wanted to wait to tell you. You know how she is. She wanted to orchestrate the perfect moment. Our father left us a few bones."

Dallas threw her arms around her bewildered husband's neck. "Surprise! We assumed we'd have to wait until our child started kindergarten. But now we have enough money to put a down payment on a house before our baby is born!"

With Bryce's back to Grace, Dallas mouthed a silent, *thank you.* Grace quietly opened her sister's bedside table drawer and shoved the plastic bottle bearing the fertility medication as far back as possible.

She grabbed her gym bag and closed the door, leaving her sister and brother-in-law in a celebratory embrace.

Chapter 13

Her Floral Cover-up

When Dallas found her sister holding the fertility medication, a panic, the likes of which she'd never experienced before, took hold of her. It only accelerated when Bryce showed up. At that moment, everything could have catastrophically gone wrong. But Grace saved the day by covering for her. The stark reality was her sister realized Dallas hadn't conceived while on Clomid. A conversation with Grace was unavoidable, but Dallas wasn't sure if she'd ever be ready for one with Bryce.

Before starting the fertility medication, Dallas took a pregnancy test. She should have screamed and run to Bryce, joyfully saying, "We did it without drugs. I'm pregnant!"

But she hadn't. For years, they tried to have a baby. Bryce might question why now. He might start probing. He might look at her activities more closely. Saying she had conceived after taking the medication was easier. No one would have to know. Why hadn't she flushed the pills down the toilet as planned? Dallas stood in front of the full-length mirror and dropped her floral cover-up. She needed to talk to someone about the Clomid issue, yes, but there was more.

Dallas was confused. Being pregnant was what she

and Bryce had wanted. Yet her body and brain started waging war the second the home pregnancy test registered positive. Already, she feared the weight gain, the stretch marks, and the loss of control over her physique. Tender breasts, nausea, and vomiting were constant reminders of what was happening to her body and the horrors of what was to come. She rubbed her hand over her abdomen and sucked in. Truth be told, when she did vomit, part of her brain said to her, oh good, fewer calories you have to worry about.

She stepped out of her swimsuit and into the shower. A white mist filled the small enclosure. Since puberty, Dallas maintained her slim stature by monitoring caloric intake and workouts–excessive exercise if necessary. That was something she could control in her life. But strict discipline would not make a difference anymore. Her body was on a predestined course of expansion. And worse than all, she second-guessed the decision to have a child. *I must be defective,* she thought. *If I hate being pregnant, what if I hate being a mother? Oh, baby, you are doomed before we even start.*

The hot, pounding water did little to ease the tension. Dallas needed help. There had to be a way to put everything in perspective. Now that Grace's perfect life was falling apart, maybe her sister would understand. But would Grace judge her as fiercely as Dallas judged herself?

As Dallas scrubbed her legs, she could still feel the sensual energy of Peter's hands as he massaged the suntan lotion into her thighs–a form of muscle memory, her body had responded.

The question was, how much would she tell Grace?

Chapter 14

Maternal Reserves

Grace pulled into the pebbled parking lot in front of the Studs-N-Suds laundromat. She'd barely turned off the ignition when her daughters flew out, racing for the workout area. Hitting a laundromat on a hotter than Hades Saturday afternoon was a surefire way to avoid social interaction. She wouldn't have to worry about her daughter's zest for life, intruding on another's need for solitude. Grace grabbed two canvas bags and followed her daughters inside.

The temporary sublet Grace was lucky enough to nab was down the road from her mom, but it didn't include luxuries like a washer or dryer. Grace used her mother's ancient workhorse for a week until it broke under the heavy load. And though Dallas offered the use of her washer, Grace didn't feel like schlepping their dirty clothes across town. The Studs-N-Suds establishment, less than three minutes from their rental, would do just fine.

Grace trudged past the 'Stud' section of the set-up, which housed a series of large, full-length mirrors and several wrestling pads. A single barbell weight bench hugged the wall. Never had Grace seen anyone who would qualify as a stud here, but her children enjoyed tumbling and dancing on the mats.

Ally, Amanda, and Ora laughed and made funny faces at each other while leaping, gyrating, and cartwheeling in front of the mirrors. Grace glimpsed her profile as she moved past the reflection but didn't stop. Full-length mirrors, like her childhood, were something she'd left behind. The image in the biker shorts revealed long, solidly defined legs. Her oversized T-shirt hid a curvy midsection and bottom.

As Grace began sorting the clothes into different loads, she remembered reading a chapter in her nursing pre-natal book about the fifty pounds she put on with Ally. It divided the average weight gain of a pregnant woman into components: baby, placenta, uterus, increased blood supply, and "maternal reserves." She smiled inwardly, instantly recognizing the soft layer beneath her belly button, the thickness spread onto her hips and thighs. "Maternal Reserves" sounded ingenious, as if she had intentionally packed this substance away for an emergency, like a songbird who builds up its reserves by forty percent in preparation for migration. *My secret tank of fuel*, she thought, while slotting quarters into the machine's thin lines. *In a time of famine, all those svelte body types would dissolve while I endured. Is this my body's secret rationale? If forced to, I could survive weeks in the African savanna– a hardy elephant whose stores make it both buoyant and impervious to the elements. Could Sabrina say that?*

There, she had finally brought *her* name to consciousness. Grace set all four washing machines off in rapid succession. Sabrina, her husband's girlfriend and possibly her children's step-mom-to-be, had no built-in reserves.

Inevitably, she compared herself to Sabrina. Would it have made a difference if Grace had been slimmer and more refined, if she had dressed or acted differently? The space of separation filled her with doubt: *if only I had fought harder, if I had done or said this instead of that, if only I had produced a living son, would it have made a difference? Would Andrew have stayed? Would my daughters and their father still be sharing the same roof?* The what-if, if-only cycle was a barbed revolution that left crushing destruction each time she looped through.

She desperately tried to be everything Andrew needed her to be. And yet, she failed. She was flawed as a woman and a wife, but she could choose to be a perfectly imperfect mother. Her girls needed her more than ever. She wanted them to grow into strong, confident women who were comfortable in their bodies and ready to take on the world. Giving them what they required was daunting–no textbook or manual explained what was needed. What if she messed this up, too?

In high school, Grace discovered the amazing things her body could do. The coach of the girls' swim team valued her strength. During the countless hours of endurance training, when the lactate build-up caused intense cramping, and her muscles screamed, when taking another stroke seemed impossible, her coach would yell through his megaphone, "Faster." And somehow, Grace would reach down into that physical reserve and push herself further. She would climb out of the pool after a 500-meter race, her face flush with exertion, a bit surprised at her body's ability to blaze through the twenty laps. During this time, she didn't feel her body let her down for not being slender enough, and her ability became more important than how she looked. As she walked off the deck, carrying her head a little higher, rivulets of water ran down her muscular thighs and calves.

Above the vibrating washing machines rose a peel of laughter. With Ally's vast appetite for life, her firstborn led her sisters in a dance-off. Sturdy and sure, she pranced before the mirror with wavy brown hair and intense dark eyes that mirrored Grace's.

Amanda, the observer, was as slight and quick as a warbler in the forest. She appeared to live on air. Amanda tried to emulate Ally, desperately seeking her older sister's approval. Her petite limbs and ginger hair flew in all directions.

Ora, lively and stubborn as a wild horse, equally wanted validation. Each time Ally told her she wasn't doing the dance right, her face scrunched with frustration.

Emotional disaster was a step away.

Grace shored herself and stepped before the full-length mirrors with her daughters. "Try this one." She performed a ridiculous sequence of contortions. Her daughters, squealing with delight, tried their best to emulate them.

Ultimately, all four collapsed on the worn wrestling mats in uncontrollable mirth.

"That's not dancing, Mom." Ally was using her let-them-down-gently voice.

"Well, this won't surprise you, but I don't dance. The first and last time I tried was with my father, at his second wedding, and even then, I had to stand on his feet so I would know what to do."

Ora shoved her Pink Pony water bottle in Grace's direction. "Here, Mommy, your face is red. Have some ice-juice."

As Ally and Amanda sipped their water, the Holden girls started giggling again. Ice-juice. Ora had coined the term when she was two. Orange juice is squeezed from oranges and apple juice crushed from apples. Ora wanted water, so she asked for something that made perfect sense: Ice Juice. The term stuck, becoming one of their inside jokes, one of the countless individualized strands that generated the fabric of their lives—a vibrantly colored wealth of shared experience.

Unable to change the past and unsure about her ability to navigate the future, Grace had only the here and the now: to be the best mother possible, to provide unconditional love and stability, yes, but also to ensure that the substance of ordinary days held glimmering moments, cotton candy strands of happiness that would sustain and endure should there be a period of drought.

Chapter 15

Sweet Tea

"Andrew, stop! You hardly had time for the girls when we lived under the same roof. You're busy with the pharmacy, and I'm sure you spend all your free time with her." As Grace spoke, spitting out the word *her*, she hated herself for bringing up the girlfriend. She promised herself she wouldn't stoop to his level. She slowed down. "Look, my support system is here. You left us, you made that decision, and we didn't have a say. Give us space. Please." Grace hit the call-end button and slammed her phone on the Formica table.

Mary placed a glass of iced tea before Grace. She pulled out a red chrome chair, leaned over it, and looked at her daughter.

Grace met her mother's eyes. Her body was rife with tension.

"He's threatening me with legal action."

Mary took a deep breath. "Give him some time. He's angry that you aren't playing into his narrative. Andrew disengaged from you and the girls a while ago. He'll become so absorbed in his new life that he won't fight for long."

"I hope you're right, Mom. I don't have the strength for a protracted custody battle."

"I'm worried about you, Grace. I wonder if you

should see a professional to help you through this tough patch."

"I'm okay. I have you, Dallas, and my friend at work, Ronnie, to confide in."

"Nothing will replace the relationship we have, Grace. But professionals offer different perspectives and have years of experience helping people navigate loss."

Grace went to the freezer and grabbed a few more ice cubes. "Are you saying I'm floundering?"

"No, quite the contrary, Grace. But you've had countless life stressors piled on all at once–a pending divorce, losing your father, moving cross country, leaving one job, and starting another. Any one of these events might push someone to the edge."

"I know these things." Grace's voice trembled. "I'm overwhelmed. But I'm getting it together. If I feel myself slipping under, I'll get help. Let this go, please."

"Fine, for now." Mary hugged Grace and sat down.

"Mom, will you go to Dad's safe deposit box with me? He said I might need your brains to help figure things out. Dallas will watch the girls. I'd be inclined to write off my last conversation with him as the ramblings of a dying man. But Mr. Richeza was overbearing and intimated that the company would reimburse me if I turned over what he claimed was their intellectual property."

"Tomorrow afternoon works."

"Dad's attorney reassured me Mr. Richeza was using pressure tactics and I should ignore him. He said Caligula Oil would have involved their lawyers if they had solid legal footing. Dad worked on his design outside of company time. From what his attorney told me, a patent is pending."

"No offense to your father, but don't get your hopes up. He was a dreamer with patents on projects that never panned out."

"I'd prefer whatever this is to be a bust. I made Dad a deathbed promise, so I must see it through. But man, my plate is full, and besides, you know me, I'm not Dallas. I'm a no-drama mama. I hate conflict."

Mary took a sip of tea. Since the funeral, her daughter struggled to keep going while holding everything together. Grace somehow persevered despite the pile of losses. Smears of sleep deprivation ash were below her eyes.

"You've accomplished quite a bit in the eight weeks since your father died."

"And since Andrew dumped me." Grace shrugged in her usual self-deprecating way, issuing a wan smile, and sipped the sweet tea. Mary wished her daughter could see how strong, beautiful, and resourceful she was.

Days after the service, operating on auto-pilot, Grace gave formal notice to the hospital where she worked in Michigan and applied for a non-patient care position at Hightop Medical Center. After two weeks, she determined the hospital needed a tightly controlled Intravenous (IV) start and maintenance team. Grace worked for days and long into the night, gathering data and developing a detailed proposal highlighting a cost-benefit analysis centered around quality patient care.

Not only was her recommendation resoundingly accepted, but she was also appointed manager of the dedicated group. Grace was directly involved in client care for the first time since working in labor and delivery.

Grace's long-term goal had been to become a nurse midwife. After graduation, she worked a year on a step-down unit, honing her assessment skills before starting labor and delivery training. Determined in focus, her pregnancy, marriage, and the birth of Ally had not detoured her trajectory. Every time Grace talked about her intent, Mary heard confidence in her voice; this was her future. Grace was steadfast, and Andrew supported her. But then, something changed. Grace switched departments and never talked about being a midwife again.

"How does working with patients again feel?"

Grace went to the kitchen window. Mary joined her. Her granddaughters were turning the weathered crow's nest of Grace and Dallas' childhood playset into a fairy castle. Behind each girl flapped sparkly wire wings they found at a rummage sale. Ally, the visionary, threw pillows up to Ora, the unreliable interior decorator, who was laughing so uncontrollably that she kept dropping them. Amanda, always the peacemaker, gathered them up before Ally got mad. Each time she bent down, the weightless wings slipped around her waist.

Grace turned to face her mother, her brown eyes soft and glowing. "Tough work being a fairy, isn't it? But to answer your question, working with patients feels great. I've missed this part of nursing."

"Then why, Grace? Why did you stop?"

Deep in her daughter's eyes lodged a sheering pain.

Grace shook her head and spoke softly. "It's better this way. Now, I work with patients and am essential to their care without worrying about missing something or causing unintended harm."

Mary fought the urge to throw her hands up and yell, *Talk to me, Grace! Tell me—I'm sure it isn't as bad as you think. We can work through this. What happened to the determined daughter who graduated with honors, who didn't let marriage or childbirth stop her?*

Mary scanned her daughter's face, looking for an edge, an opening. What caused her daughter's dreams to derail? She recalled a time when Grace shared everything with her.

A stillness settled over them. Grace exhaled and slid into the chair, her hands tenting her head. "It happened–"

The back door flew open.

"Mommy! Grammy, help!" Ally's shrill voice sliced through the day.

Grace rushed toward her oldest daughter, whose tears streaked a strained, scarlet face. "Ally, what's wrong?"

"Come! Hurry! Ora fell out of the fairy castle. She won't wake up, and she's bleeding."

Chapter 16

A Hypothesis Proved

Grace held the kitchen towel to her daughter's gashed head, trying to stay in the role of mother and not second-guess the responding emergency room staff. Her mom was in the waiting room with Ally and Amanda, undoubtedly feeding them chips and soda from the vending machines.

"I think a nail worked itself loose on the play set. It's the only thing that might have caused the laceration."

"Did she lose consciousness?" The physician assistant removed the towel, and, with a rubbered hand, gently began her examination.

"That hurts!" Ora screamed, her skinny legs kicking furiously from bright pink shorts, her fairy wings bent and protruding from her back.

Grace cradled her head and whispered soothingly, "Jill's trying to help, Ora. Let her look." She raised her eyes and met the PAs. "When I got there, Ora was awake and oriented. At first, I thought cerebrospinal fluid was coming from her nose. But it was salty."

The PA nodded and smiled at Grace as she cleaned Ora's wound. Cerebrospinal fluid was colorless and sweet. A taste test was the quickest way to differentiate the substance from clear nasal mucus—something only a mother would do. Jill had children, she understood.

"We'll get a scan just to make sure. Okay, young lady." Jill spoke directly to Ora. "I know you are strong and brave like your mother. I will give you some medicine so this next part doesn't hurt. And when I finish, you'll have a stitched-up wound so impressive that no one will want to mess with you."

Ora grinned, her loose front tooth jutting forward. Grace smoothed her tangle of blond curls and kissed her forehead, considering how devastating a fall from that height might have been.

****

Ora slept in Grace's arms. Mary, feet propped on the exam table, read a journal while Amanda pushed Ally on the rolling stool around the small room. Grace was going dizzy watching them, wondering what was taking so long for the discharge instructions, when a member of the Intravenous Team found her.

"I hate to bother you. I know it's your day off, and this is the worst possible time. But we have a situation in room 747. No one can get a line started, and he's refusing to let IR put in a PICC. Will you give it a try? The patient said we had one more shot."

"Go on, Grace." Mary took Ora from her arms. "I'll take the girls back to my place. There's a frozen pizza I can heat up for dinner."

Grace struggled. She didn't want to leave Ora. Yet she wanted the gentleman in #747 to get the medication and care he needed. Ora was stable and would be fine in her mother's capable hands.

****

Grace anticipated an angry patient and his family, upset with the quality of care. And who would blame them? Getting poked multiple times while establishing an intravenous line was less than ideal. Disgruntled patients were a way of life. Grace had learned to acknowledge their dissatisfaction while assuring them they were on the same team and wanted what was best for them. She steeled herself and entered a room full of laughter.

"Did I just die? Or did an angel fall from heaven?" A silver-haired man dressed in cotton pajamas that appeared ironed beamed at her.

An adolescent couple, arms draped around each other, giggled.

"Grandpa, did that line ever work?" asked the young woman.

"No, but one of these days, it will." He winked at his granddaughter.

Grace applied hand sanitizer and vigorously rubbed her hands together before shaking his hand. "Hello, Mr. Fresno. My name is Grace. I'm from the IV team and understand that you will let us try one more time."

"My veins are tricky. What can I say? They like to play hide and seek when they see a needle coming. But you are going to be successful. I can tell." He rolled up both sleeves. "Let me introduce you to my granddaughter, Becca, and her boyfriend."

Grace donned her gloves, applied a tourniquet, and palpated Mr. Fresno's veins while they bantered.

"They tell me they are in love." Mr. Fresno chuckled. "And I don't doubt it. Look at them." His granddaughter shifted into the boy's lap. She leaned back, and he kissed her. "Oh, how I recall that head-over-heels feeling. Don't you, Grace?" he asked, squinting intently, a glint in his eye. "Let me tell you about my first love."

Grace set up her equipment as Mr. Fresno's words wound around her, pulling.

****

After her parents' divorce, Grace retreated inwardly, keeping herself in check around her father. She tried to be the kind of girl who would make him want to return home and the sort of daughter he couldn't imagine living without.

In high school, she marveled as her sister Dallas navigated relationships with flippant ease. Before Dallas broke up with someone, she usually had another eager suitor ready to take his place.

Grace's first and only high school experience was during her sophomore year with a boy named Lee Leland.

What transpired between them couldn't be cataloged as dating or a one-night stand. It happened during a study session before their final exam, at the end of a year of being honor biology lab partners.

The familiarity, developed over nine months of working closely together, led to a relaxed, unexpected intimacy. The teenagers in a "hands-on, minds-on" class worked to generate hypotheses, then designed and carried out ways to test them. They bonded over osmotic experiments on shell-less boiled eggs and planned procedures to determine whether yeast was alive. All year, she studied him.

Grace was curious about her subject. She learned by careful consideration as she observed Lee navigate the world. For the first time in her life, there wasn't pressure to impress or be something she wasn't. He accepted the quirky, self-effacing mess of her. The idea that someone of his status would be interested in her was absurd. Lee was her lab partner, nothing more.

But in Lee's Aunt Ida's empty apartment, surrounded by textbooks and study notes on the faded multicolored rug, with the afternoon sun catching fine particles like fairy dust, Grace, a little surprised by her audacity, had initiated the encounter.

She was comfortable with him and didn't think twice about testing a hypothesis she had formulated months ago about how the fullness of one's lips correlated with the quality of a kiss. Once, during a school outing, he'd brushed her lips with his while pulling her underwater, but that didn't count. The kiss wasn't full on. When a lock of dark hair fell across Lee's face, she moved the strand, and because he was close and familiar, she put her lips against his. Hypothesis proved. He responded.

Lee was a protected secret.

She didn't tell her mother, her sister, or even her diary about him. That afternoon in late spring, when Lee asked her if she would be his girlfriend, she panicked. She cared for and trusted him in the classroom, but she appreciated how the scenario would end if played out in the real world—badly, with heartbreak. Like her father, once he saw her true colors–her deficiencies—he would become fed up and walk out without explanation.

Grace pushed him away first. "Why do you want to date me, anyway? I'm not your type."

"How do you know what my type is?" He looked at her, his green eyes alight with curiosity.

"You're a jock, a football and baseball player. Everyone knows you. I'm a nerdy nobody." And she continued provoking, desperate to protect herself, determined to be in control. "Why don't you date my sister? She's a cheerleader. Dallas, you know her, right? She just dumped her last boyfriend. You should go for it."

"Dallas Walker is your sister?"

"I know, right? We're so different. She's the best one for you."

He stood and brushed his hands against the worn denim of his jeans. "I can tell when I'm not wanted." He helped her to her feet. "I thought you were different. How did I get this so wrong?" His eyes were downcast and turbulent. "We don't need to study together anymore. You're going to ace the final, anyway. You know where the door is."

For six long weeks, Grace counted, Dallas and Lee dated. When he was over their house, leaning tall against the doorframe, lying stretched on the couch with Dallas by his side, Grace felt his intent gaze following her when she entered the room. Grace flew down the hall or outdoors, anywhere but near him.

For the remainder of high school, Grace protected herself with blinders and aloof distance. Though she longed for the ease that had become part of their lab partner relationship, Lee represented her first intimate encounter, and madness was to expect a first to endure. In college, Grace hurled from one botched relationship to the next, with a degree of desperation, searching elusively for what had been. Everything changed when she met Andrew. He saw and loved her; he was nothing like her father or Lee. He was safe.

When they graduated, Lee was off without looking back, starting a new, exciting chapter in California. He had a baseball scholarship at Stanford. Grace was equally eager to fly north to Michigan, a state fluid with promise, tightly hugged by the Great Lakes.

She occasionally thought about Lee over the years. You always remember your first. But even with the allure of social media, which promised instant information, Grace never allowed fleeting curiosity to entice her to search for him. He was firmly rooted in her past.

****

"There you go." Grace secured the plastic tubing with tape and smiled at Mr. Fresno. "Someone from our team will visit every four hours to ensure everything is going well. Tell your nurse if the IV starts to hurt or if you notice any redness or puffiness around the insertion site. I work tomorrow and will pop in to check on you. Meeting you all was a pleasure."

"Thanks for taking care of Papa." Becca stood and high-fived Grace.

Young, tender love, Grace thought as she said goodbye to the couple and dapper Mr. Fresno.

She stepped into the hall and stopped in her tracks.

There he was.

A manifestation, larger than life, Lee Leland, leaning against a wall chatting with her friend Ronnie, a sassy, intelligent social worker.

What was he doing back in Tulsa? Had his Aunt Ida been hospitalized? Was he a visitor? Did he work here? Grace slapped her forehead and shook her head. She didn't want to know. Her life didn't have a place for someone like Lee–a playboy, a player, trouble with a capital T. She ducked back into Mr. Fresno's room and ran into the adolescent couple as they left. They stared at her, bright eyes wide and questioning.

"I'm sorry," Grace stammered, the heat burning her cheeks. "I forgot to record something."

Under the amused scrutiny of Mr. Fresno, she pretended to finish charting, chastising herself all the while. Her reaction was ridiculous; she was a grown woman, a mother of three. Grace composed herself, took a deep breath, and entered the corridor.

Lee was gone.

Chapter 17

No Respite

Dallas stepped out of the air-conditioned lobby of the bank where she worked into the sweltering Oklahoma summer. Usually, when assaulted by an atmosphere as heavy as an overheated sauna, she would retreat to her car and crank up the air, full blast, before making personal calls. But today was different. She'd spent most of her break in the bathroom being sick. Now that she was cleaned up and feeling slightly better, she only had five minutes to spare.

The sun was a bonfire in the sky, a flaming container of searing heat. There was no respite. Sweat dotted her carefully made-up forehead, appearing on her neck, exposed arms, and under her breasts.

Dallas leaned against the building, hoping none of her clients or co-workers would see her and interrupt, and pulled out her cell. She had missed a speck of vomit on her slim-cut pressed slacks and silk blouse. Would she have time to spot-clean them and apply fresh deodorant before her next appointment? She opened her contacts and selected a name from her favorite novel. If Bryce saw the number, he wouldn't think twice; the area code was a local one. And if, by remote chance, he called Dallas, she had her response rehearsed. The contact was an acquaintance from one of her Community College study groups, and numbers changed constantly. But Bryce wasn't like that. He trusted her implicitly.

Relief flooded through her when a resonant male voice answered. She gulped liquid air and exclaimed before she lost her nerve, "I need to see you. Please." She hated how the last word slipped out, unbidden, as if she were still an insecure child.

****

Grace sat cross-legged next to her daughter's mattresses on the floor. What a day it had been— Andrew threatening legal action, Ora's accident, and almost running smack dab into Lee. Thank goodness she'd seen him before he had a chance to recognize her. Awkwardness averted. She hoped he'd been visiting from out of town and that he'd returned to wherever he'd come from, firmly staying where he belonged–in her past.

Although Grace had the day off, she didn't accomplish anything on her to-do list. Five hundred square feet of chaos awaited organization, including a sink full of dirty dishes. She sighed. The chores weren't going anywhere, and they'd still be there tomorrow when she got off work. She needed this moment of stillness.

After returning from the hospital and eating their grandma's frozen pizza, they retreated to their rental. Before bed, the girls pushed their mattresses beside each other, making a "fairy ship." Yet, despite the separate sectors, all three ended up on the same lifeboat. In sleep, their bodies sought the solace of sisterhood.

Grace fought the urge to touch Ora's forehead as

she slept. The thick black stitches with a knot in each center looked like a row of insects she wanted to shoo away. Ally was beside Ora, a protective arm resting across her sister's chest. Amanda was perpendicular to the two. Her body pressed into her sister's feet as if grounding them.

Grace watched her daughters breathe, noting the shifts of their chests, checking for a subtle flare of their nares. Her obsession with their respiratory status wasn't reasonable. But then, nothing about being a parent was rational. In the shadowed space where her daughters lay tangled in each other and dreams, beneath their pajamas, beneath the thin membrane of their skin, embedded in their muscle, tissue, and internal organs, connecting every part of them, was their circulatory system. Oxygenation was everything.

When pregnant, Grace inhaled and often followed that oxygen molecule until it reached the placenta, a whole new organ her body manufactured to connect mother and child. Once there, the molecule passed through the dull maternal side of her placenta into the shiny fetal side, pulsing life-sustaining blood to her unborn baby.

After birth and their first lusty cry, after the conjoined maternal-infant circulatory system was severed with one swift slice, the cutting of the umbilical cord, Grace did not forget the shared connection. When her daughters were infants, on their heads, impossibly small hands and feet, in the folds of their cubital fossa, and even as they grew into toddlers, then young girls, Grace often traced the thin pale blue veins that surfaced reassuringly skimming below their unblemished skin, before they dove back beneath their protective flesh.

If there is oxygenation, you can persevere. Breathe in, breathe out. Sometimes, that was all Grace could do.

Chapter 18

Poetry in Motion

"When you finish viewing the box's contents, press this button, and the vault guard will let you out. No one else will be allowed to enter while you're here." The no-nonsense bank manager closed the steel door behind Grace and Mary, who surveyed each other and laughed.

"This is just like the movies. Dad's sending us on a treasure hunt."

Mary waited as Grace brought the deposit box to a table covered with fabric that reminded her of a pool table.

Grace removed three sedimentary rocks that he gifted to each of his granddaughters. Each stone was polished, with the date and location of his successful drills written on the base. Next, she removed three laminated pages with writing on the front and back. "It looks like some crazy formulas and diagrams that only a rocket scientist could read."

"Or a geophysicist," Mary returned, adjusting her bifocals to read more closely. She recognized the tidy penmanship of her husband's cursive, the precise way he wrote measurements, and how he had written notes to her. "The first page has chemical composition formulas. I'll find someone in the chemistry department to help figure them out. The second page resembles a mishmash of geometry, algebra, and trigonometry superimposed over a complicated construction diagram with measurements and specifications. The third page looks like computer coding. Once we figure out the meaning of one section, maybe the rest will make sense." Mary leveled an entertained gaze toward her daughter. "What has your father gotten you into?"

"There's something else." Grace pulled an envelope from the bottom of the box. "Mom, it has your name on it."

"Go ahead, Grace. You open it."

"It's a poem." Grace began to read.

Gathering dusk, in a dress of lace, my first wife. You

Entered my life at a time and place. When

Scant else made sense. Steady, strong

Together, we structured a life, our song.

A fool I was for letting you go,

Lusting, yearning, for what I did not know. Remember

That sacred night of our first snow.

"Mom? This sounds like a love letter to you."

Mary's chest tightened, and the edge of her eyes burned, but she blinked, banishing all sentiment. "No, your father and I are ancient history. Anything he felt for me died a long time ago. This poem's a clue for you."

"I don't understand."

"It's an example of an acrostic poem, where the first letter of each new line spells a word or message. Your dad and I often communicated this way, before cell phones and text messages, before children. Sometimes, I'd find a verse tucked into the mirror, my lunch, or I'd slip one into his overnight bag before he headed into the field. But this one has no sentimental value. The message is for you: GESTALT."

"From my psychology course, I remember Gestalt means something like 'The whole is greater than the sum of its parts.' Right?"

"Exactly. The diagrams are one part of the equation. But there has to be more."

Grace grabbed her cell and started taking pictures of the pages, including a copy of the poem. She hit a button and grinned. "These may be the originals, but if they were that important to Dad and Caligula is so determined to get them, I need backup. I uploaded them to the cloud.

Grace tucked the papers into her mother's satchel. "I'm worried Brandi and the others will find out about the safe deposit box. Dad's attorney said it would take a while, but they could get an injunction and make the bank turn over the contents. The safe will be empty when they do. We'll have figured everything out. Mission accomplished. We got his gestalt message. But where do we go from here, Mom? He wouldn't leave us dangling."

Her daughter's eyes brimmed with excitement. Grace's enthusiasm was contagious. "No, your dad has given us a clue as to where our next stop should be. Come on, my daughter, how do you feel about grabbing a bite to eat at Tequila N' Tacos?"

****

How could Mary forget that night? The poem stirred emotions she thought had fled out the door with her husband all those years ago. She closed her eyes, remembering as Grace navigated the traffic.

After accepting a tenure track position at the University of Tulsa, Mary negotiated a January start time for the following year so that she and Michael could take a long-planned trip together.

"Earth to Mom," Grace punctured her reverie, "What did Dad mean when he said, 'Remember that sacred night of our first snow?'"

"After your dad and I returned from Europe, we found a rental near campus. Our move-in day coincided with a fluke snowstorm. We didn't have any food in the apartment, so we set out on foot to forage. The snow had been falling all day at an unprecedented rate–an inch an hour. The streets of Tulsa were tranquil and muted. No one else was out. The convenience stores, gas stations, and restaurants were all closed. We were about to turn around and head back to the apartment. Getting lost in white-out conditions didn't hold any appeal. But through the thick snowfall was a flashing neon sign. We ran laughing toward the haven."

"And that's the night you met Mr. Rodriguez and his family?"

"The extended Rodriguez family was celebrating Alberto's birthday at a long dining room table created by pushing all the high tops together. Even though the party was in full swing, they invited us in, offering refuge and feeding us some of the most delicious food in the world."

"And the rest is history," Grace filled in.

Mary nodded. Over the years, the cafe had been a family favorite. She had taken her daughters there even after Michael walked out on them. Mary was confident that her ex-husband, with his ever-rising status and position in life, would never lower himself to grace the doors of such a humble abode. And she was right. Not once had they run into him at Taquila N' Tacos.

The enchantment persisted as Mary and Michael left the restaurant that night. They carried enough takeout to tide them over until the streets cleared and the stores reopened. On the slow, hushed walk home amidst the lacy flakes and quiet streets, they decided they were ready to start their family. And, on the mattress, on the floor, of their new home, they made love as if the intensity of their coupling could manifest dreams. Never mind, six more years would pass until Grace was conceived–the snowy night had marked a turning point, a deepening in their relationship. And, Michael had remembered, he called the pocket of time sacred.

****

"Mary!" Alberto Rodriguez lifted her petite frame off the floor in an all-encompassing hug. "Grace!" He hugged her, then held her at arm's length. "Remember, if your nursing gig doesn't work out, you'll always have a job here. You were one of my best servers."

Grace smiled fondly. She'd earned extra money in high school by waitressing. Alberto continued. "I haven't seen those girls of yours in a while. You'll have to bring them in soon. Maybe one day, they'll work here too."

"They'd love it. And I promise, once we get settled, this will be my daughter's favorite restaurant, too."

Satisfied by her response, he led them to their preferred table. "Let me start your order, and then I'll get what Michael left for you."

Mary and Grace exchanged looks. Maybe the lock

box contents would make sense now.

They dove into the warm corn tortilla chips.

"I'm surprised he remembered Dad's name," Grace said as she dipped another chip into the homemade salsa. "I bet he hasn't been here in ages."

"You'd be wrong then." Mr. Rodriguez placed a Neiman Marcus gift bag on the table. Mary and Grace laughed. What in the world?

Mr. Rodriguez continued. "Michael never stopped coming. I think Michael's secret wish was to run into you guys whenever he came. He'd always look around with expectation and seemed disappointed, though resigned when he didn't see you. The last time he showed up, he told me he was going into hospice care. He said one of you would be coming in sometime after he died and to give this bag to you. Well, I'll leave you to it. Let me know if you need anything else."

On top of the tissue paper was a card.

Grace opened the envelope.

My girls! I knew I could count on you to make it this far. But your mission is only beginning. It's imperative that the two components, the contents of this bag and the diagrams, are never kept together. If someone gets their hands on one without the other, they will not make sense. But together, well, you know— gestalt. Store them in different spots until Grace knows what to do with the information. Guard them. You have resources at your fingertips—you are intelligent and brave, and I have never been so confident that my project will end up benefiting this world. Hopefully, this will offset the harm I managed to cause. Love, Dad/Michael

"Showtime." Grace pushed back the tissue paper

and retrieved a tube made from a substance that resembled PVC piping but had a different feel. Etched on the side in tiny lettering, it read: prototype, not to scale, biodegradable & compostable. Grace pushed forward a small sliding lever. And from the mouth of the tube slowly expanded one of the most intricate and complex gadgets she had ever seen.

Chapter 19

Closed Loop Communication

"Mr. Fresno, I hear you're getting discharged this afternoon," Grace whispered. His granddaughter was curled in the overnight chair, tucked into a shadowy corner, the morning light unable to penetrate the closed blinds. She reflexively pulled the blanket over the sleeping adolescent. "Did Becca spend the night?"

"My granddaughter, my life. She lives with me. Did I tell you that? My son, her father, a strong, strapping man who played football for the Sooners, died from a massive heart attack. He left behind a wife and four girls. Becca was only five years old. His passing was a wake-up call. I also had narrowing of the arteries and high cholesterol. I was a ticking time bomb. But my cardiologist helped me turn things around. Of course, I'm still at risk, but I need to stick around for his girls. Especially this for one, she and her mom are gasoline and fire. Becca came to live with me several years ago, and it's worked out for everyone."

Grace smiled and turned on his bedside light.

"The irony, though," he continued, as Grace assessed his IV line, "is that a darn respiratory infection, community-acquired pneumonia they call it, brought me to the Emergency Room, nothing to do with my heart."

"Your chart shows you have one more dose of intravenous antibiotics around noon. I'll swing by half an hour before discharge to remove the line."

"You bet. I can't wait." He glanced at his granddaughter, who was still sleeping. "To tell you the truth, Grace, the night was rough. I didn't sleep well, even with the pill they gave me. I have to hang in there until she graduates and starts college. Returning Becca to her home situation would be explosive."

Grace acknowledged his words while noting an increase in pallor and a sheen of perspiration across his forehead.

"Has the team been in to take your morning vital signs?" she inquired.

"Not yet." His voice was a fading whisper as Grace, without thinking, leaned over him, placing her index and middle finger over his carotid artery, palpating.

He didn't have a pulse, and his mouth slackened. He was no longer breathing. Grace's advanced life-saving training kicked in as she simultaneously yelled for help, hit the code button, and began cardiac compressions.

"One and two and three and four and…" Grace called as she pushed on the frail man's chest rhythmically and with force. Around her was a blur of activity as the critical care response team filled the room and each began their assigned tasks. She registered the voice of the doctor who was running the code.

She didn't need to look up to see that it was Lee Leland. *Great, he's a doctor, and he works here. I'll have to find ways to avoid running into him.* The thoughts flashed and were gone. Grace concentrated on the depth and rate of her compressions.

Lee called out instructions clearly and waited until the person he spoke with closed the communication loop and responded. He didn't tolerate extraneous talking or banter. The sole focus was the patient. Grace had witnessed enough botched codes where everyone shouted over each other, and a lack of leadership resulted in missing critical steps. This was an efficient and well-run code. Mr. Fresno had a fighting chance.

Grace continued her compressions, each thrust pushing two inches into his chest in a steady rhythmic beat, 120 times per minute.

"Pulseless V-Tach," a technician called after applying the sticky defibrillator pads to Mr. Fresno's chest. "All clear," he commanded. Grace stopped her compressions and listened to the charge of the automated external defibrillator. As the shock slammed into Mr. Fresno, his body performed a rag doll leap— no cardiac response. The technician upped the joules and jolted him again. As the second charge to Mr. Fresno's heart deployed and immediately before the monitor registered the response, Grace looked into the terrified eyes of his granddaughter, whose body was pressed against the wall.

An anemic sinus rhythm limped across the screen. Mr. Fresno's heart had responded to the electric shock. Even though this was a regular rhythm, the situation was still critical. At any moment, everything could deteriorate. Grace leaned into Mr. Fresno's ear and motioned for his granddaughter to join them.

"Welcome back," she said as the team raced his gurney down the hall. Grace and Becca were barely hanging on.

"What happened?" His startled eyes moved from his granddaughter to Grace.

"We are unsure what the cause was, but your heart stopped. You're heading to the Cardiac Cath lab to see what they find."

"My guardian angels, both of you."

Tears fell from Becca as they wheeled Mr. Fresno into the interventional room. She held and kissed his bony hand. "Papa, be okay!"

Grace steered Becca into the waiting room and told her how long the heart catheterization might take and what to expect. She stayed with her until the hospital chaplain arrived.

"Here's my number. Text me with questions or concerns. Your grandfather has plenty going for him and is in experienced hands."

****

Grace stretched her legs on the bench before her and rolled up her scrub pants. The warm afternoon sun felt delicious on her neck and calves. She was grateful for the solitude the hospital's serenity garden provided. Beside her, a Koi Pond with a cascading waterfall lulled. She closed her eyes, laid back on the wooden slats, and inhaled. The entire shift had been non-stop, and she hadn't found time to eat. She needed a few stolen moments to still her mind and regroup before she returned to work.

Her thoughts meandered. She reviewed the code, what she needed to make for the girl's dinner, the irony of running into an old crush when she was at one of the lowest points in her life, and finally, they settled on the gadget currently stuffed in a duffle bag in the closet of her rental home situated around the corner from her mother. Her mother kept the papers. Every night, Grace pulled out Gizmo, as she had affectionately dubbed the contraption, trying to discern his mysteries. A soft noise drew her attention back to the garden.

Opening her eyes, she was startled to find Lee on a bench across a small expanse of Dark Night Tea roses, eating a sub and reading a book.

"Are you following me?" Sitting up and pulling her pant legs down simultaneously, she smiled awkwardly. She felt exposed.

"I come here to get away." He put a marker in the book and set down his sandwich. "Usually, no one else is here." He took a swig from a water bottle before continuing. "Mr. Fresno is stable. The cardiologist did a balloon angioplasty and inserted two stents. He also got a temporary pacemaker for some abnormal rhythms, but the team is confident he won't need it for long. Good work, by the way."

Grace shrugged, uncomfortable with compliments. "I happened to be in the right place at the right time." She leaned over to run her finger over the lip of the deep red rose petals and traced the creamy ocher back. Her mother had these disease and heat-resistant flowers in her garden. Grace admired their sturdy stems and upright manner.

"If you hadn't been so observant and responsive, he might not have made it." Lee sounded sincere. His green eyes were unreadable. Still, they were focused intently on her. "Most of the team was in a room at the end of the hall, stabilizing a gastrointestinal bleed before they took them to surgery. It would have been a hot minute before Mr. Fresno's primary nurse had gotten around to doing his morning assessment."

"I was just doing my job." Grace stood, grabbed her scrub jacket, and flung it over her shoulder.

"In any event, well done, Grace Holden." He called her by her married name, the name on her identification badge, the name she had recently decided to keep even after the divorce so that she and her daughters would, at least, have this in common. He must have seen her ID while running the code, or when rushing Mr. Fresno to the procedure room, or maybe in the waiting room when he came to check on Becca. All the better, Grace thought as she walked by him, trying to act as if her heart wasn't engaged in a jumping-jack contest. Let him think I'm married. Let him stay away, as far, far away as possible.

"See you around," he said as Grace opened the fireproof door into the cooled hallway. As the ingress closed, an infinitesimal smile flitted across Lee's handsome face, or maybe, she later convinced herself, the alteration was due to an afternoon shadow.

Chapter 20

An Argentinian Malbec

"There she is, our widowed evil stepmother, in all her perfect glory," Dallas whispered to Grace, as she smiled widely and waved.

"I'm so glad you two could join me for lunch." The words were an antonym to the cool way they were delivered.

Once again, Grace was second-guessing why she and Dallas had accepted Brandi's invitation. She'd rather spend her day off from work in countless other ways. But Dallas argued, "We've never been to the Summit Club before, and chances are, since we're not membership material, we'll never get another opportunity. Let's get our nails done and order the most expensive items on the menu. Besides, aren't you remotely curious about why she wants to talk to us now?"

Grace, as always, consented to her sister's requests. Dallas was right; getting ready was fun. However, as Brandi motioned for them to join her at a table next to the floor-to-ceiling window, one with a thirty-second-story view of downtown Tulsa, Grace's stomach flipped. She could not wait to get home and put on shorts and a tee.

The waitstaff was attentive, and the food was

delicious. The experience would have been perfect if the fourth wife had been replaced by the first.

Dallas stuck to mocktails, but she didn't hesitate to order Grace an expensive glass of Argentinean Malbec. Maybe the wine made Brandi's superficial banter tolerable. Maybe Brandi didn't have any ulterior motive for inviting them to lunch. Perhaps she did miss her husband and wanted to connect with his daughters.

Dallas' sharp kick to her shin brought her reeling back.

"About Michael's lockbox." Their stepmother smiled and ran a finger around the rim of her untouched wineglass. "If you give me the contents, we can avoid the legal mess."

"Dad left us rocks, rocks, and more rocks." Grace kept her voice even, hoping Brandi couldn't tell she was withholding information. "What do you want with them? You saw the one Dad left me at the will reading. He also left one for each of my three daughters. Mementos, paper holders, why in the world would you want those? They have sentimental value for us but aren't worth anything."

"So you say. I want the stones appraised. Michael had them locked up for a reason. Of course, I'll reimburse you for your portion. I don't want to rob you of your inheritance. I just want what's due to me. And as his wife, I have more rights than you. Let's not make this into a thing, girls."

****

"Girls? Girls! Can you believe that witch, who is only a few years older than us, dared to call us girls?" Dallas laughed as she brushed her hair in the elegant Summit Club's bathroom. Grace was still trying to digest how rapidly the luncheon had turned to disaster.

Dallas stood and yelled, "The hell, you're getting your hands on what Dad left us, you bitch." Despite the explosive situation, the circumspect waitstaff and other patrons carried on as if nothing happened.

Brandi watched, amused at Dallas' display, exhibiting the tolerance one might have for a toddler throwing a tantrum. Dallas said her piece, and then they fled to the bathroom.

Grace poked her head out of the restroom–Brandi was gone. On the elevator, Dallas punched the button for the top floor. "What the heck, sister?" Grace pushed the entry-level key, but the lift was in motion.

"We'll never get another chance." Dallas danced. "I want to see the top floor. According to rumors, the outdoor patio has a 360-degree city view. Come on, Gracie, color outside of the lines. Let's glimpse how the other half lives before security throws us out."

Grace laughed and flung an arm around Dallas. They hadn't had this kind of fun together since high school.

"It looks like an episode of "Lives of the Rich and Famous." Dallas gushed as she pulled Grace from the elevator.

"Wait, stop, Dallas! Look."

The elevator door closed behind them.

Beyond the potted trees, floral arrangements, outdoor furniture, and water features, beyond sculptures, Brandi, the newly minted widow, stood by the glass railing. By her side, with one hand holding amber fluid in a crystal glass and another hand on the small of their stepmother's bare back, was the CEO of Caligula Oil and Gas company, Mr. Renny Richeza.

His thinning, clearly dyed jet-black hair was lacquered down, impervious to the wind that swirled around them. The CEO whispered in her ear, and Brandi tilted her impeccably made-up face toward him like a pert snapdragon and beamed.

****

"Seeing them all over each other when Dad's body isn't even cool yet makes me want to throw up." Grace impatiently hit the elevator call button when the floor started to tremble. "Oh, my goodness, that Malbec is making the world spin."

"I think I'm going to be sick, too," said Dallas.

"You didn't have anything to drink," reasoned Grace as the vibrations increased, rattling the paintings and crystal sconces on the wall like a semi-truck barreling past them at close range.

"Don't worry," Dallas interjected. "It's only an earthquake." She squeezed Grace's hand reassuringly.

Grace was stunned and suddenly afraid. "Let's get out of here," she said, pulling Dallas toward the stairwell. The door slammed shut behind them.

Chapter 21

Venus Flytrap

Grace's visceral response to the tremor surprised Dallas. A minor quake, a quiver lasting no longer than it took a dog to shake the water off his back, was nothing. Dallas has lived with the ongoing "Oklahoma Earthquake Swarms" since 2009. But her sister's response made sense. The tremors started after her sister headed north for college. Grace had no frame of reference, but the more than a hundred convulsions per year had become a way of life for Dallas. It was a new normal.

At the bottom of the Summit, while waiting for the valet to retrieve Grace's ancient minivan she bought off a used car lot, Grace shook her head incredulously. "I don't understand. We never had earthquakes growing up."

"It's a result of wastewater disposal," Dallas responded. "At least, that's what Dad told me. Don't worry, Grace. It's nothing. Buildings don't collapse, roads don't buckle, the earth doesn't open up, people don't die. You and your girls are safe. The most that happens here is insignificant damage; a teacup might crack, a picture could shatter."

****

Dallas slouched into the double-wide armchair of

her current therapist's office. The cheerful pattern made her want to puke. The space was friendly and inviting, unlike the stark, modern decor of Dr. Steele, her previous therapist's place, the one she had shamelessly hit on. The complete shock on his craggy face as she threw her arms around his neck and kissed him was something she wouldn't soon forget.

Dallas groaned and pulled a cotton throw over herself. "Let's cut to the chase–why I'm here. Because my last counselor terminated me."

"What was your reaction to that?" Dr. Kay sat still—her short gray hair framed a kind face.

It made me feel like a total screw-up. What do you think?

"I guess I'm more embarrassed than anything." Dallas traced the large, happy fabric flowers with a finger. If the seat had to be botanical, she wished it would be a predatory species like a Venus flytrap, one that would swallow her whole.

"Transference is normal," Dr. Kay explained with infinite patience. "The unconscious redirection of feelings and desires onto another person during therapy means you were getting close to exploring unresolved issues, usually stemming from childhood."

"If transference is normal, why did Dr. Steele abandon me as a patient?"

Dr. Kay studied Dallas with practiced ease. "Your choice of words is enlightening. You used the word abandon, and we'll get back to that soon. But you're right; the feelings of transference are commonplace. Acting on them, however, is unexpected. Dr. Steele is ethically obligated to avoid further interaction with you while providing continuity of care through another qualified psychologist, in this case, one of his partners."

Dallas walked over to a large window that overlooked the Arkansas River. The blanket, still draped around her shoulders, trailed the wooden floor like a worn-out wedding gown.

The river, low in its enormous bed, struggled to find purchase. A dry spring had bled into a summer where moisture refused to fall.

"Dad left when Grace and I were eight," Dallas' whispered.

"And how did that make you feel?"

"Abandoned, of course. Abandoned and vulnerable, like the Walker girls weren't enough. I promised never to let someone make me feel that way again."

Breakthrough.

Dr. Kay's quiet tenor continued. "From what you told me in our past few sessions, it sounds like once you reached maturation, through adolescence and into young adulthood, you never let anyone get close to you again. You used your sexuality to prove to yourself that you were enough."

"That might be an understatement. I went through boyfriends like a dust storm in the panhandle. When they became clingy, or I got bored, I'd dump them."

"That's called an avoidant attachment style, which is understandable given your vulnerability and perception of abandonment as a child."

Dallas faced Dr. Kay, the blanket falling to the floor in a pool, a wave of defensiveness rising. "I've been with Bryce for six years. I'm pregnant. I'm not avoiding anything."

"Let me ask you this, Dallas. And you don't have

to answer this minute. Have you ever cheated or had an affair? Have you kept secrets from your husband? Do you find yourself distancing yourself from him by creating drama around an issue or focusing on his flaws and imperfections?" These are all deactivating techniques to avoid true intimacy. And I don't mean detached sexual encounters."

"I have to go." Dallas slipped on her strappy sandals and grabbed her purse from the coat rack. "I'm taking my nieces to lunch, and we'll spend the afternoon swimming before I meet up with my mom and sister. As you can see, I'm engaged in my life. I'm not avoiding anything."

Dr. Kay stood, the folds of her floral dress clinging to her round, stockinged legs. "Without question, you are fiercely devoted to the women in your family—women you have learned to trust. But I want you to consider your relationships with men, specifically your husband. We'll talk more next week."

Don't count on it, sister. I'm the one paying you, and I don't have to put up with this shit. Dallas exited through the back door, leaving Dr. Kay with her sensible soft-soled shoes and look of perpetual concern in her wake.

Chapter 22

The Gathering Place

An internal warning system. Grace didn't understand how Dallas could be so calm about the earthquake. Their childhood was earthquake-free. A quick online search revealed that the surge in seismic activity was directly related to human activity. Wastewater disposal sounded innocuous enough, but force-feeding the fluid from oil and gas production deep into the ground was an assault.

Convulsions in Oklahoma were a way for the earth to sound an alarm. Wake up, pay attention. What you are doing is not okay. As much as she wanted to, putting her dad's deathbed wish on the back burner was not an option. But when was she going to find time to figure everything out?

Grace was fumbling with her car keys in the hospital's underground parking structure when a bulwark of a man in a suit and tie stepped in front of her, blocking the security camera.

"I'm not here to hurt you." The deep voice stopped her from doing what her body implored her to do–run. "Consider me a private process server, Graceland Walker Holden. Only you will not get a written missive, so listen closely." His titanic body coiled with a forbidding menace. His hands were enormous anchors soldered to bulging arms.

Grace gripped her key like a makeshift weapon and willed herself to remain calm, committing every feature to memory, anticipating the need for a police sketch. Buzz cut, tiny dark eyes, about six feet six inches.

"You have material Michael Walker worked on while employed with the Caligula Oil and Gas Company."

The lock box, Grace's mind raced. The bank called last week, saying they had an injunction to open the box and reveal the contents to the petitioning parties. But she hadn't worried–the compartment was empty.

The man advanced, his bulbous nose pushed toward her. She stepped back, ready to flee. "If you return the contents of the safe deposit receptacle, you'll be handsomely compensated. If you choose not to comply..." His words dripped with menace. "We will do whatever is necessary to secure the items, and you will regret not cooperating with us." To emphasize his point, tiny spots of spittle sprayed from his mouth. "I've left my business card beneath your windshield wiper. Remember how precious your three little girls, pregnant sister, and mother are to you. Call me when you're ready to negotiate."

And as quickly as the articulate bully had appeared, he was gone, behind a cement scaffolding, into the enclosed stairwell. Grace grabbed the slim card with a hand-printed phone number, jumped into her beat-up minivan, and gunned out of the parking spot, scanning for a vehicle bearing the man and a visible license plate number. Just as she reached for her phone, it started to ring.

"Grace," her mother's voice was agitated. Had she

been threatened, too? Per her father's directives, they never kept the puzzle pieces together. Grace retained Gizmo while her mom discreetly stashed the formulas in a secured cabinet in her office on the university campus.

Had involving her mom put her at risk? "Mom? What's going on? Are you okay?"

"I know what the chemical composition page means. Meet us at the Gathering Place. Dallas is on her way with the girls. I'll grab some carryout for dinner. We'll talk then."

****

The girls assaulted Grace with hugs. "It's so hot," Ally said. "Can we get something, please?" Amanda nodded in vehement support.

"We're parched," stated Ora, her stick-thin arms akimbo.

Grace and Dallas tried to control their laughter.

"Parched? Why, my darlings," —Dallas curtsied toward her nieces— "in that case, a thirst-quenching treat is necessary. It's an aunt's prerogative to ruin dinner. How happy I am to have you all living in the same city with me!" Dallas kissed the tops of their heads, then turned to her sister as she pulled out her wallet. "That goes for you too, sister."

Ally, Amanda, and Ora each clutched a popsicle and skipped in front of them as they headed toward their favorite part of the park.

"Grace, your daughters are adorable. Maybe having a little girl wouldn't be so bad."

"Children are life-changing, that's for sure."

In a few moments, their mother would join them. Now wasn't the time or place to bring up the fertility drug incident. Instead, Grace broached another subject, which had been nagging her. While trying to sound casual, she asked Dallas, "Do you remember Lee Leland from high school?"

"Doesn't ring a bell."

"Really?" This surprised her. "Football and baseball player–you dated him for a little while," Grace replied, thinking about the six long weeks of summer after their sophomore year. The specifics of that time were seared into her memory.

"Grace, our high school was huge, and I dated so many guys, some longer and many shorter than that. I don't remember him. Why?" She gazed at her sister intently, suddenly very interested in the conversation.

"He works at the hospital. I was wondering if you know anything about him."

Dallas's affectionate smile and light blue eyes danced. "Why Graceland? Miss, I'm never going to date again. Do you have a love interest?"

"No, it's nothing like that." Grace's face heated up. She should have kept her mouth shut.

Dallas threw her head back and laughed. "Oh, sister, you have it bad." She slipped her arm through Grace's and continued, "I can ask Peter what he knows about him. Do you want me to?"

"No, please don't."

Dallas leaned her soft blond head into Grace's arm, saying, "Fine, have it your way. But this subject is far from over."

The girls crammed their treat sticks into the trash can.

"Hey, kids," Grace called as they squealed with glee and flew amuck in three directions. Each head momentarily turned to look as they ran. "Make sure you can always see me. A sixty-six-acre park—maybe this wasn't such a good idea." Grace found an empty table beneath a shading elm, where she could monitor the entrance and exit of the Skywalk Forest while tracking her daughters.

"What's up, sister? You and the girls love this place. Why so tense?" Dallas inquired as she slipped off her sandals, digging brightly painted toenails into the sand.

Grace told her about the man in the garage and his veiled threats. At the end of the story, their mother showed up toting a picnic basket.

"Whatever your dad was working on is a hot commodity," she said, spreading out the worn checkerboard tablecloth and unpacking cartons of Indian cuisine. "He'd invested significantly in a green IQ tech company. His gadget is biodegradable and compostable. The chemical compositions confirm this."

The sisters exchanged astonished glances. Grace opened a container and spooned some carrot curry and rice onto a paper plate. "Well done, Dad! I thought Gizmo was a pipedream," she said, taking a bite while clocking the girls' location. "Next up is figuring out what the math and computer code mean and what Gizmo is supposed to do. We have to see the big picture."

Grace gazed skyward at her three daughters, navigating a floating pathway twenty feet off the ground. The corporate thug's words reverberated in her mind: *you will regret not cooperating with us.* It was extortion. They could target her, and she would fight them to fulfill her father's dying wish. She, however, was unprepared for threats to her mother, sister, or daughters.

How could a single mom, a nurse, stand up to an International Oil and Gas Company? She needed backup; Caligula had crossed a line. She'd file a police report and keep Dallas and her mom in the loop, but she wouldn't say anything to the girls–no need to scare them.

Grace pushed her plate aside, her appetite suddenly gone.

Chapter 23

Goodnight Moon

"Good night, Ally. Goodnight, Amanda. Goodnight, Ora," Grace said, smiling at her three daughters tucked in their beds.

"Good night, Mommy," they sleepily replied.

Grace leaned in and kissed each forehead one last time before turning off the light. And as tradition dictated, she whispered, "Goodnight, moon."

She paused in the doorway, her hand on the knob, and turned to face her girls. "Remember, when you get up in the morning, Grandma will be here. I must be at the hospital early."

Never satisfied with the status quo, Ora found a second wind and piped up, "Why?"

"One of Mommie's patients needs an IV before having an interventional procedure. I promised I'd be in to take care of them."

"What's a procedure?" Ora asked, her voice curious but fading.

Grace sat on the edge of Ora's bed and stroked her hair. "The patient is getting a filter to catch tiny clots before they go into her heart and lungs."

"And that would be bad, right?" Ora's voice drifted as her eyes fluttered.

"Yes, that would be very bad," Grace confirmed

with a smile. "You are so bright, my little one. Sweet dreams, my loves." She stood up and turned on the nightlight before padding down the hall in her sleep shorts and favorite cotton T-shirt, worn to transparency.

As she settled into bed, her mind swirled. Their sublet, a two-bedroom duplex a block from her mom, ended in fourteen days. Grace would miss the proximity to her mother, who was an enormous help. She hated putting her daughters through yet another move, but the horizon was getting lighter. Tomorrow, she was meeting her sister and brother-in-law after work. She hoped they would be receptive to her ideas and that Bryce would have good news.

Once Grace programmed her cell alarm for 4:30 a.m., she leaned back in her bed and, for the hundredth time, pulled out the object of her obsession.

"Hello, Gizmo, you handsome fellow." Running her fingers over the intricate, interconnected spheres, tetrahedrons, and cubes, she tried to understand what her father saw when he looked upon his creation. He was counting on her to figure this out. The mounting pressure from Caligula compounded the urgency. She was terrified to discover what they meant when they said she would regret not cooperating with them.

She was keenly aware that while she had copies of the formulas and equations, she only had one Gizmo. She photographed the prototype from every angle and downloaded the pictures. But if Gizmo were lost or stolen, she'd never discover his true purpose.

Grace cataloged what she knew about the device. The cylindrical tube was a delivery system. When she slid the lever forward in the restaurant, the apparatus emerged, expanded, and disengaged. Her father had designed the object to remain underground, or had he? *I need some help here, Dad. I'm not catching on. Some muse, right?*

She slid Gizmo under her pillow, hoping, through osmosis, she might understand. Though bone tired, her mind raced. Only five hours until she had to be at the hospital. Thoughts took her back to that sun-drenched morning when her quest started. She felt her father's cool, weathered hands grabbing hers with surprising strength for his condition. Grace closed her eyes and heard his voice as though he was alive and sitting beside her. "Remember my visits when you were in nursing school? When I had a connecting flight through Detroit, you'd drive to the airport to meet me. I found our exchanges about implantable medical devices particularly fascinating. Replay these conversations. You'll find useful information in them."

Years ago, she explained in detail to her dad the concept of a retrievable inferior vena cava filter, the kind her patient was getting. For individuals who couldn't take blood thinners and needed short-term protection against pulmonary embolisms, a filter snagged tiny clots before they reached the lungs. The device stayed in the body until it was no longer needed. Then, the doctor would percutaneously retrieve the apparatus.

Grace tried many times and in different ways to get Gizmo back into his delivery pod, but to no avail. Every detailed aspect was interconnected, so the shape of the device was unalterable. She assumed that once deployed inside the earth, the device would remain in place until degradation was complete. But what if her father had fashioned a recovery system like the retrievable filter?

"Remember," his voice faded, and Grace bolted up, grabbing Gizmo by his sharp, polyhedron top. Grace slid the lever forward to the end, and a hook popped out. It can't be this simple, she thought excitedly. With focused dexterity, she attached the hook through a small loop on Gizmo's apex, held her breath, and slid the lever back to its original position. And just like that, the device collapsed coaxially as it slid back into the housing sheath. Gizmo was retrievable!

She stashed the reunited team in a duffel bag, shoved it into her closet, and flicked off the light. Her body relaxed while images of her father bent over drawings she had made on a restaurant napkin flashed before her. He whispered, "You are getting closer, my girl. Stay the course." With his words in her mind, Grace drifted to sleep.

Chapter 24

Broken Steps

Grace's daughters skipped through the afternoon light across an expanse of tall grasses and late summer wildflowers. "What do you think, Bryce? Will this work?"

"I'll get someone out here, see if the land perks. If so, I don't see why you couldn't put one of those prefabricated modules here. Where were you thinking of putting the house?"

Grace didn't realize she'd been holding her breath. She grinned at her sister and brother-in-law. Bryce smiled back, but Dallas appeared preoccupied. She clung to Bryce's arm, concentrating on not breaking her heels as they navigated the rough terrain.

Refusing to be detoured, Grace quipped, "I'm not going to need a pre-fab. I want to show you something. See that cluster of trees? They'll help buffer us from winter winds and, in the summer, provide cooling shade. Once I found this unexpected shelter, I was sold."

"Just hope you don't find a toxic dump on the backside." Dallas was half joking. Her sister was still mad that Grace hadn't moved closer to them in town. Even now, she was still trying to argue her point. "It's not too late, Gracie. I checked. Down the road from us is a beautiful complex with two condos for sale, a pool for the girls, and workout facilities for you. The place is close to your hospital and has excellent schools nearby."

Grace didn't expect Dallas to understand. She and the girls needed space and time to re-group and start healing. They had recently returned from an end-of-summer excursion to Michigan. Grace had flown with Ally, Amanda, and Ora. After dropping them off with Andrew, she hung out with her college roommate in Ann Arbor while the girls spent time with their father, his fiancé Sabrina, and paternal grandparents at their cottage on the shores of Lake Michigan.

In December, when Ora turned five, Grace wouldn't have to accompany her daughters on these trips. One more time to practice over Thanksgiving, one more time to ensure they felt comfortable with every aspect of the direct flight. After that, her daughters would be old enough to fly under the "Unaccompanied Minor Service" the airline provided. Grace's stomach lurched at the thought. How could she send them into the air while she remained tethered to the ground? She brushed the rumination aside.

Grace was overwhelmed by the heavy load on her shoulders. As if establishing the hospital's first intravenous team with her future riding on the program's success wasn't enough, Caligula's threats exacerbated her urgency to ascertain the connection between her dad's gadget and the formulas. She also needed to create a functioning home for her daughters, who would start their new school soon.

Grace pushed through the dense overgrowth. "*Voila*," she said as she opened her arms wide. Long shafts of amber light fell from the sky onto a discarded mobile home. Looking through the foliage, which was swallowing the unit in an act of reclamation, seeing beyond the crumbled front steps, the slanting shingles, and the scabs of missing siding, Grace saw potential. She envisioned a home.

"You have to be out of your ever-loving mind." Dallas' hands were on her hips. "No way are you moving into that trailer! Come on, Bryce. Talk some sense into my sister, who has gone off the deep end."

"It's not a trailer," Grace asserted. "It's a grounded, double-wide modular, with two acres of land for the children to run around. The interior needs cleaning up, of course. But everything seems intact, and in the back is an overgrown yet charming courtyard. This place just needs attention. Fixing this up would be cheaper than erecting a prefab. The realtor told me the older man who lived here before had a functioning well and septic system. Come on, let me show you. This way, the back steps aren't as fractured."

For the next forty-five minutes, Grace tailed Bryce as he thoroughly examined the trailer, took measurements, looked beneath carpets, sinks, and closets, and paused to annotate his notebook. When he finished, they stepped outdoors where Dallas, newly appointed fairy queen, twirled on the overgrown pavers around intertwined wisteria, unruly bushes, and roses. A chorus of early evening crickets, making music with their bodies, rose and fell around them.

Dallas held a twisted branch as her wand, granting wishes to her nieces. "You are hereby transformed into a sparkling unicorn." Ora screeched with delight, pranced, and neighed, her blond hair a wild plume around her. The look of love on Bryce's face as he watched his wife was unmistakable. Grace felt a pang. Did Dallas know how lucky she was? What would it feel like to have someone look at her that way? In all their years together, had she ever seen an expression like that on her husband's face?

A hand tapped her shoulder. "Earth to Grace. The answer is yes. I can get the materials needed for repair using my builders' discount. I'll get some of my guys out here. We'll have this place up and running within a week." And Grace was off, hee-hawing and flipping her dark mane, capering alongside Ora. Peals of laughter rose as Ally, Amanda, and the fairy queen joined the parade.

"Shoot," Bryce pushed his cell back into his pocket. "Grace, will you give Dallas a ride home? I have to get to the construction site. My guys can't leave until a foundation issue gets resolved."

"I'll come with you." Dallas' words came in a rush.

Was Dallas trying to avoid being alone with Grace? Dallas had to know Grace would eventually ask her about the unused fertility medication.

Bryce kissed Dallas. "This'll take a while. You've been working all day. Go home, get something to eat, and put your feet up." He jingled the keys.

Grace squeezed her sister's hand. "The girls would love some extra Auntie Dallas time. And so would I."

Bryce walked across the craggy expanse. Before climbing into his truck, he smiled broadly, with undisguised affection, and called, "Don't get into trouble."

Dallas reluctantly smiled at her sister. "You look like the cat who swallowed the canary." Her pale face suddenly contorted, and she began to wretch.

Grace pulled back strands of her sister's hair as she bent over. "And you look like the cat throwing the fool bird up."

Dallas looked like she wanted to laugh, but the contents of her stomach prevailed. They hit the earth, splattering on her stylish high heels and Grace's hospital clogs.

"I thought this morning sickness was supposed to stop after the first trimester." Dallas wiped her face with a tissue from her purse.

"Not always." Grace handed her a bottle of sanitizer from the pocket of her scrubs. "Sometimes pregnancy-related nausea lasts until the twentieth week, or even longer."

"Great." Dallas found a rock and sat down. Ally, Amanda, and Ora were picking wildflowers, laughing and chattering with each other, their voices intertwined like musical notes.

Dallas finally faced Grace, her blue eyes clouded with turbulence. "What will I do?"

"Eat less at a time, eat more frequently, and stick with bland foods. Some pregnant women say a ginger supplement helps. But you should check with your obstetrician first."

"No," Dallas interjected and rested her hands on her swell. "What will I do with this pregnancy, Bryce, and everything? Grace, I'm in trouble."

The tears began to fall.

Chapter 25

Grand Rounds

Wherever Grace turned at work, Lee was there. He became an inescapable part of her daily routine. Lee appeared in interdisciplinary care team meetings, patient rooms, corridors, the cafeteria, the serenity garden, the resource library, and Grand Rounds. At first, Grace tried ignoring him, hoping to manifest his disappearance or at least send him the message–stay away. This strategy, however, was untenable. Everyone on a patient care team must communicate to provide the best outcome for each client. Once Grace recognized that interaction was unavoidable, she resolved to keep their communications strictly professional.

Grace's work friend, Ronnie, waved her to the cafeteria table, where she was video-chatting with her daughter. "Maya, say hi to Grace."

The adolescent, dark curly hair framing an oval face, grinned. "Hi, Grace!" Then she returned, "Gotta run, Mom. My shop class is working on the 3-D printer, and I don't want to be late."

"I love you, kid," Ronnie said, though her daughter had already hung up. "I guess I'm still lucky she calls on her lunch break. Most parents don't get that. She's in this summer program for nerds–her words, not mine."

"She sounds like my kind of gal. I can't wait to

meet her." Grace unpacked her leftovers from last night's meal and began eating.

"When you get settled, Maya is a terrific babysitter. She took a child CPR class and first aid course to prepare for anything."

"My girls will love her."

Grace was grateful for Ronnie's friendship. "We're peas in a pod," Ronnie said to her one afternoon as they shared a cup of coffee. "You know, kindred spirits, single moms. Don't get me wrong, married women are great, and a girl can never have too many pals. Still, unless you're swinging in our boots, you can't understand the logistical and emotional calisthenics of being a solo parent. I'm here for you, Grace, whenever you need a hand."

Ronnie made her transition to the hospital seamless, introducing Grace to everyone from food workers to janitors and filling her in on their backstories. Through her friend, Grace learned that Lee was a hospitalist–a dedicated in-patient physician–and everyone, clients and staff alike, thought the world of him.

As they continued eating and chatting, she spotted him. Grace tracked him through the cafeteria line, talking to an Intern by his side. Ronnie leaned over and whispered, "Lee Leland is an enigma. As far as we know, he's not married. He doesn't wear a ring. And heaven knows enough women, and men for that matter, have tried hitting on him, but other than casual dating, he doesn't seem interested in anything long-term. Not only is he as yummy as a pie supper, he's also down to earth." They followed his progress as he headed to a table across the room. Ronnie sighed. "Perhaps he has a secret family we know nothing about."

"Or maybe he's an alien?" Grace quipped, eliciting a chuckle from Ronnie.

"Finally, a man with brains," Ronnie said.

****

"I'm sorry Bryce couldn't come with you today." Dallas' obstetrician peered over her bifocals as she scanned the ultrasound report and handed her an image of the baby. "Your baby is growing splendidly. Its development is right on track. Do you want to know the sex?"

Did she? Dallas was trying to stay engaged and remain optimistic about what was turning into the worst months of her life. Bryce's unending enthusiasm and obliviousness to her internal turmoil were more than she could handle. Sometimes, she grew annoyed by his constant plans for their burgeoning family. *Stop it. Can't you see nothing will be the same after the baby is born?*

Bryce tried to hide his disappointment whenever he realized Dallas had seen the doctor without him, but his despair was apparent. So she'd stopped telling him about her visits. Maybe Dr. Kay was onto something with this avoidant attachment style; was it a thing? And if so, was there a cure? She'd have to explore this further. But, for now, at least, she could offer Bryce an olive branch–he would be thrilled to know the gender of their baby. Maybe learning more about the life form displacing her internal organs, expanding like a greedy tapeworm inside her, would help Dallas feel more connected to her infant, more like a mother.

****

"My private physician is older than the hills and

not nearly as handsome. Will you be my forever Doctor?" Ms. Ponyo's tightly curled locks framed a powdered face. She batted artificial lashes unapologetically.

Grace finished her assessment and turned her back to Lee and Ms. Ponyo to conceal a smile.

"Your primary care doctor will resume your care upon discharge. I've sent him all the reports. I explained everything when we first met." Lee was kind yet firm.

"Oh, bother." Ms. Ponyo's voice rose with great expectation, "You mean if I want to see you, I have to go and get myself admitted again?"

Lee's laugh was deep and sincere. "Unfortunately, it's not like ordering carryout. I'm not always here, and hospitalists are assigned based on many factors."

Grace finished charting on the computer and started to leave the room the moment Lee stepped back from the bed and bumped smack into her.

Quickly, he turned, and grabbed her shoulder to steady her.

"Sorry," they both said simultaneously, amusement in their voices.

Grace couldn't look away from his deep jade eyes, which danced with curious vitality even though he wasn't smiling.

He was at the hospital, everywhere, and then he wasn't—two weeks on, two weeks off, a pattern. And with increasing dismay, Grace noted how her spirit lifted on days he would be there.

****

It took Dallas several seconds to understand. Then, as she took the filament-thin piece of paper in her hands, with an arrow pointing to a nether region of anatomy, she heard while simultaneously registering the words printed on the slip, "It's a boy!"

Boy–a three-letter word that cracked open the earth beneath her feet, creating a crevasse threatening the stability of the ground upon which she walked. The concept was as simple and terrifying as a plane hurtling toward that abyss—a male child. Oh, good lord, a girl she could have probably handled, but a boy? She sucked at male-female relationships. What did she know about nurturing the sapling of a man?

****

Seated in the hospital auditorium, Grace waited for the weekly brown bag Professional Development Lecture series to start. The assembly hall's seats were filling. Grace moved her day pack from the chair beside her to the floor. Someone slid into the vacancy. It was Lee.

"Must be nice," Grace began without thinking.

Lee pulled the stethoscope from around his neck and raised an eyebrow inquiringly.

She continued. "Two weeks of work followed by two weeks off to play."

"I'm flattered. You noticed." He flashed one of his easy, broad smiles.

She tried not to respond, but his grin was contagious, like when they were adolescents.

"It's kind of hard not to. You're everywhere, in everyone's business, and then you're gone."

"That is one of the perks of being a hospitalist. I negotiate the terms of my employment. Working a few weeks here enables me to spend the rest of the month doing other things."

"Like jet setting to Paris, rock climbing in Colorado, skiing in the Alps, gambling in Vegas, racing cars in Monte Carlo?"

His smile was bemused. "Something like that."

Lee took a bite of his sandwich. "You seem to have me figured out. But what about you, Grace? What do you do on your days off? What brings you joy?"

The question surprised her. Lee appeared genuinely interested. *Rein it in, Grace; remember who he is. Keep everything on the surface.* Dimmed lights and the sudden appearance of a stage four bed sore–a gaping open wound so deep that the patient's muscles and bones were exposed–flashed on the amphitheater screen, saving her from answering.

The lecturer adjusted her microphone. "Not the best picture for a brown bag lunch, I know," she quipped. "But, one way or another, we chose this field. Now, let's talk about how to protect our patients from these diabolical decubitus ulcers."

Halfway through the lecture, Lee's cell vibrated. He glanced at the message and said, "Gotta run. Room number 222 is tanking. See you around." He winked and promptly left.

****

Grace entered the patient's room, awash with bright lights, artfully arranged flowers, and a mixture of hard rock, funk, and hip-hop playing from a plugged-in phone on the bedside table. Each space had a different atmosphere, and every patient had their story. This twenty-year-old had been in a horrendous car accident, was ventilator dependent, and hadn't regained consciousness.

Grace gathered the materials needed for the

patient's sterile dressing change, and the respiratory therapist, who just finished suctioning the patient, greeted her. He looked familiar.

"I'm Peter, remember? I live in your sister's condo complex."

Speedo Suntan Lotion Man, she thought, and politely smiled.

"I usually rotate between the second and third shift."

This explained why she hadn't seen him recently. She waited as he finished giving an aerosolized breathing treatment. Peter took his time packing up.

"I haven't seen Dallas around lately. I usually run into her at the pool or gym. Is everything okay?"

Since discovering the unused fertility medication in her dresser, Grace hadn't found the right time to dive into what was going on in her sister's life. Superficially, other than struggling with her pregnancy symptoms, she appeared to be okay. Beneath the surface, though, Grace had no idea. But she certainly wasn't going to say anything to Mr. Handsy.

"We're getting together soon. I'll let Dallas know you were asking about her."

"Sure, that would be great," he stammered.

After Peter left the room, Grace hung a "Sterile procedure in progress. Do not enter" sign on the door. Though her patient hadn't been conscious in weeks, Grace chatted with her, explaining what she was doing, talking to her as if she understood.

Chapter 26

A Bridge

"Would you guys stop fighting?"

Grace was at her wit's end. All morning, her daughters had been at each other. They relentlessly teased one other, fighting over the iPad, the same stuffed animal. The object didn't matter; the others wanted what they didn't have.

Monday, Bryce and his team would start working on the double-wide, and Grace hoped bringing the girls to the house over the weekend and having them do some cleanup would help them feel invested. Maybe this wasn't such a good idea. A headache started to form as yet another shriek shattered the day.

The morning started with burned toast and not enough of the girls' favorite cereal to go around. To make matters worse, Andrew called on the way to the property, and the girls fought over who would talk to him first. With all the pushing and shoving, Grace pulled off the rough road.

Putting Andrew on speakerphone hadn't helped. A screaming match erupted, with each child trying to be heard over the other and vying for their father's uninterrupted attention.

Grace held the phone aloft, saying, "You can talk to your dad when you get it together." She tried to control her frustration, telling Andrew, "I'll have them call you back." And she hung up.

Ora flung open the door in outraged defiance and cast herself onto the flinty shoulder. Everyone else clambered out, surrounding her. Ora's meltdowns were epic.

"Somebody woke up on the wrong side of the bed," Ally observed as Ora's arms and legs moved like stranded starfish in the dirt. Amanda started to giggle, and Grace bit the side of her mouth.

Hearing that, Ora screeched and flailed at an accelerated rate, "I DID NOT WAKE UP ON THE WRONG SIDE OF THE BED!"

The expression's injustice infuriated her daughters, as it had Grace and Dallas when their mother said it to them when they were young. But as adults, Grace and Dallas found it hilarious. Would there be a day when her daughters felt this way, too?

****

"This place is a dump." Ally kicked the broken steps. Tears gathered anew in her eyes. "Why can't we go back home? I wanna go to my old school." Strands of dark hair escaped her ponytail, caught in the dry wind, and spun about her face like an unmoored spider web.

"I miss my bedroom. I miss my daddy." Ora's blonde hair was matted and riddled with dirt and small rocks from her roadside tantrum.

Amanda's thin shoulders shook. She tucked her hands under her chin like a chipmunk. Grace's peacemaker was trying to stay strong.

Even though Andrew abandoned them, the girls blamed Grace for the breakup. "If only I had done this differently" was a repeated tagline scrolling at the bottom of her life. There wasn't a reset button. She was here, now, on a tough patch of Oklahoma, with a house falling apart behind her and three struggling children.

"I'm so sorry for everything. You didn't ask for any of this."

Her daughters looked at her quietly. Their heartache made Grace want to destroy Andrew and paint him with an ugly meanness. But something so simple and pure in their love for their father made this impossible. She suggested a bridge instead.

"You know your daddy loves you, wants to be with you, and would do anything for you." Her daughters listened. "So, let's make a pathway leading to him."

A trellised archway sat behind the trailer, near the back of the overgrown pavers. "Look, this is where we'll start."

Grace and her daughters worked diligently through the morning and into the afternoon, bringing load after load of rock in an abandoned rusting wheelbarrow. They lined the trail with stone–erecting a passage in their hearts and minds, connecting them to their father, pausing only once for lunch and ice cream.

When they finished, Grace stood with them in the opening where the path ended and regarded what they had done. They held hands on the banks of a scorched creek, forming a chain—the Holden girls. Fireflies flickered in dusk's plumb glow.

"See, all you have to do is to open your heart to your father, and he will come. Whenever you feel alone or miss him, walk down this path, and hold him close."

Chapter 27

The Name He was Due

Grace and Andrew had agreed that one of the most exciting parts of the birth experience was the surprise of not knowing the baby's gender until the day they were born. Anytime the ultrasound technician asked if they wanted to know the sex of their child, even when Andrew wasn't there, Grace refused, honoring their tradition.

Between Amanda and Ora existed another.

"My baby hasn't moved in over twenty-four hours," Grace told the obstetrician.

The sharp intake of his breath told her what he was thinking: *another pregnant, hormonal woman overreacting.*

"No, you don't understand. Something's wrong."

"How far along are you?"

"Twenty-eight weeks gestation." She threw in the gestation part, hoping he would appreciate that she was a healthcare professional.

"Look, I know you're concerned, but it's not unusual for women at this stage to go for long periods without feeling the fetus move. It's not that the baby isn't moving. It's just that the mother doesn't perceive every motion."

She fought to keep her voice even, not wanting him

to think she was getting hysterical. "This isn't my first pregnancy. I know my baby's patterns."

A long pause ensued. "All right. Call the office if you still haven't felt anything by the morning, and we'll fit you in."

****

Grace's water broke in the middle of the night amidst an unrelenting Nor'easter blizzard.

"You're going to have to drive yourself to the hospital." Andrew's straw hair was plastered down on one side; the other side waved in all directions as he pulled a flannel robe over his sleep pants. "We can't take the girls out in these conditions. It's too dangerous. I'll call around and find someone to come and be with them. That might take a while."

"I'll be there as soon as I can," he called as Grace stepped into the driving snow and wind. With all visual cues obscured, able to see only a few yards in front of her, she navigated using memory and instinct. But that was all she needed—a few feet at a time, then a few more. As the car's headlights perforated the darkness, giving the illusion she was driving through a tunneled meteor shower, the contractions started.

****

In the triage room, Grace scanned the ultrasound technician's face. No light-hearted banter or frivolous questions were forthcoming.

"I'll be right back." The tech left the room briskly without meeting Grace's eyes.

Grace didn't need to hear from the doctor. She already knew. For as vividly as her child's complete form filled the monitor, head tucked down, perfect arms and legs folded together, the infant was lifeless–with no heartbeat.

****

Two hours later, as Grace held her stillborn son in her arms, Andrew came flying into the room, his winter boots caked with snow. "I've been calling and calling. Why didn't you answer me? The nurse wouldn't give any information over the phone, even though I told her I was your husband. This privacy nonsense has gotten out of hand."

From her swollen eyes, the warm tears started again. Andrew registered her countenance. A baby blanket covered her chest.

"Oh, Gracie." He came to her and held her.

Grace pulled the blanket back, and they looked at him together, counting his fingers and toes. Grace traced the soft skin of his limbs and the contours of his face, memorizing them.

"He's perfect." Andrew's voice cradled the question.

"The doctor said he couldn't see an obvious reason this happened. But they'll do some studies. Maybe we'll have answers then."

Andrew nodded and grabbed the box of tissues to hand to Grace. His fingers knocked a piece of paper onto the bed. "What's this?" he asked, picking up the death certificate worksheet. His face blanched; controlled anger flickered on his face.

"No, no, no!" He ripped the paper in half.

"This is the name we decided on. I won't have 'Baby Boy Holden' inscribed on his gravestone," Grace said firmly.

"No, this is the name my *living* son will have." His mouth was a narrow slit, pinched with displeasure.

"Look, I can't. Grace, this is too much. You can pick whatever name you want, an 'A' name, a 'Z' name, any name in the world but not this one." To emphasize his point, he tore the worksheet again into quarters. "I need to get back home. The sitter can't stay long. Let me know your discharge time. If you don't feel up to driving home, call me, and I'll arrange for someone to come and get you." The hard edge of his expression left no room for negotiation–the subject was closed.

Overwhelmed and shaking, Grace pulled her baby to her. She inhaled his simple, earthy scent, held him close, and whispered in his ear. "I'm sorry, Andrew William Holden the Sixth. I'm sorry for how my body failed you and for the remarkable life you'll never know. But above all, I'm sorry I couldn't give you the validation you deserve–the name you were due.

Chapter 28

Code Pink

"Hey, Grace, do you mind?"

She glanced up from her novel and started to forage for an excuse, but who was she kidding? She never minded when Dr. Leland interrupted her.

She scooted over and motioned to the spot on the bench beside her. "I only have a few minutes of my break left. But you're welcome to join me."

"Thanks." He sighed heavily, leaned his head back, and closed his eyes.

"Rough morning?" she asked. Lee nodded. As his breathing regulated, his body relaxed.

Grace returned to her novel. If he didn't feel like talking, that was fine. Reading, however, was impossible. She glanced at his handsome face, serene in the afternoon light. One of these days, we'll talk about what happened in high school.

He opened his eyes. She quickly turned a page in her book, embarrassed.

"That second day in honors biology," —his voice was easy— "You probably don't remember this, but I told you I forgot my textbook and asked if I could share yours."

Grace nodded. "You didn't want to get in trouble."

She recalled the feel of his fingers grazing hers as

he pulled the volume between them. They leaned, heads bent together, their breath blending, looking at cell growth and replication diagrams. He was the best-looking boy she'd ever seen. How had she been so lucky that he had chosen to sit beside her?

"Well, Graceland, you'll be shocked to learn I lied. My textbook was in my backpack all along." His eyes were mischievous. "Mr. Cast was assigning lab partners that day and I figured my chances would increase if I sat next to you, sharing a book."

Grace laughed. "Well, your diabolical plan worked."

Their phones vibrated at the same time. *CODE PINK. CODE PINK. NOT A DRILL! All personnel not involved in patient care—cover exit points. Stay until the all-clear signal.*

Grace and Lee raced through the serenity garden entrance in response to the hospital code indicating an infant abduction was in progress.

"Stay here. I'll cover the next exit," Lee called as he ran down a quarter flight of stairs and planted himself by the door.

Visible from Grace's vantage point, was the top of his dark hair, which hadn't been trimmed in some time, and his white lab coat protecting his hospital scrubs. Was he about to bring up what had happened at the end of their nine months together as lab partners? She would never know.

At every door and elevator throughout the whole hospital, staff members were vigilantly watching for any suspicious activity. Grace couldn't fathom the terror of having your child abducted, and she fervently hoped this was another false alarm. They usually were.

Security chips embedded in the infant's ID bands triggered alarms when a new mother on the postpartum unit wheeled their infant too close to the sensors. But in case an abduction was in progress, Grace's body remained alert while her eyes, taking in the whole of him, merged the man before her with the boy of her past.

On a sweltering day in May, when the school's air conditioning stopped working, Mr. Cast announced an impromptu field trip to the river. He said the generic permission slips the honor biology students had on file would suffice. Students who thought their guardians would object should stay and do homework. No one remained. The goal was to get water samples to examine macro and microscopic specimens. Each year, the class counted the living organisms found in the river and compared them to the years before, trying to ascertain the trending health of the estuary.

Mr. Cast must have known. The excursion was probably his annual spring experiment: pick the hottest day possible and watch how quickly a group of hormonal teenagers granted sudden freedom transformed an organized field trip into a wild celebration.

The afternoon was close to a hundred degrees, and the water in the alcove where they waded, their bare feet sinking in muck, gathering samples in large buckets, was still and cool. Grace never imagined Lee being interested in her, so the pressure was off. She'd been herself. Within sixty seconds, Lee was wet up to his T-shirt. She couldn't take her eyes off him as he scooped water. Tall and graceful, the cotton fabric clung to his lean muscles.

He and his Aunt Ida had eaten at the restaurant where she worked over the weekend. Without hesitation, she dumped her bucket of water over him. "A bucket of protozoans for you," she said in her best waitress voice.

Lee howled with delight and furiously splashed her in return. A class-wide frenzied free-for-all ensued. The water churned and flew in all directions; bodies dove and were dunked; they swam and sank; screeches escalated into the hot afternoon. The shorebirds took flight.

Lee pulled Grace underwater so swiftly that the sun shrunk to the size of a lemon. Silt rose from the bottom, and then he was before her, their limbs entwined in a lucent, fluid embrace. Smiling, he brushed his lips on hers, giving Grace her first kiss. He held her briefly before letting go. Grace pushed upward through the water, guided by luminous rings of light.

CODE PINK IS ALL CLEAR. The announcement came over the intercom system. Thank goodness he's only a good doctor and not a mind reader. Grace glanced in Lee's direction, where two female fourth-year medical students had cornered him. One of them was wildly gesturing. Grace took the stairs, two at a time, escaping the scene of her thoughts, and headed toward her office. She reminded herself to keep everything in perspective. Lee was a flame, drawing all around him to the light. He dated as much as Dallas in high school and likely had kept the trend up through college, med school, and his current life.

Do not let his seemingly sincere way of interacting deceive you. Remember, he is off gallivanting every two weeks. He has another life you know nothing about. Be wary, Grace. Be careful.

Chapter 29

Too Shy for a Tea Party

"Before I forget…" Dallas clutched her stylish handbag as they trudged across Grace's property on the outskirts of Sand Springs. "I showed Bryce the pictures of the documents Dad gave you."

Grace nodded. "And?"

"Well, the second page, the one with the mathematical mish-mash of formulas, the one with measurements?"

"The point, Dallas, get to the point."

Dallas grinned, enjoying seeing her sister trying to act cool but unable to contain herself.

"According to Bryce, it's construction through mathematics. Algebra, geometry, and trig all play crucial roles in architectural design. They're applied to plan blueprints or sketch designs. So, what you have on page two–"

"Is the way to replicate Gizmo?" Grace interrupted her sister. "To scale and to the exact specifications the way Dad intended."

"Not so fast, sister. Bryce says Dad purposely omitted some information. Having the physical prototype will fill in the missing pieces for the manufacturer. Dad didn't want the design to be replicable without Gizmo."

"But with both, it's possible. We are getting close!"

Grace yelled into the sky, "Hear that, Dad? Your girls are figuring this out." She hugged her sister and sent Bryce a thank-you text as the school bus barreled into sight, a cloud of dust kicking up behind the rattling wheels.

"The next step is determining what the computer code means and what Gizmo does," Grace said as her daughters emerged from the dilapidated bus. They called goodbye to the driver and schoolmates, dragging their backpacks behind them. Their joyful voices filled the afternoon air as they sashayed down the dry and dusty drive.

Dallas stopped before the reconstructed double-wide and pushed up her designer shades. "Okay, I must admit, this looks better than I imagined."

"Bryce and his team are miracle workers." Grace's excitement was impossible to suppress. In a week, the construction crew stripped the modular home down to its studs, ripped out the ratty old carpet, and put in drywall and durable laminate flooring. New navy blue siding, doors, and white-trimmed windows went in. The broken steps were repaired. Everything was neat and orderly, and Grace was involved in every step, choosing deeply discounted, builder's-grade kitchen countertops, cabinets, and light fixtures—who was she fooling anyway? Rural Oklahoma was a world apart from Birmingham, Michigan.

"If you think this is nice, wait until you see inside." Grace put in her key, but the door was already open. Maybe she'd forgotten to turn the lock as they rushed out of the house that morning.

Grace, Dallas, and the three girls stood, staring, their mouths agape. The interior looked like a wedge tornado had moved through, leaving a path of destruction in its wake. Couch cushions and chairs dotted the floor. The coffee table was upended.

Every drawer and cupboard was emptied. Not even the refrigerator was spared—frozen peas mixed with slices of bread. Raspberry preserves tenaciously clung to all matter within the shattered radius.

"Who would do such a thing? Why?" Grace's voice trembled with the violation. Then, a realization hit her: the man in the parking garage, the not-so-veiled threats, Gizmo. She raced to her bedroom closet and pulled back her hanging clothes. The duffle bag was open. The contraption was gone. Grace began to cry.

"Mommy, what's wrong?"

A small hand slipped through hers. Grace scanned the upturned face of her youngest child, light freckles scattered across milky skin. In the doorway, Ally had her arm solidly around Amanda's quivering shoulders.

"I can't find what Grandpa gave me." Grace's heart sank.

"You mean the rocks?"

"Gizmo."

Ora tugged Grace's hand, pulling her into the hallway. Standing on her tiptoes, she whispered in Grace's ear as Grace leaned down.

Ora led Grace into the girl's shared bedroom. Even though the trailer had enough rooms for them to have their own, her daughters still wanted to sleep together. Amidst the wreckage was a child-sized table with four chairs. Three seats sported each child's favorite stuffed animals: Alouette, Bur Bur, and Clowny. "Remember our fairy tea party yesterday? You made crustless sandwiches for us." Ora pointed.

The girls had placed little tea cups on saucers before them, and in the fourth chair, in plain sight, sat the porcelain fairy queen, Veronica, in all her majesty, holding her magical wand. The scepter had an abundance of hair ribbons lovingly tied around the shaft and a cascade of tulle protruding from the top.

"Gizmo was too shy to come out of his house," Ora solemnly explained as she handed Grace the wand. "This was his first tea party, so we didn't force him. We wanted him to feel comfortable, so we dressed him up."

Relief flooded Grace as she drew Ora close to her. "I thought Gizmo was stolen," she said as she bent to kiss her daughter's forehead.

"But he's safe and sound in his little tunnel house." Her youngest daughter grinned and padded down the hall to find her sisters.

****

Grace pulled a soapy rag from the bucket and started wiping down the cabinets while Dallas swept debris into a pile. "Thanks for staying and helping me."

"That's what sisters are for, right?" Dallas looked up. "Helping clean up each other's messes."

"Speaking of which." Grace's smile was anemic. Though shaken by the violation of her home, she couldn't put this off any longer.

Dallas didn't try to pretend she didn't know what her sister meant. "So, it turns out I didn't need the fertility medication after all."

"I don't understand why you didn't tell us."

Dallas thew a trampled loaf of bread into the garbage can they'd hauled in from outside. "I don't know. Everyone was so hyped about me starting Clomid. Letting people think the medication was a success was easier."

"Bryce doesn't know?"

Dallas swept trash into a dustpan, her hair shielding her face. "No, he doesn't."

Each sister concentrated on their task. A shielding silence fell around them. The girls had taken their after-school snacks onto the overgrown patio. Grace listened to her daughters' voices through the open screen door.

"Oh, Dallas, before I forget, I ran into that respiratory therapist from your condo complex–what's his name again?'

"Peter."

"Right. I ran into Peter at the hospital. He wanted to know if you were okay. He said he hadn't seen you in some time and appeared genuinely concerned."

Dallas' face paled, and her head lurched forward. Fortunately, the trash receptacle was directly in front of her.

Her sister was holding back, but Grace wouldn't push. Dallas was having a rough go with this pregnancy. Her job as the older sister was to protect and support. What did it matter if Dallas conceived with or without the aid of a fertility medication? What difference did it make if Bryce knew? The important thing was her health and that Dallas and Bryce's dream to start a family was coming true.

Dallas found an unbroken glass and filled it with water from the sink. "I hate this. I hate feeling like I can't tell you everything."

"Why can't you?"

"Because you'll look at me differently."

"I'm your sister, Dallas. Besides, this is a no-judgment zone."

Dallas inhaled as if to say, fair enough. "Where do I start? Okay, here is one cold, hard truth: I'm defective. According to what I've read, I should love being pregnant. I should feel like a life-giving goddess sporting a flower crown, glowing with femininity and feeling one with my body and baby. But I don't enjoy a single thing about the experience. I'm ashamed to admit this, Grace. I despise being pregnant."

"Is that all?" Grace smiled as she flicked a puff of soapsuds in her sister's direction. "I thought you were going to tell me you're having an affair and that the baby isn't Bryce's."

Grace didn't think her sister had any remaining stomach contents. Dallas proved her wrong. As she finished retching and opened her mouth as if to reply, the girls burst through the back door, a whirlwind of energy and excitement.

Ally was holding a scraggly apricot and white, mewling kitten. "We found her hiding in the bushes. She told us her name is Tinkerbell, and we're her long-lost family."

Chapter 30

Forever Is a Long Time

Dallas continued her appointments with Dr. Kay, though, week after week, when she asked annoying, probing questions, she vowed never to return.

"How do you feel getting weighed at every doctor's visit?"

"I hate it. Stepping on the scale reinforces how out of control my body is getting."

Dr. Kay's eyes did the probing.

Dallas sighed. "My obstetrician's office is great. I was a mess, crying and throwing a mini tantrum each time I had to weigh in. Now, I close my eyes and hop on the scale. The assistant makes a note in my chart but doesn't say anything. My doctor doesn't want me to fixate on weight gain. The goal is to have a healthy baby, so I count my nutritional intake instead of calories. I track what I eat and review the content with a dietitian at every visit."

"It sounds like you have a supportive team."

"I would have fallen apart without them. Every visit, I learn what part of my baby is growing. That way, I can visualize how my healthy habits contribute to his well-being. It's the only way I can tolerate my body expanding to accommodate a sprouting pumpkin. Don't get me wrong. I still despise every aspect of pregnancy. I hope this doesn't mean I'll hate being a mom."

With the help of Dr, Kay and her penetrating questions, Dallas was gaining insights into her behavioral patterns. If only she could talk to Grace about everything, seeing Dr. Kay might not be necessary. And why did she hide from her sister and husband that she was seeing a professional? Her life was crumbling and the people she cared about the most were unaware. How messed up was it that her ex-psychiatrist and now Dr. Kay's numbers were in her contacts under a pseudonym, yet Peter's number was out there for all to see? An old friend she had known longer than Bryce, an acquaintance. If only they knew, they would see her flawed core. She was nothing like Bryce or her sister, loyal to a fault.

Her sister's response to the news that she hated being pregnant wasn't what Dallas expected. Grace was understanding. "There's no right way to experience pregnancy. I remember feeling miserable at times; the weight on my bladder made me feel like I had to pee, and the pressure on my diaphragm made eating and sleeping difficult." Dallas was ready to share more when her nieces exploded onto the scene, holding the newly found Tinkerbell.

While Grace's comments were reassuring, Dallas remembered the conversation with her sister that changed everything. After Bryce proposed, Dallas called Grace, hoping she would help her determine why she was reluctant to accept Bryce's offer.

Bryce's marriage proposal was sweet and unassuming. He tucked the engagement ring in the pocket of her favorite fleece robe. When she looked at him in surprise and didn't answer immediately, he didn't become defensive, angry, or hurt. He simply said, "I want you in my life forever. And forever is a long time, so take as long as you need before answering."

But when Dallas called Grace, she hadn't been able to ask. Grace was over the moon, flush with the pregnancy of her second child. She had a husband she loved, who loved her, and she likened the bearing of children to being in a constant state of life-altering meditation. Dallas swallowed. A relationship that took existence to the next level, stability, someone who loved you beyond comprehension and would never walk away, that was what she wanted. And having children sounded downright glamorous.

Count me in. What am I so afraid of? Even before she ended the call with Grace that night, she texted Bryce, —*I'm all in! YES!*—

****

Grace breathed a sigh of relief as she sat on the bench beside Ronnie in the hospital's serenity garden. No one else was around.

"I can't tell you how much this means to me." She retrieved Gizmo from her work bag. "Having 3-D copies of Gizmo will make me feel better. Thank Maya and her shop teacher for doing this."

Ronnie took the contraption from her, looking at Grace skeptically. "You think this is what they were looking for when they looted your home?"

"I'm not exactly rolling in dough, Ronnie. They didn't toss my double wide, looking for money or jewelry. They took the sedimentary rocks Dad gave me and the girls, a lot of good that will do them. But they don't know that. No, Gizmo is the only reason that makes sense. Here, let me show you how he works." She pushed the lever forward, and from the sheath, Gizmo emerged in all his complicated glory.

"What in the world is that?" A masculine voice behind the bench made Grace jump.

Since the break-in, she felt on edge, like someone was watching her. She rode an emotional roller coaster. One moment, she'd feel angry at the violation, then worry and fear crept in. Nightmares interrupted troubled sleep. Often, she'd jump from bed, turning on the lights to check the doors. Then she'd inspect the windows, listening carefully to every sound, the wind pulling its fingers across the trailer's siding, a truck speeding down the gravel road. Everyday noises startled her, making her believe the thugs had returned and were coming in to harm her family. Since the break-in, she had not left Gizmo alone. She even brought him to work.

"Oh my gosh, I didn't mean to scare you, Grace. I'm sorry." Lee's eyes were deep emerald in the garden light, mirroring compassion and concern.

"It's okay." She relaxed as he slid next to her.

"Can I look?"

Lee reached across Grace, the hair curled on the back of his head, whispering close to his neck.

Ronnie handed him the device, and Grace leaned in, showing him how Gizmo worked.

"This part looks like a complicated energy converter or generator," he said as he ran his fingers over the model. As if to answer a question she hadn't asked, he said, "My dad used to tinker a lot. He'd get all sorts of gadgets that didn't work from the dump or scavenge them on trash days. He'd jerry-rig, then sell them."

Grace absorbed the information. In high school, Lee hadn't talked about his parents. He was ten when he'd moved from rural Oklahoma to live with his Aunt Ida in Tulsa, but that was all she knew.

"I've got to go work on some discharge planning." Ronnie stood, took Gizmo, returned him to his hidden state, and placed him in her oversized purse. "Grace, I'll get the original and duplicates to you as soon as possible."

Grace nodded, instantly afraid as she tracked her friend's departure. She hoped today wouldn't be the day some random purse snatcher ran off with Ronnie's bag. Replication was needed. Her father's legacy depended on Gizmo, but Grace almost lost him in the burglary. She had to be vigilant.

****

After stopping for groceries on her way home, Grace called Ronnie. Gizmo was safely locked in the storage closet of Mr. Mills, the shop teacher. Reproduction was going to start tomorrow. Grace breathed a sigh of relief as she eased onto the busy thoroughfare when a pickup abruptly swung into the lane before her. She responded, slamming on her brakes, stopping a few inches from his bumper. She had the minimal car insurance allowable by law, and affording her ancient vehicle had been difficult enough. Grace glanced into her rearview mirror and clenched the steering wheel as a shiny BMW approached. *Look up, Mister, please. If you don't slow down, you're going to–.* The force of the impact pushed her into the stopped truck.

She leaped from her seat and raced to the driver's door behind her.

"Are you okay?"

Grace scanned him, doing a cursory assessment. She had to fight the urge to reach in and take his pulse.

He exited his vehicle, seemingly stunned. Noticing Grace's dangling bumper, he moved closer to inspect his front end. His gait was steady. He didn't appear injured. Not a mark was on his car.

The impeccably dressed man smiled. "Wait a second, and I'll get you my insurance info."

After a few minutes of rummaging through his glove compartment, he returned and handed her a slip of paper. "My name, phone number, and insurance company." I'll call them right away, don't worry. I'll take care of the repair costs. I was distracted. This was my fault."

Grace gave him her contact information. He took a picture of her bumper with his cell. She reflexively felt her scrub pocket. Her phone nestled next to a few alcohol wipes. She paused. "Shouldn't we file a police report?"

"For a minor fender bender, the cops might take an hour or so to respond. I'm sure we both have better ways to spend our time."

Grace nodded assent. She had fifteen minutes until the bus dropped off her girls.

Grace slid into the front seat and turned the ignition. Only then did she realize the driver in front of her, the one she had tapped, hadn't exchanged his information. Maybe he didn't have insurance and didn't want to get involved. The truck was long gone.

But also missing from the passenger seat was her

hospital bag, where she usually kept Gizmo and her purse. A glance in her rearview mirror confirmed what she already knew. The BMW was gone, too. She didn't think to get his license plate number in her rush to exchange information and ensure the man wasn't hurt. She didn't need to call any numbers on the paper he had given her to know the man behind the wheel had not only deceived her but was part of something bigger. While he was keeping her busy, someone had stolen her personal belongings.

She willed herself to remain calm as she drove home. The parking lot bully, a break-in, and now an orchestrated accident–she did not doubt that the Oil and Gas Company was behind everything. The only advantage Grace had was that Caligula had no idea what they were looking for.

Maybe now the police would believe her. The officer who had taken her initial report was kind but stated they didn't have the human resources to follow up on a parking lot threat or the theft of rocks. Grace wasn't optimistic that a stolen work bag and purse would bump her case any higher; nonetheless, she would try.

She promised her father she would see this through, but the threats were escalating. Caligula was becoming desperate. Grace's resolve wavered. How far would they go? A rise of panic choked her. Cars whipped around her on the congested four-lane thoroughfare. In the distance, a train horn blared, and a siren grew louder as a fire truck approached. Try as she might, she could not find a spot to pull over.

Chapter 31

Her Predicament

Dallas followed her obstetrician's exercise parameters and threw in some additional butt exercises for good measure. Side lunges came while she brushed her teeth, calf raises, and leg lifts while waiting for the microwave to heat up. Nothing was better than a series of thirty-second gluteal squeezes while sitting at her desk in the bank or at a red light. Her persistence paid off. Friends told her, "From behind, you can't even tell that you're pregnant." That was her intent.

She stood with her back to the gym entrance in form-fitting workout attire, performing her light weight lifting.

As the electronically controlled door opened, Dallas held her breath. She didn't need to turn around to see who was there, so she persisted with arm curls until he was behind her.

"Hello, stranger. I've missed you." His breath was familiar and intimate.

Putting this off any longer was untenable. Dallas took a deep breath and slowly turned around. Her eyes locked on Peter as he took in the whole of her—six months pregnant. His smile faded, and shock registered. Yet he didn't back away or turn with disgust, as she had predicted.

"You're pregnant?"

Yes, Captain Obvious. She watched him simultaneously digest the information while performing internal calculations.

"Is it…?"

He couldn't bring himself to ask more.

"I don't know."

Then the very thing she promised herself she wouldn't do transpired: her eyes welled with tears.

Peter drew her into a hug.

He let her cry.

The gym was a safe place. Bryce was not a fan of regimented workouts, saying he got enough exercise at the construction sites. Since their marriage, he had yet to access the workout area.

Dallas had held everything in for so long that she couldn't stop. This predicament was something she'd never meant to happen.

When she first met Peter, before she knew Bryce, he made it clear he was a bachelor for life: no wife, no kids, no complications. Dallas, taking him at his word, had been happy with the arrangement. She, too, didn't want encumbrances. Her pattern, established in high school, had continued into adulthood. *I'm just like Dad, always looking for the next best thing.*

Undeniable was the thrill of starting new relationships. Oh, how Dallas relished the sweet spot where intrigue and passion consumed everything before the monotony of routine stole the magic. Opportunity led to a fantasy world where each encounter jolted awake her numb system. She and Peter shared the same molecular makeup. Never had jealousy or attachment been an issue. When one needed the other, they were there. And arising from this arrangement rose an unexpected friendship.

After Dallas accepted Bryce's proposal, she was determined. There would be no one else. Peter respected her decision, and though they'd run into each other at the pool, a barbecue, a mutual friend's gathering, or a planned workout in the gym, Dallas had remained faithful, at least for the first four years of her marriage.

"Is this something you wanted?" he whispered into her hair.

She stepped back and scrutinized him, this friend, sometimes lover, someone who appreciated the unorthodox parts of her and never made her feel trashy or less valuable. "I thought so." She tried to smile, aware of how her mascara had probably streaked her foundation and how puffy her eyes must look.

"Does Bryce know that, maybe?"

"No! No one knows. Not even my mother or sister." She inhaled a deep breath. "But I'm seeing a therapist, and she's helping me work through things."

Dallas picked up her weights and resumed her routine.

Peter picked up a bulkier pair of dumbbells and began to exercise alongside her. "You're going through some heavy stuff," he said.

"No shit."

"If you need help with anything, to talk, scream, whatever, I'm here."

She looked in the mirror before her. Peter stared intently at her reflected image. Dallas's nod was barely perceptible, but it was an acknowledgment. Side by side, they worked out and engaged in a form of communication—one without words.

Chapter 32

Security Codes

Bryce talked Grace into getting a surveillance system. But when the bundle arrived on her doorstep, with detailed instructions on installation, her brother-in-law was away at a remote construction site.

"It's no big deal waiting another week until Bryce returns." Grace took a bite of her sandwich as Lee slid into the chair beside Ronnie, directly across the cafeteria table from Grace. She continued talking, trying to maintain her train of thought, "I'd try installing it myself, but I don't think I have the right tools, and I'd hate to mess it up."

Lee peeled the cellophane off the top of his microwaved lunch. "Hope you don't mind me joining you." He took a bite of the macaroni and cheese and swallowed before continuing. "I've been thinking about your 'accident,'" he said, addressing Grace while making air quotes around the word accident. "Caligula has someone following you or a tracking chip on your car. How else would they have been able to orchestrate stealing your purse and bag? There's no way they could predict you would stop for groceries at that time and place."

Grace was incredulous. "A tracking device on my car? You can't be serious. This is the stuff of television shows, not a boring single-mom nurse's life."

Yet, since her first run-in with the man in the garage, she was constantly on alert, looking around and furtively peering into her side and rearview mirrors as if someone was watching her. "What can I do?"

"A friend of mine, Brian, owns an auto repair shop. He'll go over your car and search for hidden devices." Lee scrolled through his phone and scratched a number on a paper napkin. "Here you go. And as far as your security system goes, I'll help you set it up. Handyman is my middle name."

Ronnie raised an eyebrow.

"It's all good, Lee," Grace replied. Glancing at her watch, she started packing her lunch bag. "You're leaving tomorrow, anyway. Bryce will be back soon. He'll help me."

"You have tomorrow off, right?" He took a bite of his apple and waited.

"Sure. But at the end of this shift, your two-week break starts."

"I don't have to leave until the afternoon. I'll help you get the system up and running and be on my way."

Grace stood, pushed her chair in, and was about to protest when Lee touched her arm. "Friends are supposed to help friends. Come on, Grace, let me in."

His face was open, expectant in a hopeful way.

"Okay, thanks." Apparently, her brain had already decided. "I'll text you the address."

"Grace," he called as she was walking away. *He's already having second thoughts.* She turned.

"If you're going to text, don't you need my number?"

Grace hoped he didn't notice the flush in her

cheeks as she handed him her phone. He typed in his contact information.

"Smooth, you two. Smooth." Ronnie grinned.

"Whatever," Grace said with a smile. She couldn't believe she had succumbed to what she had sworn not to do. She had Lee's number, and soon, he would have hers.

****

"I told Bryce this complicated system is unnecessary." Grace held the ladder while Lee mounted a camera on the side of her double-wide. The vast Oklahoma sky shone like a polished blue gemstone, a backdrop to October's burnt oranges and apple red foliage.

"Regaining a sense of peace and control after a break-in is important."

"I felt this was a safe place for my daughters. Now, I can't let my guard down. I keep telling myself I shouldn't make such a big deal out of it. Thankfully, no one was home or hurt. Caligula should back off once I figure all this Gizmo stuff out."

"Your responses are normal." He reached down. "Can you hand me the drill?"

Wearing a gray heathered T-shirt and faded jeans, he made a hole for the power cable confidently and efficiently, as if he lived there. "All done." He climbed from the ladder, a sense of relief lacing his words. "Let me see your phone." With a quick gesture, Lee showcased the security app on her device, revealing a world of possibilities. "Here, you have full control over the system remotely. You can monitor your camera feed, adjust your interior lighting, and lock or unlock doors." Leaning in closer, he showed Grace the features while she tried to focus on his instructions.

"The motion sensors and smart cameras will alert you to any activity in and around your house. If something happens, the surveillance service will notify you."

Grace shoved the phone into her back pocket. "Thanks again for helping out." She paused and rolled a pebble with her toe. The sparkling lavender nail polish Ally had applied three nights before was already starting to chip. "You want a water, soda, or Capri Sun pouch before hitting the road?" The offer was the least she could do.

He stared, taking her in. "I have a little time. Water will be fine."

"Ice juice it is. I'll meet you on the back patio."

Exiting through the back door, Grace picked her way over the rough pavers and handed him a glass. As he took the water, a raised circular area of lighter-colored skin rose in the middle of his right palm. Grace remembered seeing this in high school and was never comfortable asking him about it. Now, she recognized the aberration for what it was–scar tissue. The past was seared into his flesh. She sat in the deck chair beside him.

He tilted his head back and drank half the glass. "As time goes by and with these safety measures in place," he began, a note of assurance in his voice, "coping will become easier. You'll regain peace of mind, and your home will feel safe again."

She smiled. "How did you get so smart?"

"Honors Biology."

Grace laughed. Sitting next to an old friend, in chairs so close she could reach to touch his hand, was good and a little unnerving.

The whimsical back garden chock full of hidden fairy houses and mythical creatures, with twinkling lights strewn along the trellis, tucked among the overgrown rose bushes and foliage, was a glimpse into their lives, a sacred space shared only by those in their inner circle.

"A magical space where childhood dreams flourish," he said the words so softly that Grace wasn't sure she heard correctly.

"I beg your pardon?"

"Nothing…" He shook his head as if embarrassed. "One peril of living alone is sometimes you say inner thoughts aloud. Hey, is that a magnolia warbler?"

That's one way to change the subject, but why push? Grace followed his gaze—a bright yellow and black bird perched on the tip of a conifer branch. An edged white band spanned its outer tail feathers.

"Do you remember seeing a bouquet of warblers at Oxley Nature Center when we were studying fall migration?" Grace asked.

"I do. It seemed unfathomable that such a tiny creature could make such an arduous journey from Canada to Central America."

"Amazing, isn't it?" Grace wondered. "I saw a magnolia warbler at Tawas State Park in Michigan one summer. I'd just finished swimming in Lake Huron, and there he was, chirping away. What if this guy is the same one? You never know."

The bird flew away as an orange and white kitten sauntered onto the pavers and jumped onto a cushioned bench. A queen on a throne—the creature regarded them and issued a pathetically reproachful meow.

"Lee Leland, I'd like to introduce you to Tinkerbell. She's incredibly tolerant, allowing the girls to dress her in doll clothes and colorful socks. But she also gets her fill of whatever we're eating, milk from cereal bowls, bites of a sandwich, chunks of pizza."

The cat tilted its head, listening for a reasoned response. It blinked yellow eyes, then shamelessly groomed her outstretched limb.

Lee leaned back in his chair and extended his legs. "Aunt Ida had an old tortie. She was a sassy old thing, kind of like my aunt."

"I remember her," Grace responded.

"The cat or Aunt Ida?"

"Both."

"She liked you."

"The cat or Aunt Ida?

"Both, actually."

Grace laughed.

He took another draw of water. "Without her, Aunt Ida, not the cat, I don't know where I'd be."

Without fail, Lee appeared exhausted at the end of his two-week work stretch. But today, in the circles of fatigue around his eyes, under the surface of his skin, pulsed a pain she hadn't seen before.

"She was clairvoyant, you know." His voice was distant.

"The cat?"

He chuckled, low and rumbling. "Haha. My grandmother, my mom, and her sister, Ida, had it. Though a lot of good it did anyone. I kept asking Aunt Ida what was going to happen. And she told me my future would be different than I imagined. Of course, as a teenager, I thought I'd make the big leagues."

"You went to Stanford on a baseball scholarship. What happened?"

"I graduated with a degree in biology, was drafted by the Padres, and played one season of A-Ball. When Aunt Ida was diagnosed with stage four colon cancer, everything changed. I came back to care for her. I studied for the MCAT, and after she died, I enrolled in med school."

While talking, Lee absentmindedly rubbed the fingers of her hand between his own, the way he would gently palpate an appendage for broken bones.

"And what about you, Grace? You were all fired up in high school to be an obstetrician or nurse midwife."

"You remember?"

"Of course. We were together fifty minutes a day, five days a week, for nine months. We got to know each other."

"We did, and we didn't." Grace paused. "You know the platitudes, life happened. Things don't always turn out as planned." Why was she feeling vulnerable? She started to say more, to disclose what transpired, something she hadn't told anyone, even Andrew. But she stopped. Would he look at her differently? Would he understand? Besides, time was running out. The school bus was due in half an hour, and Lee had to get going.

"I don't want to keep you from your other life." Grace stood, took his glass, and walked with him toward his truck. A sudden gust of wind caused sleeves of bumblebee yellow and rich merlot leaves to fall around them.

"You'll have to come with me sometime."

Was he kidding? Surely he was. *Play it cool, Grace. Shrug it off.* "Nice as that might be, I can't drop everything and go gallivanting for two weeks. My life doesn't work that way."

"You mentioned your daughters will be with their father over winter break. You could come then."

"I can't take two weeks off from work. I haven't worked long enough to accrue vacation time."

"But you could take a day or two and hook them onto your scheduled days off."

"And jet-set back to Tulsa from wherever you are?"

"I'd ensure you were back when you needed to be."

"Sounds tempting." She smiled. The divorce papers were waiting in Michigan. She and Andrew had a joint appointment with their attorneys to finalize the terms. Grace would sign the document when she flew with the girls over Thanksgiving break. She wouldn't take Lee up on his offer even though a few days with a drop-dead handsome man in an exotic locale might be what the doctor ordered.

Grace stood by the truck's door as he climbed in.

"Think about it." He took her hand and softly kissed the pulse point on the inside of her wrist. The feathery nerves linked to her brain fired on all cylinders.

As if aware of the impact of his solitary kiss, he smiled. "Take care, Grace. Get your car into the shop. Brian will check it for bugs. See you in a couple of weeks."

She waited until the sound of his wheels on the road dissolved into silence. The powder kicked up by his truck settled like a delicate sprinkle of fairy dust all around her.

Chapter 33

The Sandman

"Special delivery." A hospital volunteer knocked on the side of Grace's cubical and brought in a brightly-hued, whimsical floral arrangement featuring tulips, daisies, and lilies. "There's a card tucked in the side." The silver-haired woman winked conspiratorially before pushing her delivery cart off in another direction.

"A secret admirer?" Ronnie's workspace was adjacent to hers.

No one had sent Grace flowers since the birth of Ora. Who would send them to her now? "I don't know who they could be from." Maybe a name mix-up or the bouquet had been misdelivered. Grace's fingers trembled as she slid open the small envelope and retrieved a card.

"To my guardian angel. Thanks to you, I'm alive. I even got rid of the temporary pacemaker! Fondly, your earth-born mortal, Frank Fresno."

"Too bad Lee isn't around to see your flowers. It might make him jealous." Ronnie sat in the wheeled chair in front of Grace's desk and spun around. "I'd bet my bottom dollar that man's got something for you."

Grace leaned in to smell the fragrant arrangement, hoping Ronnie wouldn't see the heat rising in her face.

"Your imagination is in overdrive." She didn't mention that he'd asked her to accompany him on one of his monthly excursions. Ronnie wouldn't let her hear the end of that one. "He doesn't see me as more than a colleague and an old friend."

"Oh, sister, that's where you are wrong. I've been observing how he acts around you. If you were a movie, he'd watch you over and over again."

Grace laughed, saying with unconcealed affection, "You're off your rocker, you know that?"

Ronnie stood to leave, still grinning. "I may be crazy as a Betsy Bug, but anyone can see he's happier than a hog in mud when he's around you."

Grace crumpled her 'to-do' list and threw the ball at her friend as she left the cubicle.

Ronnie had one foot in the hall when she stopped. "Before I forget, I have Gizmo and his clone ready to give back to you. They're in my car. After your shift is over, I'll get them for you. The shop teacher, Mr. Mills, kept a copy, and I have one, too."

"So if my main squeeze gets stolen, his progeny will live on to tell of his legacy. Thank you, my friend!"

Grace glanced at her creased worklist. She had to start two more IVs and had ten lines to check. Additionally, she had to submit her monthly audits by the time she left work. All doable, provided some emergency didn't crop up. She felt lighter than she had in days. Gizmo had duplicates, Mr. Fresno's flowers had given her insight into what the final page of computer code might mean, and tonight, she and the girls were celebrating her mom's birthday with Bryce and Dallas. Still, more importantly, tomorrow, Lee would be back after his two-week hiatus. She could not wait to see him.

****

Ora was dawdling, as usual. Distracted by the contents of her backpack, she showed her sisters the drawings of Tinkerbell she'd worked on that afternoon in her Pre-K class. Five minutes after the final school bell rang, their bus was still nowhere in sight.

"Come on, Ora. We must get going. The bus will be here any minute. You know Ms. Emwah hates slowpokes," Ally said in her bossy, older sister voice, pushing the papers back into Ora's pack as fast as Ora pulled them out when the massive man with a nose in the shape of a light bulb appeared under the sugar maple tree and smiled at them.

Ally stepped before Amanda and Ora, trying to look as big as possible. "Mommy says we shouldn't talk to strangers." The school bus rattled around a distant bend. In a few minutes, they'd be on board. The other children were already waiting in line.

"She is smart, that mother of yours. But, you see, we aren't strangers at all."

"Yes, we are," Ora piped up, though maybe he was right. His voice sounded familiar and deep, like the father lion from her favorite movie.

"We've never seen you before," Amanda chimed in, feeling emboldened by her sisters, though her knees wobbled. The man was so big that he blocked her view of the late afternoon sun. He was taller than her father.

"I know your mother. I also knew your Grandpa Walker before he died. I'm looking forward to getting to know your Grandma Mary and Aunt Dallas too."

Ally processed the information. She slung her arms protectively around her sisters. Something didn't feel right. What he said seemed friendly, but his black eyes didn't match his words.

"I don't want to scare you, girls. I only wanted to say hello and let you know you can trust me. I'm a friend of the family. Look, I brought you a present." He pulled a bejeweled collar with a tinkling bell attached from his suit pocket. "This is for your kitten. Only a friend would know about your kitty cat. See, the collar has your phone number and address on the tags in case she gets lost. You can never be too careful."

"Thank you," stammered Amanda. She stepped forward and shook his hand before taking the gift. Her mother told them that kindness didn't cost anything and acts of consideration might make a difference in someone's life. She hoped he was one of those people. His haircut did remind her of the astronaut from the toy movie, so maybe they could trust him. Something in his face softened as she grasped his meaty fingers. What if he had a daughter her age? He certainly knew how to choose a perfect kitty collar.

Ally took charge. "If you're not a stranger, why don't we know your name?"

"Forgive me for not properly introducing myself." The family friend stretched a smile with teeth that didn't fit his face. "Call me the Sandman." He solemnly shook Ally's outstretched hand. "I'm planning a big surprise for your mommy. And it would wreck the surprise if you told her about me. You know how to keep a secret, don't you?"

The three girls nodded. "Well, I look forward to seeing you again, young ladies."

The Sandman slipped away when the bus pulled in front of the school. Ally, Amanda, and Ora scuttled like jackrabbits up the steps and pressed their faces to the large windows, trying to see where he had gone. But like the character in their grandma's folklore book, who sprinkled moon dust into children's eyes at night, had seeing him just been a dream?

Chapter 34

To You

Everyone Mary loved was gathered to celebrate her birthday in her favorite Mexican restaurant on the edge of campus. The woven textures and rich colors felt like the fabric of her life. The boisterous party was in full swing when Alberto Rodriguez walked in with a piled-high plate of golden-brown sopaipillas. As he placed the dish before her, the assemblage burst into unrestrained song, "Happy Birthday To You." Though there were no candles, Mary closed her eyes and made a wish.

Her granddaughters, Ally, Amanda, and Ora, squealed with delight. Each grabbed a pastry and put it on their plates before wrestling over the solitary plastic honey bear. They settled down when Alberto seized two more receptacles from behind the counter strung with chili peppers.

Grace ripped a corner of the doughy delight and poured a smear of honey into the pocket. "I think we're close to figuring out the Gizmo Affair." Her eyes were eager and shining.

Mary nodded. "Do tell."

Her oldest daughter continued. "We have a biodegradable, retrievable, modular energy converter slash generator. Everything supports that hypothesis."

Though in the process of devouring dessert, all adult attention riveted on Grace. "The third page of formulas is computer coding. One of our information tech guys at work says it looks like an API, or application programming interface, which is software that allows applications to communicate with each other."

"English, please," Mary interjected.

"I think this code is a way to monitor Gizmo remotely. One of my patients with a pacemaker reminded me of a conversation I had with Dad."

"Go on." Dallas pushed back her plate; she'd eaten half a sopaipilla. Bryce put a hand over Dallas's and squeezed. They were all invested.

"An implanted pacemaker continuously monitors its own function, recording information about the efficacy of the leads, battery life, and heart rhythm. The pacemaker stores the data. Remote monitoring allows the device to communicate with the clinic, saving the patient from repeatedly going in for an implant check. This concept fascinated Dad. With a pacemaker, the patient comes in for a replacement when a battery has a certain amount of juice left. So why would Gizmo be any different? The engineers can tell if Gizmo is operating optimally through remote data transmission. And when the data shows his functioning decreasing, there'd be a point when retrieving him from the earth and deploying a new unit would make sense."

Mary clapped her hands excitedly. "Grace, you've done it!"

"We've done it, Mom. All of you guys had valuable input, and I've had help from some friends along the way."

There it was–the word 'friends,' accompanied by a glow in Grace's face that Mary had not seen in a long time. Dallas peered conspiratorially at Grace and smiled knowingly. Mary had all the information she needed. Who did her daughters think they were fooling?

Dallas was another story. The pregnancy was taking its toll on her, but an additional layer of tumult simmered below the surface.

Her daughters were close growing up. Even though time and experience had distanced them, Mary was grateful to see them closing the gap.

"I'm still unsure what Gizmo's function is or what we're supposed to do with the information once we know everything," Grace continued.

"We know Caligula is hell-bent on getting Gizmo and the formulas," Mary interjected. "This gadget has the potential to bring in a boatload of money."

"It's not about money," Grace exclaimed, looking to her family for support and confirmation.

"Of course not," Dallas replied.

"The money isn't important to us, but it is to them," Mary furthered.

"Dad had something bigger in mind." Grace paused. "He said this was his gift to the earth and humankind to compensate for the harm he caused. And besides, we know what will happen if we're suddenly swimming in cash."

"The vultures would swoop in, saying the money belongs to them. They'd argue that it's their property," Dallas said, "tying us up in a courtroom for years."

"The break-in and the accident prove they're getting desperate. Caligula's actions are escalating." Flanked by her daughters, Mary grabbed their hands.

"One of the university's top geophysicists returns from sabbatical after Thanksgiving. I say we get the information to him in pieces, of course, and see what he thinks."

"Perfect." Grace stood and started stacking the dinner plates. Having worked as a Tequila N' Tacos server throughout high school, Grace's reflexes were programmed. "I'll be back with the girls from their break in Michigan." The muscles in Grace's face tightened, even as she tried to act brave. This trip would be the last time Grace flew with them. Over the winter holidays, they all would be old enough to fly as unaccompanied minors. Having no way to ease her adult daughter's angst was difficult. Their problems were easier to fix when they were children.

Grace handed the waitress her collection of dishes and continued helping clear the table. After all, Leticia was Mr. Rodriguez's granddaughter and was like family. Mr. Rodriguez nodded in appreciation as he walked in bearing a gargantuan-sized bouquet of brightly hued sunflowers and red roses.

He placed the arrangement before the birthday girl, whose eyes widened with surprise. "My favorites! You guys already gave me a present. You didn't have to do this." She beamed.

Dallas and Grace looked at each other quizzically, then at Bryce, who shook his head.

"Mom," Dallas started, "I wish we'd been that thoughtful."

Mary felt the blood leave her face. "Alberto?" She regarded her longtime friend, who shrugged.

"The florist who made the delivery said I was to give them to you. And if you didn't show up, I promised her I would drop off the arrangement at your house. She didn't say anything more than that."

"The card, Mom, the card!" Grace pointed to an envelope taped to the cellophane. The girls stopped playing with Mr. Rodriguez's great-grandchildren and perched on the adults' knees. Amanda snuggled next to Bryce, who had one arm around his niece and another around Dallas. Ora leaned against her grandmother, trying to read her expression upside down, while Ally had her mother all to herself.

Mary read the typed letter inside the card. "I don't understand." She considered Grace and Dallas, softly saying, "You probably don't know this. Why would you? But my birthday was also your father's and my anniversary. He said he never wanted to forget either day, and you know how he'd get when involved in a project."

"Wait. These flowers are from Dad?" Dallas asked incredulously

"He's courting you from the beyond!" Grace, a cheerleader for a happy ending, smiled and hugged Ally. "I told you that the first poem was a love letter to you, but you wouldn't believe me. He must have made arrangements before he died to have these delivered. And knowing we came here for your birthday, even after he left us, means he never stopped caring. How romantic!"

Bryce stared lovingly at Dallas, who returned his gaze. She leaned against his shoulder and sighed. "Did he sign the letter?" Dallas reached out, asking to see. Mary, uncharacteristically, folded the paper and shoved it in her purse.

"He did," was all she said as she gently extricated

Ora, placing a kiss atop her golden locks, and stood. "Thank you all for a memorable birthday celebration."

****

Mary waited until Grace buckled her children into their car seats, until Bryce helped his seventh-month-pregnant wife into the car, and until the vehicles bearing her family pulled from the near-empty parking lot and were on their way home before retrieving the poem from her purse. Tears gathered in the corners of her eyes as she read the words amidst an overwhelming wash of fresh roses and unearthed grief.

HAPPY BIRTHDAY–HAPPY ANNIVERSARY

To my first love, to my first wife. I apologize. It took an eternity for my

Orbit to return. It took another life. For me, to see

You, fully. And what could be. Wisdom, laughter, articulate insight. You are an

Orchid. Standing alone in the dark of night. Always shining true.

Understand. I can no longer fight gravity. Pulling me forever back to you.

And, as always, he signed the poem, *Eternally yours, Michael.* She traced the cursive of his closing salutation repeatedly until she could feel his hands move over her body, hear his breath in her ear. *What are you doing, Michael? I promised myself I'd never give you that power again. Yet here you are, even after death, inserting yourself into our lives, changing everything.*

Chapter 35

What You Can Give

Dallas rubbed her eyes and peered into the darkness. "Where are we?" The car's motion, the heater's warmth, a belly full of baby, and food must have caused her to doze off. Her mother's birthday party had been an eventful topping to a long and tiring day.

"I want to show you something." Bryce opened the car door and helped her onto a cobblestone drive. "This house isn't on the market yet, but it will be soon." He pulled a key from his pocket.

"Where did you get that?"

"Mr. Titan," Bryce responded.

"He's the owner of the new boutique store you're building on Memorial, right?"

Bryce nodded. "He and his sister grew up in this house. He'd love for a young family to move in. If we want the place, he said he'll sell it at the list price so we don't have to get into a bidding war."

"And you're getting the inside scoop because you are a brilliant builder with honor and integrity, doing such a quality job that he views you like a son." Even to herself, the words sounded sarcastic and cold, but the truth was, she meant them. Bryce was all those things. *Damn it, Dallas*, she chastised herself. This *is your husband.* Maybe *this is what Dr. Kay was talking about—a distancing technique.* She squeezed his arm.

He smiled wistfully, accepting. "Something like that."

Bryce ran his hands across the stucco exterior as they approached the front door and looked up at the tiled roof. "She's a beauty, isn't she? Built in the 1920s, Mediterranean style."

He let her into the Spanish-tiled foyer. "It's a three-bedroom, two-bath, 2000-square-foot home. Perfect for our family."

"Can we even afford this?"

"If we use the money your dad left, we can put enough down so our mortgage would be about the same as we're paying now. And we've built enough equity in our condo so that we can make any changes you want. By the time our baby is born, the renovations will be complete."

As Dallas followed Bryce through the meandering home, she couldn't stop thinking about the party's surprise ending. What had her father's enormous bouquet of roses and sunflowers been about? Flowers from the grave? Did this mean he never stopped loving their mother, or did his feelings return as he was dying? Was this his way of saying he'd made a mistake and had regrets? Dallas's reaction to the events surprised her. She'd always identified more with her father. This gesture shattered what she believed to be true.

With the house tour complete, Bryce and Dallas stood in the updated kitchen, looking through the double casement window to a charming backyard with a fountain in the center. "Can you see us outdoors in the spring, having our morning coffee and watching our little one run around? Old-world elegance meets modern-day living. What do you think, Dallas?" The excitement in Bryce's voice was palpable, but she was overwhelmed with heaviness.

She sank into one of the upholstered chairs. "I don't know."

He sank before her, taking her hands and looking directly into her eyes. "I thought this was what you wanted. You told me you wanted a house the day you learned about your inheritance."

"I know."

"But anytime I show you pictures online, suggest meeting with a real estate agent, or talk about going to an open house, I feel you shutting down." His voice was gentle and non-accusatory. "Dallas, what's going on?"

"I don't know." And she didn't. The house was lovely; why wasn't she flush with enthusiasm? She brushed aside a strand of hair from his face and peered intently at the face of a man she had married, trying to read his feelings. "Are you mad?"

"Confused, yes, but not mad." Bryce handed her a water bottle. She uncapped it and took a sip. "Look, we can stay in the condo for as long as you want. We can raise Sprout and grow old there. I was operating on what you said. There certainly isn't a rush, and I never want you to feel pressured. For the record, Dallas, I don't care where we live. What will make *you* happy?"

That was the million-dollar question.

Bryce was patient and kind. "Any baby would be lucky to have you as their father," Dallas said, returning the water. She looked him in the eyes, unwavering. "Do you ever want more?" she asked, "From me, I mean?"

He rose and dropped a kiss on top of her head. "I want what you can give."

Chapter 36

Georgia Gray

After unloading the car in the Tulsa International Airport departure lane, Grace embraced her sister.

"Happy Divorce Day," Dallas whispered in Grace's ear. The children were already wheeling their carry-on suitcases up the curb.

"See you in five days," Grace said, placing her palm against her sister's pregnant swell. "You behave yourself, mister."

Dallas paused as if in an internal debate. "I'm calling him Mark for the time being."

Grace grinned and gave a tiny whoop. "You have a story. Tell me, sister! Don't leave me hanging."

"When you get back. We'll get together, you'll tell me about the divorce, and I'll fill you in on everything else. You gotta get going."

"That sounds good. Listen to me, nephew Mark. Don't give your mommy any trouble. And don't get any bright ideas about coming early. Auntie Grace wants to be here for your birth."

****

Five hours later, in a high-rise divorce attorney's office in downtown Detroit, with November ice particles battering the window, an eight-year marriage dissolved. Looking at Andrew across the large polished table, she saw flashes of their lives together: their first encounter, their first kiss, football games, their wedding, and the birth of their daughters. She remembered celebrations, holidays, and moments in the sand.

Now, though, she was painfully aware of the hidden cracks between those memories. She heard the subtle criticism of things she did wrong and the way he sometimes corrected her while she was talking. She noted his growing resentment manifested in the little things he said. And when he became irritated, she took mental notes and tried not to repeat the same mistake. Most of all, though, she felt the loneliness seep in as he drifted away, working more and more under the guise of doing it for the family.

There was a time she could tell what Andrew was feeling and thinking simply by looking at him. Doing so was impossible now. During the divorce procedure, Andrew focused on his attorney, the papers before him, the weather outside–anywhere except on Grace. He had already surgically excised her from his life like a dermatologist would do with a cancerous growth on the skin. How can our time together and his feelings have been distilled to a point where he summarily discards them with the flourish of his signature? And yet, when her turn to sign the divorce decree came, she picked up the pen and did the same.

A couple near the conference room engaged in a volatile exchange of words. They headed toward the elevators, fury palpably linking them. Grace envied them their acrimony. At least they still have passion, she thought. The past eight years of her life were relegated to little more than a marginalized footnote.

Grace finally caught his eye as Andrew and his attorney waited for the lift doors to close. Inside, she carried an overwhelming sense of sadness, of loss, but in his arctic eyes, she saw nothing, not even a flicker of light against the ice.

****

Grace fastened the top button of her wool overcoat and pulled her knit hat over her ears. She stood alone in front of her son's gravestone. The sleet was heavier than when she'd left the attorney's office. With gloved hands, she tried unsuccessfully to clear the Georgia gray granite encased in a glaze of ice.

The traffic by the cemetery was already slowing as wheels began to slide and spin. The roads would only worsen, yet still, Grace stayed. She wanted to spend more time with him.

Grace had given him an 'A' name, after all. And a 'Z' name. Aziz was a name that meant beloved and cherished. She had also given her son the name of his paternal grandfather–Aziz Michael Walker Holden, the first and only. From deep inside her coat pocket, her phone vibrated. The call could wait. She didn't want to talk to anyone at this moment. Her girls were safe with their father, Grace's now ex-husband. Eight years, four children, Grace stood in silent grief, her head bent, until the crystal pellets falling from the dark sky transformed into snow.

****

She listened to the message when she returned to her college roommate's spare bedroom.

"Grace, this is Brian from Captain Auto's Repair. I found a GPS tracker in your car's wheel well." A long pause followed. Grace was about to delete the message when Captain Auto started talking again. "I also found an audio surveillance device inside your vehicle. My guess is if your car has bugs, your house does too. When you get back, we'll check it out for you. In any event, I have the car and the devices waiting for you when you return. Call me if you have any questions."

Chapter 37

Searching for Bugs

With a sense of urgency, Grace's mother yanked her into the secret world of the anthropology conference room. She cast a wary eye down the silent corridor before slamming the door shut and securing it with a sound that echoed like a gunshot. Whirling around, she locked her gaze with the room's other occupant, a man of diminutive stature who, despite his size, dominated the cavernous space—his three-piece suit lending him an air of unassailable authority.

"Dr. Brody, I'd like to introduce you to my daughter, Grace. Thanks for meeting us on such short notice."

He nodded, silver hair falling across his forehead. "Anything for a respected colleague. And please, call me Hiram."

"I don't think Caligula followed me," Grace said to her mother. "Brian from Captain Auto's Repair Shop agreed to keep the tracking and audio device he took off my car. That way, it looks like my vehicle is still in the shop."

"Innovative thinking, Grace. But they'll figure it out."

"I'll put the devices back on when I go to work. If I don't want them to track me, I'll leave them at home, giving the impression my car is parked."

Dr. Hiram Brody, a luminary in geophysics, scrutinized the two women, his intelligent eyes alive with curiosity. "If Caligula has set their sights on this project, it means Michael was onto something groundbreaking." He smiled. "His insights sparked animated debates at our university gatherings. It is high time we uncover what he left in his wake."

He put on his wire-rim spectacles and gasped in appreciation as Grace introduced him to Gizmo's intricacies and told him the working theories.

"We just don't know what he does. Dad told us never to keep the gadget and the formulas in the same place. One without the other doesn't make sense."

Dr. Brody stood. "I'm leaving tomorrow for a week. Are you free to meet me in my office next Wednesday evening with the paperwork? After I review the blueprints, I might be able to help you."

Grace accelerated onto I-244 West and hit her sister's speed dial function, but her sister didn't pick up. They were knee-deep in fairy play or outside, roasting marshmallows in the fire pit. She left a message. "Dallas, I'm heading home. I have another favor to ask. Can you watch the girls again for a couple of hours next week? This time at your place. I'll drop them off after dinner. My car still has problems, so can I borrow yours?"

****

"Grace!"

He called her name across the hospital's lobby. She stopped, her heart airborne, and waited for Lee to catch up. She took a swig of coffee, trying to act nonchalant. Though Grace was aware, her smile had given her away. She hadn't seen Lee since she left for Michigan to finalize her divorce. She missed him more than she wanted to admit.

Lee broke the silence. "I'm heading to the medical-surgical unit if you have a minute. Brian filled me in on the tracking and audio devices he found." They fell into step together as they walked side by side down the long corridor.

"It's unnerving to think they've been following me. Your friend was going to help search for any bugs Caligula might have planted in the house during the break-in, but he's swamped." Grace paused and opened her cell. "He sent me images of what I'm supposed to look for."

Lee peered at her phone and nodded. "I'll help."

"You've already done plenty, setting up the surveillance system and everything."

"Those devices can be difficult to detect. Two sets of eyes are better than one. Come on, Grace. You aren't in this alone."

He stopped short of the nurse's station, away from prying ears.

"And while I'm pestering you, have you considered my invitation to go with me on my next trip?"

"I didn't think you were serious." She took another sip of coffee.

"I'm not in the habit of saying things I don't mean."

She hesitated. She would be without her daughters for ten days over the winter break, the longest she had gone without seeing them, and an excursion would help ease the pain of separation. Plus, she was deeply curious about what Lee did between his two-week rotations. A barrage of self-rebuke followed–what was she contemplating? Considering his offer was ludicrous–entanglements were the last thing she needed. As her head vehemently shook in refusal, her mouth, acting as an independent entity, betrayed her better judgment. "Okay."

He laughed, looking surprised. "Okay, to what? Bug searching or trip taking?"

"Both, if I get the time off approved."

****

That afternoon, Lee poked his head into her office. "Well?"

Grace made sure no one else was around. "I got a few days off. What should I pack?" she asked playfully.

"Use your imagination."

"A swimsuit? Trekking gear? Evening gown? A motorcycle helmet?"

He chuckled. "That's a good start." The fine lines around his eyes crinkled.

"Do I need my passport? Should I give you money for an airline ticket?" She kept her tone light.

"Not this time." He winked. "See you tomorrow when we scavenge for bugs."

Chapter 38

A Taste of Single Malt Scotch

Parents don't tell their grown children everything.

The birthday flowers were long faded, the petals turning crisp and brown. But still, they remained on the dresser in Mary's bedroom. Tucked in her underwear drawer was the poem. One she didn't need to retrieve to read, for she had it memorized...*I can no longer fight gravity, pulling me...forever back to you.*

Michael had written this while confronting his mortality, surrounded by a trophy home, a trophy wife, a trophy life. And yet, even with death's fetid breath on his cancer-ravaged shoulders, the compulsion to expend precious energy and leave a future message to her meant something.

There is peace in knowing you've left nothing unsaid. Had she made a mistake all those years ago?

****

Between wife number two and three, he came back.

First, she saw the shadow, then the man. Mary's hands were deep in the loamy earth, weeding, next to her night tea roses.

He leaned into the velvet-cupped buds and inhaled. The high-centered blooms caressed his rugged face. "The fragrance is subtle, unassuming, yet exquisitely beautiful—like you."

"Michael." Mary stood, getting her bearings. It was twelve-thirty. Dallas and Grace were at school. Since their divorce six years ago, Mary had only seen him when exchanging the girls for visitation. Today was not a "Daddy Day."

She wiped the earth on her gardening apron, her body firing, all cylinders in motion. She took a step toward him. "The girls are not here."

"I didn't come to see them." He closed the distance and took her face in his large hands, his eyes burning with ultramarine intensity. "I'm recently divorced, not because I have someone else."

He bent to whisper in her ear, "I came to see *you*. I've missed *you*."

Chalk it up to years of loneliness or muscle memory. Mary did not hesitate. She threw her arms around his neck; he swooped her up and carried her inside. There, she gave in to the rhythms of the past. The passion, the tenderness, the frenzy all rose unbidden, uninhibited, pure.

****

The water from Mary's shower-damp hair soaked the shoulders of her cotton blouse. She handed Michael a glass of sweet tea as he surveyed the backyard.

"You have a gazebo." He sounded surprised, that life without him continued. "We used to talk about how nice sharing a drink in a gazebo would be after the girls were in bed. We never got around to building it. Let's take our tea out there."

"I don't think so, Michael. This afternoon was lovely," she said, her fingers grazing the coarse stubble of his cheek, "but that's all this was–an interlude."

"I don't understand. I thought our getting together meant you wanted to try again. Everything will be different this time, I promise. Remember what we had? We started together from nothing. We created a life, a home. Mary, you keep me grounded in a way no one else can."

The father of her children spoke with animation, caught in the intensity of what he felt, the here and now. And that was the crux of the problem. The pulse of–*this is bigger than both of us*–the gestalt was what drove him. Michael embraced fate with headlong abandon, rushing into her extraordinary embrace, thus erasing any memory of having been there before. Michael lived with enthusiasm and zeal–a corner office with a hundred-mile view, luxurious cashmere suits that caressed his legs like the soft fingers of a Geisha, explosive success on his core drills, a nubile palm on his chest, a taste of smoky noted single malt scotch, a young stockinged leg on his thigh. Each delirious experience was a case of 'I've never been like this before,' as if every prior experience was merely an audition.

Mary did not doubt his sincerity, which was infectious. How easy it would be to dive into his vivid narrative, where he convinced himself his feelings were real this time and that he was alive in ways he hadn't been before. This was part of Michael Walker's charm, a component of why she had fallen for him, a piece of what she loved about him still but also feared. She wavered.

During their divorced years, he'd sampled the earth's delectable upper crust. Life at that elite level was an alluring seductress. Every time he turned around, she'd be there flirting–with a platter of sensual offerings to choose from.

When the school bus arrived and her children, full of buoyant life, floated into her field of vision, he was gone.

She kept the afternoon rendezvous to herself. Even during one winter break, when sharing a bottle of wine with her young adult daughters, who pestered her for the dirt on her life as a single woman, she remained silent.

She made the right decision.

Mothers don't tell their grown daughters everything.

Chapter 39

An Accelerated Course

Grace kneeled before her pots and pans cabinet with a flashlight. She nearly jumped out of her skin when Lee touched her shoulder. She hadn't heard him coming. This searching for bugs had her on edge. He put a finger to his lips before guiding Grace onto her back patio. He bent his head to hers, whispering, "I found two mics–in the family room and your bedroom."

She waited until they were twenty-five yards away from her mobile home, halfway down the path, until she blurted out, "My bedroom. Are you kidding me?" Grace was shocked but tried to downplay her response. "How boring for them." She hoped her voice sounded calm, even as she struggled to remember if she had talked to her mom or Dallas about Gizmo and the paperwork in her double-wide. As far as she knew, Caligula still had no concept of what her father was working on.

"You have to decide what to do with the audio equipment." Lee took her hand. "If I remove them from the house, they'll know you're wise to their game."

"How long will it take them to figure out I'm taking the GPS off my car when I don't want them following me? This must stop. Living in fear isn't what I agreed to. I can't keep looking over my shoulder and having to censor what I say. I can't subject my daughters to this. Dad would understand."

They were at the end of the path, where her daughters stood when they wanted to connect with their father. Autumn's rain had given the scorched creek purchase. A thin, persistent stream gurgled over the rocky base. Lee faced her. Their eyes met. "What do you want to do?"

She didn't want to give up but wasn't sure she had the strength to keep going. Could Lee see this? Did he know how close she was to the edge of holding everything together? How the slightest Oklahoma wind might cause her to shatter, sending pieces of her skittering across the horizon. Grace tilted her head toward the sky. A fine tremor ran through her. Lee stepped forward and wrapped his solid arms around her in a protective, warm, all-encompassing hug. One with pressure in all the right places that said you are cared for, you are not alone. Grace's body responded. At first, with relief, *you can let your guard down and rest for a moment.* But then, on a deeper level, her neurons fired, sending impulses to parts of her body that had long been dormant. *Oh no, you don't,* she sternly reprimanded herself, pulling back. *Don't go getting me into more than I can handle.* Why did her prefrontal cortex turn to mush when this man was around? She slipped from his arms before he could read her body's ridiculous response to his friendly embrace.

"An accelerated course." She gulped.

His verdant eyes asked the question.

"The truth is, I would never forgive myself if I didn't see this through. I made a deathbed promise to Dad. What kind of example would I be for my daughters to give up when the going gets tough? I have to jump this into overdrive. The girls leave for winter break with their dad soon. My goal is to have everything resolved by the time they return." Grace paused and locked onto Lee's gaze. "This means I might be unable to go with you on your magical mystery tour."

He pushed a strand of hair from her face. "You have to do what's best for you and your family. I get it. I go every two weeks. You're always welcome."

Grace smiled wanly. She knew as well as he did that this opportunity wouldn't come again until the girls left for their summer vacation. And by then, who knew what life would serve up? He might not feel the same.

****

"What do we have here?" Professor Brody bent over the downloaded forms on Grace's phone. "These formulas support your theories. Something is missing, though. Here, on this page, the one with the poem, there's a date at the bottom, but the camera doesn't capture the month or year. I have a feeling this is important."

They had debated whether showing Dr. Brody the poem would have any evidentiary value beyond telling him what they could say in person: the whole is greater than the sum of the parts. Grace won. "Mom, he has to see everything if he's going to help us." Her mother reluctantly agreed.

"I'll get you the originals. They're locked in my office upstairs." Mary stood and headed toward the door.

Grace called after her. "Mom, I must get going. Dallas is watching the girls, and I don't want them riling up their unborn cousin. Keep me posted."

"Of course." She turned and hugged her daughter. "I'm keeping my fingers crossed that the original documents will give us a clue."

Grace waited until her mother locked the conference door before turning to Dr. Brody and shaking his hand. "Thanks again."

"It's my pleasure. This is fascinating. Your father's work might represent a sea change. I'll let you know if we figure things out."

"Remember, when you call, I'll say something like 'Hi, Andrew' and chat for a minute until I get outside. The ears don't care about a conversation with my ex, but they might be interested in one with a world-renowned geophysicist."

Dr. Brody smiled and put a single finger to his lips.

Chapter 40

The Gestalt

"Good night, Moon," Grace said under her breath as she turned on their nightlight. The girls were fast asleep. Tinkerbell strolled into the darkened room, her fluffy tail upright. The feline wound its tapered body between Grace's feet, rubbing her ribcage against her legs, a low and rumbling vibration rising. Grace scratched her behind the ears. The cat stood momentarily, as if contemplating, then leaped into bed beside Ally. The girls considered having Tinkerbell sleep next to them a badge of honor. And the uncanny creature always appeared to know what child needed her ministrations the most. The cat, purring softly, made her nest on the pillow beside her oldest daughter, her tail curled around Ally's head, a fluffy fur hat. Grace shook her head in quiet wonder.

****

Speeding tires crunched on the pebbled drive outside her daughter's bedroom. Glancing at the security camera feed on her phone, Grace rushed outdoors, away from the audio tracker.

"Mom! What the heck?"

Her mother jumped from the vehicle and swayed, pressing the door to steady herself. "Gracie, they can't hear us out here, right?"

"No, what's going on?"

"Good and bad news. What do you want first?"

"Mom!"

"Okay, okay." She took a deep breath. "The date that your father wrote at the bottom of the poem, November 15th, 2017, a powerful earthquake devastated Pohang, South Korea."

"Dad told me the working theory was that a geothermal project triggered the quake."

"That's exactly right. Dr. Brody explained that enhanced geothermal technology pumps water into the well at high pressures, opening existing fractures and creating new ones that tap into the hot rocks below. Sometimes, these fractures cause earthquakes."

Her mother was still talking, but Grace only heard her father's voice and saw his blue eyes dance as he beamed at her as if she was the only person in his world. "The problem, Gracie, is when the earthquakes get too big." He took a bite of his grilled cheese sandwich. "There must be a better way to tap into this sustainable, renewable energy source. The goal is to minimize the risks of such quakes when harnessing the earth's heat for energy."

At the end of their lunch, he hugged her close before he went through the security screening line. "I wish you lived closer. I enjoy our talks. Mark my words. I am going to figure something out. Oil is a finite resource. Once the earth's reserves are depleted, it's gone. But heat is continually produced in the earth. If done right, geothermal power can supply humanity's energy needs for as long as this beautiful planet exists." Her father went through the TSA precheck line. He made the security guard laugh. He bent to tie a shoe. He helped a woman pick up a tipped suitcase on its side. But not once did he look back.

Grace tucked the memory away. Her mother had stopped talking and was staring intently at her.

"Sorry. Flashbacks. Dad believed geothermal energy was the answer. He wanted to find a way to help humankind without harming the earth."

"Well, Grace, he's done exactly that! Instead of the earth being force-fed cold water pumped at high pressure and having the heated fluid drawn back through wells to its surface, Gizmo converts the heat on the spot into geothermal electricity. Gizmo is a mechanism making the earth's internal energy recoverable. Dr. Brody confirmed everything else we thought. Your father's creation is biodegradable, retrievable, and has an internal monitoring system. Not only does the contraption communicate the amount of energy converted and its well-being status so you know when to replace it, but it will detect earthquakes."

"Mom, this is incredible. What can the bad news possibly be?"

"I got a call when we were in Hiram's office and stepped outdoors to take it. I wasn't gone for more than two minutes. A reporter wanted to interview me about a recent article I wrote for *The Anthropology Times*. After twenty seconds, I realized he hadn't even read the article. I ended the call–"

"Mom!"

"When I got back to Hiram's office..." She took a deep breath and ran a shaky hand through her messy hair. "I opened the door and found him on the floor, unconscious, with a visible head wound, and the original copies of Michael's blueprints gone. They got them, Grace. All Caligula needs is Gizmo."

****

Grace knocked before poking her head into Dr. Brody's hospital room. "Are you up for a visitor?" He sat upright in the adjustable bed, wearing suit pants and a starched button-down shirt, reading a journal. A bandage wound around his head.

"Grace! Come in, come in! I'd like to introduce you to my daughter, Dr. Hawthorne."

"Holly, please." The young, open-faced woman stretched a hand to shake Grace's.

"Holly flew in from San Diego this morning. Though her doctorate is in the Fine Arts from Oxford, she thinks her old man needs someone to monitor his cerebral function."

"Dad, please. You just had your head bashed in."

"That's a bit of an exaggeration." He winked at Grace. "You'd never guess that my overprotective daughter was once rebellious." He gestured to a second chair. "Join us, Grace. Maybe you'll convince Holly that her old man doesn't have one foot in the grave."

"I'm sorry I got you into this mess, Dr. Brody," Grace said, pulling her chair closer. "I feel terrible."

"No, my girl." He patted her hand. "I am the one who should apologize. You entrusted me with your father's documents, and now they are gone."

"We've got copies, but there's only one of you. What's your prognosis?"

"The scan showed a fracture in my skull but no bleed. I gather that's a good thing."

Grace smiled. "You're correct. Did you see who did it?" She envisioned the man who confronted her in the parking garage. He had enough heft to hit a grand slam; she was grateful Dr. Brody wasn't hurt worse.

"No, they hit me when my back was to the door. The police are reviewing our security cameras and are hoping to get an identification. And Gizmo…"

Grace regarded Holly.

"It's all right," interjected Dr. Brody. "My daughter is trustworthy and an ardent Mother Earth advocate."

"He's in a secure location," Grace disclosed. "I'm not telling a soul where he is. I don't want to put anyone else at risk."

Dr. Brody leaned forward, his visage full of animation. "Grace, your father's invention is a game changer. The earth's internal heat provides an essentially inexhaustible supply of energy. The reason why geothermal power makes up less than one percent of electricity generation worldwide is twofold. The first one is because the construction of large geothermal power plants creates surface instability. The second reason is that it's capital intensive. In other words, in addition to sinking money into constructing a massive power plant, you must send electricity over costly transmission lines. These cables can cost from one million to thirty million dollars a mile. Getting energy to isolated regions in rugged terrain is exceedingly difficult and cost-prohibitive. Gizmo, however, addresses those two main drawbacks. He is streamlined; you plug him into the earth with minimal disruption to the surface, and he converts the heat to electricity on the spot so that you won't need a massive power plant or those million-dollar-a-mile transmission lines. Instead, you'd have a small substation above where Gizmo is seeded. Homes, medical facilities, and businesses who didn't have access to power before would get their electricity from this station via distribution lines, which are significantly less expensive than transmission lines."

Grace tried to follow everything he told her, her mind tripping on the details.

"Oh, fiddle, never mind the technicalities. They're not critical at this point. The important thing is that your father has created a revolutionary way to harness geothermal energy at a fraction of the cost." He peered at her over his wire-rimmed glasses. "What is your next step?"

"The gestalt of Dad's invention is overwhelming. I'm still processing everything."

"When you decide, give me a call. I have connections and will point you in the right direction. I will be around campus until the last week in December. Then, I'm flying to New York City to attend a global conference on renewable energy."

"Thanks, Dr. Brody. I may take you up on your offer. Two brains are better than one. And even with head trauma, your brain is worth about fifty of mine. Nice to meet you, Dr. Holly Hawthorne." Grace stood and checked her phone. No emergencies. "I need to check on another patient who was admitted this morning. Dr. Brody, I'm glad you're doing well."

****

Grace walked down the polished hospital floor and put a hand to her mouth, covering a yawn. The night was a long one. After her mother arrived, they spent an hour of huddled planning on the back patio. Grace then returned inside the double-wide, sat on the couch near the remote audio device, and called her mother, as she did every night.

"Hey, Mom, sorry my call's late. I fell asleep on the couch." She listened to a response, which the mic would never be able to pick up, and went over to the window, pulling the curtain back. Her mother sat on one of the deck chairs with her phone pressed to her ear and a blanket over her knees. They chatted for a few minutes. Grace faked a yawn. "I'm tired and have to text Dallas before I go to bed, or I won't hear the end of it. Everything's fine here, Mom. We'll talk tomorrow."

She ended the call, texted her sister, and quietly opened the door for her mother. Wordlessly, Grace placed a pillow and blanket on the couch and took her mother's car keys. She hoisted the duffle bag from her closet over her shoulder and entered the night.

Ninety minutes later, she returned. Her mother was awake, keeping vigil, a sheen of worry and lines etched her face. Advancing her father's legacy was taking its toll on everyone. With a silent thumbs-up, Grace returned her mother's keys. They hugged before separating.

When Grace started nursing school, hospital access was wide open, like a shopping mall or an expansive farmer's market. But things had changed. A response to the pandemic, increased attacks against healthcare workers, and workplace violence spurred hospital access to become highly governed. With a focus on identity management, strict visitor screening and restrictions, and even metal detectors, Grace felt like she was entering a nuclear power plant every time she came to the hospital.

She retraced her steps from last night. She swiped her hospital-issued ID badge at the locked employee entrance and waved at the monitor—step one. A guard was looking at a screen to make sure the face that appeared on his security feed matched the employee's photo they had on file. The secured door swung open– step two. Grace walked through the halls, whose polished linoleum floors gleamed until she reached the restricted surgical corridor. She ran her ID badge through the reader to gain access–step three. Grace strolled past the pre-op anteroom and the employee lounge before stopping in front of another locked door. She punched a controlled numerical code on an electronic keypad, granting her entry into the staff locker room–step four. And finally, three rows down, Grace found her locker, with the steel padlock whose combination only she knew–right, left, right–click. She double-checked to ensure she was alone before reaching into her locker and touching the duffle bag to reassure herself that all was well. Her patient, whom she had admitted last night, still decorated with ribbons and tulle, was sleeping.

Chapter 41

'A' Team Restructured

Grace pressed her body against the shatterproof glass until the plane carrying her three children disappeared into the Oklahoma sky. A hollowness beyond the whiteness of the morning engulfed her. The day she dreaded, the first of her daughters' solo trips to see their father without her had arrived. They were old enough to fly with an attendant's supervision on a direct flight, unaccompanied minor tags around their necks, and pilot wings on their chest. According to the divorce and child custody terms, Andrew would get his daughters for six weeks during the summer and over their winter break. Andrew wouldn't fight her decision to stay in Oklahoma and be close to her support system if she agreed. Grace had never been apart from her daughters this long. Today, she'd immerse herself in activity–finish the laundry and clean. After lunch, Dallas insisted on dragging her to do some "shopping" for her trip. Grace would have to rein her sister in but was grateful for the distractions.

Lee would pick her up for their mystery excursion at the end of her work week.

****

"Mommy?" The voice was small and distant.

"Ora, my sweet pea! How are you?" Grace placed

a spray of Winter Daphne on the counter and grabbed a clean jelly jar below the sink. "How was your trip? Did Daddy pick you up?"

"Ally threw up on the plane. Daddy was at work, so Momma Sabrina picked us up."

Grace's stomach tightened. *Momma Sabrina? I know you married the week after our divorce was final, but you're moving in rather quickly.* Grace stood motionless, aware of dusk's presence and how still the evening had become.

"Is Ally feeling better?"

"She's great. We're spending the night at an indoor water park. It's fun! Daddy's ordering barbecue, and we get to eat at a table by this waterfall. Momma Sabrina's going down the slides with Ally and Amanda."

"You called by yourself?"

"Daddy got us a family phone to share. We just hit the phone symbol by your picture whenever we want to talk to you. We can also call Grandma Mary, Auntie Dallas, and Grandma and Grandpa Holden. Dad said we can reach you whenever we want. He knows I'm talking to you. He's giving me the thumbs-up sign."

"I miss you, Ora." Her name was an exhalation, a puff of air. Last night, as Grace carried her youngest to bed, she felt Ora's perfect weight in her arms as she had on the day she was born.

"What about our 'A' team, Andrew? I thought we had this worked out." Grace hated the desperation in her voice. He was pulling away, already distancing himself from her and his children. She stroked the infant, who nestled against her chest, trying to still her breathing so the panic wouldn't flow through her breast milk. "We agreed if it's a boy, he'd have your family name, and if it's a girl, you'd finish your 'A' team."

"I know what we said. But it's not a boy." A hardness permeated his face with a cold determination she hadn't seen before. "And frankly, I've run out of 'A' names. It was a stupid idea, anyway."

"Andrew," she said from her gut, a primal utterance.

He turned his hand on the hospital door. "You want a name? Is that it?" Grabbing the birth certificate worksheet, he scribbled three letters. "There, her name is Ora. In Latin, it means coast. Her name carries infinite possibilities–shorelines encompass every land mass worldwide. That's what you want, something meaningful?"

As he crossed the threshold, he stopped. Grace grazed her lips against her third daughter's forehead. Her softness smelled like clean earth. "It's not an 'A' name, but at least it's a vowel." His laughter, low and rumbling, echoed inside her long after he left.

"Mommy? Mommy?"

"I'm sorry, honey."

"You okay?"

"You bet I am."

"Have you been down the path?"

Grace paused in response. "No, sweetheart, do you want me to?"

"It works the same for you, right? When we're far away from Daddy, we walk down the path, and he comes into our hearts. So if I'm in Michigan and you're in Oklahoma, if you walk down the path, I'll be in your heart, too. Right?"

Grace's fingertips moved over the laminate counter, replicating the thin fishhook scar on her youngest daughter's forehead, resulting from the fall from her fairy nest. "You're always in my heart."

"But it's not the same as when you go down the path. There's a difference. Will you do that? Please. You walk to the end, and I'll meet you."

"All right, sweetie, I'll go the moment you hang up. Give my love to your sisters, okay?"

"Okay."

"And Ora?"

"What, Mommy?"

"Encourage Ally and Amanda to use the family phone too."

A waxing gibbous moon rose over a distant grove of trees. Grace's bare feet were comfortable treading upon the cool earth. The stones lining the trail's course, erected by her children, were a shoreline of faith and expectation. At the end of the path, she stopped. Before her were the banks of a river that dried up long before they moved here but now held a gurgling stream of hope, and above to the east shone Sirius, the brightest star in the night sky.

Chapter 42

Rolling Hills

"Sorry I couldn't leave earlier." Lee secured Grace's carry-on suitcase in the bed of his pickup. "Last night was one emergency after another." His face was somber, and his eyes rimmed with dark circles. A slice of coral stretched across the eastern horizon. The day for their getaway had finally arrived.

Grace handed Lee a small paper bag and put the thermos of coffee between the driver's and passenger's seats. "Hand me the keys. After you eat, close your eyes and get some sleep. Just tell me where to go."

"And reveal our secret destination. What if you change your mind and want to bail?"

"Fine, plug in a landmark along the way, and I'll wake you when we get there. Friends don't let friends drive delirious."

Within minutes of finishing his breakfast sandwich, Lee leaned over and grazed Grace on the cheek. His lips were warm and dry. "My angel of mercy, that was delicious. Thanks." He leaned back and fell asleep.

As Grace navigated the open stretch of highway, she relaxed. Her daughters were safe, having a blast with Andrew and Sabrina. Twice a day, she'd check in with them. Gizmo was hiding in the equivalent of Fort Knox. Ronnie had a copy in the trunk of her car, and

Mr. Mills, the shop teacher, had one locked in his classroom closet. Caligula couldn't connect Ronnie or the teacher with Grace, for they were never together outside of the hospital setting. The Oil and Gas Company had the original formulas, but without Gizmo, it wouldn't do them any good. Bryce was keeping an eye on the security feed from her home. Dallas, though still having a hard time with her pregnancy, was healthy and counting down the days to delivery. Her mother was watching Tinkerbell. Dr. Brody was discharged and healing at home. Her car with the tracking device was in her driveway. But she'd had enough of the audio mics in her home. Monitoring her words and hoping the girls didn't accidentally slip was stressful. Bryce helped her disengage and dispose of them in an active construction site that would give Caligula something to think about.

For a few days, Grace could unwind and try to determine her next step. And she wasn't going to lie; the prospect of unraveling the mysteries surrounding the gorgeous man sleeping beside her was tantalizing.

****

They had long abandoned the highways and paved two-lane roads. Lee easily navigated a dirt tract that would have been hard-pressed to allow two full-sized vehicles to pass. The cab shuddered every time the truck hit a rut, of which there were many. Yet he stayed relaxed, skillfully manipulating the vehicle over the divots and stones with effortless attention, his right arm slung along the back of the seat.

The small brick building was in an open expanse. The parking lot consisted of matted grass and had a sign that read 'Rolling Hills Rural Family Clinic.'

She tried not to look incredulous. "This is where you go…"

"Every two weeks," he filled in.

"No jet setting to the Swiss Alps, South of France, African Savanna?"

He shook his head, dark hair brushing his shoulders. "Disappointed?"

"No, not at all, just surprised." And she was. In all her imaginings, she had never visualized Lee volunteering at a facility in a medically underserved area.

"Disabusing you of your preconceived mindset will be difficult, but I believe I am up to the challenge," he said with a wry smile, mocking himself and Grace simultaneously.

Grace shook her head, embarrassed. He saw through her. She tried to recover, "You must like me, Lee Leland, sharing your top-secret getaway with me."

His thumb brushed the nape of her neck. "You are one of the smartest girls I've met. And the answer is yes, I do like you, Grace. I like you a lot." He smiled, jumped from the cab, and swung his medical bag over his shoulder. "Ready, Nurse Holden? We have a full schedule and could use the extra help. Doors open in thirty minutes." He flung a stethoscope from his bag. She caught it mid-air and put it around her neck.

A boombox stood on the check-in window's ledge. From the speakers blared a tinny rendition of the Music Man's seventy-six trombones. Around the corner marched a spritely man with long white hair twisted in a ponytail, his arms waving as if leading the parade. When he spotted Lee, he stopped, put his imaginary conductor wand down, and broke into a grin that deepened the wrinkles in his tanned face. "Lee!" He pulled him into an unabashed embrace. "Always good to see the reinforcements come to town. And who do we have here?"

"Dr. Jenner, I'd like to introduce you to Grace Holden. I roped her into helping at the clinic for a few days."

"The father of immunology?" Grace smiled as she shook his weathered hand.

His chortle was soft. "You were paying attention in class, but I'm unrelated to the English scientist. I'm flattered anyone would think of me that way, and I'm honored to make your acquaintance, even if only for a few hours."

"We take turns running the clinic, two weeks on, two weeks off," Lee countered.

Dr. Jenner handed Lee a stack of charts. "I only stay until I've given my report. I spend my two weeks fishing and living a life of semi-retired leisure while this young man–"

"Works his tail off as a hospitalist in the big city so he can afford to volunteer at a rural clinic during his time off," Grace continued, though she wasn't aware she had said this part aloud. She was starting to get a more complete picture of Dr. Lee Leland–a portrait that didn't match what she had imagined.

The clinic was small yet efficient, with two private rooms and a break area doubling as a food and clothing pantry. Each checkup room had an examination table, scale, and small credenza; the top held cotton swabs, a thermometer, and a blood pressure cuff. Everything was orderly and pristine.

Lee and Grace worked through the busy morning

docket without incident. The secretary was a retired school teacher who checked the patients in, answered the phone, scheduled appointments, and triaged walk-ins. "I don't know how we'd manage without you, Lois," Lee said as he turned the clinic sign to "closed" for their lunch break.

"For you and Doc Jenner, I'd do anything. Working keeps me from turning into a lonely loon." She grabbed a romance novel and propped her swollen ankles on the desk.

"Thanks, Lois. We'll eat our sandwiches out back. Holler if anything comes up."

"It never does," she answered, her nose already buried in '*The Electric Embrace.*'

Lee sat down at a weathered picnic table behind the clinic and handed Grace a gourmet-looking sandwich he'd grabbed from the break room. After his first bite, he paused. "It's no secret Lois has a crush on Doc Jenner. Her work ethic is unmatched, and she's one of the best cooks on this side of the Mississippi. The refrigerator is chock full of her delicacies."

Grace surveyed the gently rolling acreage behind the clinic. The cerulean winter sky with moving white clouds prevailed. A large field lay barren, untilled. Hugging the perimeter of this land and undulating for as far as the eye could see were rows and rows of equally spaced saplings. "You have an impressive number of apple and peach trees here."

"You should see this place in the spring. It's full of vegetables, fruit, and flowers. People from the community come and work side by side. The produce is accessible to all. On the weekends, when the clinic is closed, I get out here with Lois, digging with anyone who wants to show up. Lois holds gardening, cooking, and jarring sessions. Any produce not eaten in its prime is turned into stock, frozen or jarred, and goes on our food pantry shelves. The dream is to build a separate food and clothing facility."

"What you are doing is pretty amazing." Grace was humbled.

Lee stretched his legs and drank water from his thermos. "I hate to admit this, but my initial motivation for volunteering was selfish. Naively, I somehow believed if only my parents had access to a clinic like this when I was young, things might have turned out differently."

He only talked about life after Aunt Ida. Grace was about to take this opening and gently probe when Lee stood up and offered her his hand. "Usually, we're too busy for lunch, but thanks to you, Grace, today we got ten minutes, which is over. Back to work, we go."

The afternoon flew in a coordinated rhythm. Before Grace had a chance to catch her breath, the last client had checked out.

Lee helped Lois slip on her lightweight jacket and kissed her on the cheek. "See you tomorrow."

Lois beamed. "He's the son I never had." She brushed her bright purple hair off her shoulders. "I made you some dinner. It's in the office fridge." She took Grace's hand conspiratorially. "Doc Jenner and Doc Lee would starve without me. I assume you're staying at his house, right?"

Does Lee have a home here, in the middle of nowhere? And if he does, is that where they'll stay? Grace shot Lee an inquiring look; he nodded once, a slight smile on his lips. Grace's stomach did a slow flip.

Lois continued, seemingly oblivious to the nonverbal exchange, but Grace didn't doubt that she saw everything. "When you get to his place, check the refrig. I bet he doesn't have a lot. And don't worry, sweetie, I have enough food for you, too. Enjoy." She jiggled the keys in her hand and gulped air.

Must be the steamy novel she's reading. I'll ask to borrow it as soon as she's finished.

Chapter 43

On the Roof

Like the heroine in the pages of Lois' novel, Grace's heart jackhammered as gravel crunched beneath the truck's tires. The next part of their adventure was starting.

Late afternoon rays slanted sideways, unfiltered brightness, without the warmth. She touched her phone, but its signal was nonexistent. Lee warned her about the dead zones. Only moments ago, before they left the clinic, she finished talking to her girls–their laughter and words wound through her, mitochondrial DNA strands of connection.

Now, her mind raced as she reviewed every patient she had seen that day, hoping she hadn't missed anything. "You promise you'll review the charts and ensure I didn't overlook something?"

"I don't know why you're worried," he shot her a sideways glance. "Your assessment skills are spot on. Remember, I've seen your charting at the hospital. But if it makes you feel better, I'll review them."

"I can't believe you guys still have paper charts," Grace said, patting the stack on her lap.

"The clinic didn't have internet access until recently. Our service isn't always reliable, and handwritten documentation doesn't disappear when the power or the internet is out. For those reasons, Doc. Jenner is reluctant to change."

Grace touched his thigh. "Paper charting also makes it easy for you to review my notes remotely."

Reassured that her work would be checked, Grace allowed herself to feel the moment's excitement. Before long, she would see where Lee lived–not a temporary studio apartment one block from the hospital. This was his home, where he purposely put down roots, a reflection of the person he was. "Are we close?" she said, her voice a soft lilt reminiscent of Amanda's.

Lee pulled off the road and drove up a bumpy, rock-strewn passage resembling a dried river bed. The ascent was steep. "We're officially in the foothills of the Ozarks." Rugged trails punctuated the bare-branched stands of white oak interspersed with short-leaf pine, like they were in a national park.

Lee turned off the ignition.

"Are we going for a hike first? I did bring my trekking boots."

"And what else did you bring?" His eyes were shining, curious.

"You'll laugh. Hardly seems appropriate for where we are, but I have a wetsuit and a fancy dinner dress." She didn't tell him about the new nightgown, the one shoved at the bottom of her suitcase, the one she bought last week at Dallas' insistence. "You are not going to wear those ratty old sleep shorts and cotton tee if you're sleeping anywhere near him. Trust me, sister, you'll be glad you got this." And Dallas held up a blush slip, so light that it felt like she was wearing nothing.

"You'll get to wear the hiking boots, wetsuit, and dress, I promise. But first, let's get you settled." Lee grabbed her carry-on suitcase and his backpack and headed to the base of an ascending incline.

"Ah, we must hike to your murder cabin in the woods."

He guffawed. "Still trying to figure me out, I see. Sorry to disappoint you, Grace. I'm not that complicated. What you see is what you get."

If only, she thought, as the muscles in his arms furled in the late afternoon light.

Grace extricated her carry-on from his hands and headed up the trailhead, embarrassed as the wheels tripped and spun over the earth, causing the suitcase to keep listing to the side. She should have thrown her belongings in a backpack like she wanted. Dallas had been the one to insist on a stylish carry-on. Who had she been trying to impress, anyway?

"Where are you going?" His words took a moment to register.

"Up, I guess. This is the way, isn't it?"

"Well, right now, you're standing on my roof."

Lee stood at the base of the hill, staring up at her.

"What? I didn't see…" She started back down the slope, losing her grip, and the suitcase careened ahead. So much for being suave and sophisticated.

Grace sighed; she'd never been good at pretense.

"All right, what did I miss?" Even as she was saying the words, she saw clearly what her mind hadn't registered. There, tucked into the side of the hill, with a grass berm around it, was a shelter, an earth home. The stone exterior was whimsically stacked in all shades of rainwater and sand, as if pulled from the river. A deep rust stain covered the wooden front door, and two black-framed oval windows stared unblinking eyes on either side.

"A Hobbit House!" Grace's excitement was uncontainable as one part of her brain asserted, *The girls would love being here*. The other hemisphere reasoned that they *would never visit because that would mean something serious was going on*. "How in the world did you find something like this?"

"My mom ran off with my dad when she was seventeen and pregnant. Even though I never met my maternal grandparents they left me these five acres in their will. My backyard is the Ozark National Forest." Lee unlocked the door.

"Was the house already here? Or did you build it?"

"This place was in rough shape when I inherited it. One weekend after I started working at the clinic, a bunch of people with a pickup full of recycled material showed up. They helped me fix it up. Though she denies it, I'm sure our friend Lois had a hand in organizing the repairs. Many of our patients don't have health care or can't make the co-pays if they do. Doc Jenner and I don't turn anyone away and use a flexible sliding scale for services. But pride is involved, and if our clients have a skill set the office can use, we accept their help. This summer, the clinic needed a new roof. Doc and I bought the material, and several men volunteered to replace our old one."

Lee opened the door, transporting Grace to a magical place of soft lines and curves.

"The soil and foliage protect the shelter, maintaining a constant indoor temperature."

Grace was charmed. She ran her hands over the stone interior and followed a sloping path down. At the base, a semi-circle arched outward. To one side was a bathroom, and to the other side, a bedroom. In the heart of the home was an efficient kitchen, a table, and a small living area with a cast iron wood stove and couch. Natural light cascaded through a sliding glass door.

"If we're underground, how can there be light?" Grace asked as she slid open the portal. The small backyard was enclosed; stretching upward shot a rock retaining wall, holding back the moss-covered soil on the higher elevation. When the doors were open, the interior fell outside, forming one continuous, protected space.

Lee stepped next to her, looking upward. "A natural crevice created this. Human resources alone wouldn't have been able to forge something this exquisite."

The notion of a home grounding one, giving life, was new to her. "Lee, this place is magical. No wonder you come back after two weeks looking recharged and ready to take on the world." She paused and ran her hand over the rough stubble on his face. "Then, the two weeks of working at the hospital takes everything out of you."

"It's a small price to pay to be able to live here and help a community with little access to health care. One of these days, I hope to make this my permanent home, but that's in the distant future."

He led her back inside and put her suitcase on the house's only bed. "You can sleep in my room. I'll take the sofa."

Grace started to protest, but he stopped her. "No arguing, please. It's only for a few nights."

After settling in, Lee told Grace to prepare for a hike and swim. As the winter afternoon waned, they trekked side by side along an undulating trail that wound through a heavily wooded thatch of black walnut, hickory, and oak.

"Tell me again why you have a wetsuit."

"So, I have a confession to make. While the University of Michigan is a terrific school, I picked Michigan over my other choices because the Great Lakes hug the state. How cool is that? I made it my mission to swim in all five of them, and I have. I learned quickly, though, that all northern bodies of water are not warm. Hence the suit, a bit of an extravagance, I know. But, once my dad learned what I was up to, he bought it for me. I never banked on having to wear a wetsuit in Oklahoma."

"Well, it's December. The river is bound to be cold. Now I have a confession to make." The path narrowed, and Lee moved closer.

"Do tell." Grace's pulse quickened when he pushed a mop of chestnut hair from his eyes, which were mischievous in the fading light.

"When you were on the high school swim team, I attended the home meets."

"I know."

"You noticed me sitting in the stands?"

"Of course. Even before we were lab partners, I'd seen you around school wearing your football and baseball jersey on game days. Ignoring your cocky swagger was kind of hard."

Lee grinned–irresistible and self-assured. Oh lord, what was she getting herself into? She continued. "First year, I figured you had a girlfriend on the swim team. When we were in Honors Biology, I was afraid to ask. And after we, well, after our sophomore year, I knew you didn't come to see me. You were in the bleachers with a different girl whenever I turned around."

Lee veered off the main footpath and led Grace down a narrow deer trail. He stopped before a swiftly flowing tributary. "I went to those swim meets to see you. That is my revelation."

Her eyes widened.

He laughed. "There you go, Grace, swim to your heart's content. It's deep enough to plunge in from here and doesn't get shallow again until the bend."

She was suddenly self-conscious. The wetsuit clung to her like a second skin, as though her naked form was dipped into a vat of neoprene. Grace didn't want to shed her protective covering. He would see every imperfection, the ones covered up by scrubs and everyday clothes. *You can't escape this without making yourself look more like an idiot.* She tentatively walked to the edge of the bank.

In one fluid motion, hoping Lee wouldn't have time to see her flaws, Grace dropped her coat to the ground and flung herself forward. She pushed off the earth with her legs. Her body exploded upward and outward. How she loved this part of the dive, her body streamlined and flying, feet close together, toes pointed, head tucked between outstretched arms with the thumbs hooked together—a missile diving into the swiftly moving water. The water churned and bubbled around her. She blasted to the surface and vigorously started swimming upstream. He had gone to the meets to see *her.*

Charging against the current was difficult, but still, she persisted. Every time she paused and looked back, allowing the water to carry her downstream, Lee was there, arms around his knees, patiently waiting, watching. Her.

She swam until her arms and legs were exhausted, and her lungs were about to burst. Then, hauling herself onto the rock where Lee sat, she smiled. "I needed that, pent-up emotions, you know."

"Missing the girls?"

"She nodded, her wet hair dripping as she toweled it dry. "Do you know that Ally can do a handstand for twenty seconds, Amanda can turn cartwheels across the field abutting our house without stopping, and Ora can ride her bike the length of our driveway, even around the bend onto the dirt road, without touching the handlebars?"

Grace swallowed. "I've never been apart from them for this long, and I'm desperate to resolve the Gizmo affair before they come home. Thinking about jeopardizing them or anyone I care about is terrifying. I have to figure this out."

"You will."

"How can you be so sure?"

"Because I know you. Graceland Walker Holden, you are smart and kind and have more strength than you realize."

Grace did everything to keep from throwing her arms around him and planting a kiss on his lips. She shoved her feet into her hiking boots and began lacing them up. "Thanks for bringing me here."

"It's one of my favorite spots. I come here in the summer after work to cool off. Though I don't swim, I wade in the shallow parts."

"Wait, why?"

"I never learned. No one taught me."

"I'll teach you." Once out, her words were non-retractable. What was going on, anyway? They both used the *F* word freely. If that's what they were, a friend could teach another to swim.

****

Lee heated Lois's delicacies as Grace changed into loose-fitting sweats and a long-sleeved cotton tee, dismissing Dallas's high fashion expectations in favor of comfort.

"This lighter-than-air asparagus quiche is delicious." Grace made a conscious effort to keep her legs from brushing against his. The round kitchen table was compact, offering little room beneath its surface.

"She's relentless, doesn't think Doc Jenner or I can fend for ourselves. But her efforts are greatly appreciated." As if to emphasize the point, he took another bite.

Grace took a drink of water and swallowed. It was time to jump off another cliff. "My sister doesn't remember dating you in high school," she said.

"I'm not surprised. We didn't go out that long. And, from what I recall, Dallas dated quite a bit."

"As did you."

"As did I."

"But you remember her."

He put down his fork. His expression was intense, with a glint in his eyes. "I remember Dallas only because she was your sister. I was the one who kept suggesting we go to your house. The truth was, I wanted to see you. But you hightailed out of there whenever we showed up. You told me that afternoon…."

Here it comes. Finally, we are going to talk about

it.

"When we were studying at my Aunt Ida's, you said I should date your sister."

And no, we're not discussing our first time.

Lee continued. "I wanted to understand why you thought I was better off with Dallas. Because you're so smart, I figured you knew what was best. I figured I must be more like your sister than I realized because you wanted us together. I trusted you and assumed what happened between us meant something to you, too. When you pushed me away, I was confused."

"When we were eight, my dad left us. If you love someone, you give them the power to hurt you. I wasn't ready to take the chance."

"I see that now."

****

After cleaning up, they moved to the couch, where they drank herbal tea and talked for hours.

Refreshed yet suddenly drained, Grace rose from her seat. "Thanks for today, Lee. I needed this."

"I'm a good distraction?"

"The best." She leaned over and kissed his forehead.

His face betrayed no emotion. "Sweet dreams, Grace. I hope you get a good night's rest. We have another packed schedule tomorrow. Afterward, you'll get to don your hiking boots and party dress."

"I can't wait." To her astonishment, she truly felt that way. If she couldn't be with her girls, this was where she wanted to be.

Chapter 44

Exam Room #2

Open-toed slippers padded toward her. Grace asked, "Lois, why are bunnies on your feet?"

"My feet are too big for my shoes today, and walking around a healthcare facility barefoot would be unsanitary. I usually reserve these comfy gems for breaks and when we don't have any clients in the office. It's rabbits or nothing. Your next patient is in room two." Lois handed Grace the chart. "This is her first baby. She's eight months pregnant–"

"Stop. Lee never said they deliver babies here. I thought this was a preventive care and minor emergency clinic."

"Grace, take a deep breath." Lois put a hand on her arm. "We only provide prenatal care. All our moms drive to the city to deliver."

"It doesn't matter." Grace vehemently shook her head. "Have Lee examine her. I don't do–"

"He's not available."

Grace knocked and opened the door to exam room one. "Lee, I can't...." She stopped when he scrutinized her, a needle in his right hand. The boy he was stitching up had sustained a five-inch gash to his leg. He was around Ora's age. His face was crimson, and tears filled his eyes. Suturing the wound closed was going to take some time.

Grace tried to quiet her alarm. "I'm sorry for interrupting."

His face said everything. "What's going on? I want to help, but I can't leave this boy." Grace took a breath. *Get it together, girl.* "My next client is thirty-six weeks gestation."

Lee nodded. "I know who you mean, routine prenatal exam."

"Nothing more?"

"Nothing more. She's had an uncomplicated pregnancy. There's no reason to expect anything out of the ordinary." His eyes were kind and accepting. "You've got this, Nurse Holden."

She swallowed. "Okay, thanks." Grace closed the door behind her.

Lois peered considerately through her bifocals. The magnifying section enlarged her rheumy gray eyes. "The client's name is Sue Ann, and she has to be at work in an hour."

You've done hundreds of assessments before—no need to stress over this. She took a deep breath and opened the door.

"Hello, Sue Ann. My name is Grace, and I'll be your nurse for this appointment. Dr. Leland is tied up, but I assure you I'll give him all the information, and he'll call you if he has any concerns."

The young woman visibly relaxed. "This is my baby's father, Ian." Her partner slouched in the chair, his baseball cap pulled low over his eyes, peach fuzz consuming the lower part of his face–had he even started shaving? He looked up–unmistakable apprehension reflected on his young face.

"Sue Ann, your vital signs are within normal limits, your weight gain is what we'd expect this close to delivery, and no ketones or glucose were detected in your urine, so that's good. Next, I will listen to your little one's heart rate, measure your fundal height, and check the baby's presentation. Do you know if it's a boy or a girl?"

Sue Ann lifted her smock as Grace put some warmed jelly on her protruding abdomen and adjusted the volume on the doppler.

"We want it to be a surprise."

Grace checked her watch and counted as the loud, swishing beats filled the air. "Your baby's heart rate is 140 beats per minute. Perfect. And are you doing kick counts?"

"Yup, twice a day. Peanut is incredibly active. I usually get the ten kicks in less than twenty minutes."

"Terrific." Grace gently palpated the young woman's abdomen, tracing the outline of the baby. "The last time you were in here, did the doctor say anything about which way your baby was facing?"

"No. Dr. Jenner said everything looked good."

"Well, Peanut may have done some flipping. Let me get the ultrasound to confirm. I think your little one is in a breech presentation."

Grace grabbed the machine from the equipment alcove and began to scan. "Your little one has done a somersault. See here, pressed against your cervix, where the head usually is, is your baby's bottom. Give me a few minutes to consult with Dr. Leland and call your delivery hospital. I'll be back in a flash."

****

Grace found Ian sitting beside Sue Ann on the

exam table, his arm draped around her shoulders. She understood how worried they were.

"Sue Ann, I've talked to Dr. Leland and called Tahlequah's labor and delivery department. You've got an appointment in ten days. They'll check your baby's lung maturity. If everything looks good, they'll do an external version. A highly qualified obstetrician will try and turn your baby into a vertex position, making a vaginal delivery possible. If they can't turn Peanut, since this is your first pregnancy, they'll probably do a C-section."

Sue Ann's eyes filled with tears.

Grace allowed her time to digest the new information.

"Our goal is to have a healthy mom and baby. I printed some information for you to read. Call me or return to the clinic if you have any questions."

Sue Ann took the literature, managing a half-hearted smile. "Thank you, Grace."

"I read in your chart that you attended childbirth classes. Things are a little different since we know your baby is breech. You must immediately head to the labor and delivery unit when you start having regular contractions. Don't wait until they're three minutes apart. And if your water breaks, even if you're not having contractions, call this number and tell them you're coming in."

Sue Ann sobbed. "This isn't how I imagined childbirth would be."

"I know." Grace stayed by her side and let her cry.

After five minutes, Sue Ann surveyed her watch, stood, and hugged Grace. "Time to get to work. I'm glad you were here. Don't get me wrong, the guys are great. But it's nice having a woman in the mix."

As Sue Ann was checking out, Grace texted Dallas to see how her prenatal check-up had gone. Dallas and Sue Ann shared the same due date.

The reception room was empty. Lois' brow had deep creases like plowed soil as she intently read her novel, almost at the climactic end. She breathed heavily with her cottontail feet propped on the desk. Every time she exhaled, a small, high-pitched whistle punctuated the air.

Lois broke away from the page as Grace approached the desk. "Our last patient canceled their appointment. Hence, you guys are free to go when Doc Leland finishes."

"I'm not done yet. Lois, when was the last time you had a physical?"

"I'm as healthy as a filly in a Horse Show. No complaints in that department."

"That's not what I'm asking. Yesterday, your shoes fit; today, they don't. And is the ending of the Electric Embrace getting exciting?"

"No, actually, it's a bust, a complete let-down."

"Indulge me then. Let me draw some blood and do a quick assessment. It won't take long." Grace guided Lois toward the empty exam room.

Her apprehension was unshakable, even as Lois tried to dismiss her worries.

****

In the reception area, Grace spotted Lee who was seated behind the desk with a basket of brown eggs on his lap.

Lee smiled as she approached. "Did Lois go home? She wasn't around to check Mr. Agilar and his son out."

Grace shook her head.

"I have her in the exam room." Grace leaned over the counter and whispered, "Lee, she has plus four pitting edema, shortness of breath, and an audible expiratory wheeze. I want you to listen to her heart sounds. I haven't heard an S4 since the recordings in nursing school. I think she has one."

"Congestive heart failure?"

Lee was putting the stethoscope into his ears as he smiled broadly and entered the room. "Causing trouble, Lois?" His light and teasing voice did not fool Grace or Lois. His shoulders carried tension, a taut wishbone pulled in two directions, ready to snap apart.

Chapter 45

Tell Me More

"Four weeks to go, Dallas. How are you feeling?"

"To be honest, Dr. Kay, I'll deliver this baby in prison if one more person tells me, 'Sleep while you can,' while giving me an obnoxious wink. I want to scream at the top of my lungs–if I could sleep, I would, you moron!"

Dr. Kay was unable to suppress a smile. Dallas grinned in response. Venting to her therapist was a welcome relief compared to bottling up everything. Dallas continued. "I've replaced my husband with pillows, trying to get the sleep I'm supposed to get, but I can't get comfortable. My back pain is unrelenting, and the pressure on my bladder makes me pee every fifteen minutes. Being reminded that you have years of sleepless nights to look forward to is not helpful.

"But to answer your question, I detest being pregnant so much that I'm looking forward to the body-torturing ordeal of labor and delivery." She paused, briefly grazing her abdomen, and continued, "I'm more afraid of what will happen when I bring him home."

Dr. Kay folded her hands in her lap and remained quiet. Dallas understood what this meant. When she first started therapy, the encouraging silences infuriated her; she had stormed out of many sessions, swearing it would be her last. Dallas sighed. "I went to dinner with a friend last night. The evening was wonderful. For a moment, I forgot about the daddy dilemma, the looming 'birth experience,' everything. We'd been talking about shopping, working out, or something like that. Then my friend leans in and says, 'Well, once the baby comes, you won't have time for that anymore.'

"I lost it, Dr. Kay. I don't know why, but I stood and yelled. 'Tell me more, please. Go on. Tell me how my life will dissolve into a hopeless pit of despair with nothing except sleepless nights, copious amounts of bodily fluids, and time that's no longer mine. I can't wait!' I threw sixty bucks on the table and walked out."

Dallas moved to the window and turned in despair. "What is wrong with me, Dr. Kay?" Her palms opened as if in supplication. "Help me–please. If I lose control with a rational adult friend, how will I handle a howling infant? If I can't remain faithful to my husband, how can I guarantee my son that I won't walk out on him one day? And I'd be hurting him the same way Dad hurt us. I can't help but think that this whole pregnancy, baby idea was a colossal mistake."

****

An hour after Lee confirmed Grace's suspicion, Tahlequah Hospital's cardiac unit admitted Lois. She refused to let them stay with her, saying her sister was on the way and was a fighting mother hen who would make everyone's life miserable. She didn't want them around to witness the blood bath. "I'll be back at the clinic before you know it, fit as a fiddle. Don't worry about me. You two go on and have some fun. Tomorrow will be extra hard without me." She retrieved a novel with a cover featuring a shirtless, muscled man and a swooning woman with a ripped bodice. "If my heart can stand this steamy romance, it can handle anything." She winked, waved them away, and immersed herself in the novel, as the technician took her vital signs.

****

Dallas left Dr. Kay's office with thirty minutes to spare before her obstetrician appointment. The session had been difficult yet good. She glanced at her phone. Bryce had texted her about getting carryout for dinner. He still didn't know she was seeing a therapist. There was also a message from Peter.

Since learning about the pregnancy, Peter was inquisitive and present. He asked about her check-ups and how she was doing. She ran into him at the condo complex at odd times and out-of-the-way places and always when she was alone. Peter was purposely seeking her out. But why? It wasn't because they were planning hook-ups. Did the fact that she might be carrying his son mean something? Dallas recently admitted to her therapist that, despite the boundaries of their "arrangement," she felt something for him, but she wouldn't call it love. Peter accepted her unorthodox sides. He didn't judge. They both willingly accepted the terms of their relationship. From the start, he made it abundantly clear that he was a lifelong bachelor. And Dallas, never once, wanted more from him. But surprisingly, he didn't run away once he learned the news. As a confidant, he listened to her misery without telling her what a horrible human she was. At this point, she needed all the support she could get.

What was she going to do? Raise her son as if there were no question about his paternity, keeping Bryce in the dark forever? Have the DNA test and let Bryce know she had been unfaithful. Then she risked the chance of him walking out, of being a single mom. How would that work out?

Dallas pulled her car keys from her purse. She had time to respond to Bryce's text and stop by the convenience store. As she rounded the corner to the parking structure, she thought about her next therapy session. Dallas promised Dr. Kay they would discuss the daddy debacle in-depth. Paralyzed with uncertainty, Dallas couldn't put it off any longer. Before deciding what she would do, she had to weigh all the options with someone she trusted, a trained professional.

Out of the dim parking garage came a deep voice that rattled her like the tuning fork her obstetrician used to check her reflexes. "Did you hear that bang at night? That startled you from slumber with shock and fright. That, my pet, was me." The man advanced toward her, his heft filling the space. His voice increased in timbre. "Did you feel that grasp at night? Around your neck relentlessly tight. Understanding your soul's doomed plight, that, my pet, was me."

Then he was on her, like an excavator, pushing Dallas' upper body against her car, his meaty hands tightening around her windpipe.

He increased the pressure. "I want to make sure your sister sees the bruises on your throat when she identifies your body. The game is over. We warned Grace–she didn't listen. If she doesn't turn the rest of Michael Walker's invention over to us, someone else she loves will suffer. Dr. Brody was a test run. You and your baby are the escalation. Think of it as a two-for-one sale."

Dallas struggled, frantically clawing, digging her tingling nails into the sausage fingers around her neck, but the man did not loosen his grip. As nausea mounted, her world tunneled in. Tiny white lights flickered as darkness grew. Dallas was on the edge. The strength to keep fighting was fading.

Chapter 46

Skeletons

The small city's outline receded in the rearview mirror, giving way to the vast, sprawling countryside. Grace had spoken with her daughters. But from Dallas? Silence. An unease settled in her stomach, a persistent gnaw in the back of her mind. Dallas always responded; every minute without a text felt heavier than the last.

Soon, Grace would be out of range. Thinking of Sue Ann and how rapidly complications developed, she craved a simple sign—a voicemail, a two-word text, a ridiculous emoji—anything.

"Everything good?" Lee's inquiry broke her reverie.

"I can't reach Dallas. She's not responding to my texts, and the phone goes straight to voicemail. Give me a second. I'm going to call Mom to check. Oops, I guess I'm not. No bars." Grace turned off her phone–no reason to run down the battery. She threw it into her purse. "First thing tomorrow, when I get to the clinic, I'll touch base with everyone. I have to stop worrying."

"Speaking of misgivings." Lee shot her a sympathetic look as he drove. "What's up with you being terrified of a thirty-six-week pregnant client?"

Grace was silent in her response.

"Anything to do with why you didn't go the midwife route?"

Lee touched her upper arm. "Grace...." She turned to him. The compassion in his eyes, a response to the pain reflected in hers, undid her.

"You don't want to talk about it?"

She nodded and looked out the passenger window.

Lee was taking a different route home than he had the afternoon before. Winter's stark glare created a strobe light effect as they passed through a dense thicket of barren trees.

The truck slowed to a crawl. "I want to show you something," he said. "It's not far from here."

Grace turned her full attention to him.

He turned off the dirt road onto tracks in the rutted ground and braked. Lee took Grace's hand as she jumped from the truck. "Be careful. All sorts of hazards await."

It was a junkyard. The skeletons of abandoned cars in various stages of rusting degradation and piles of tires rose and fell around them, a silent army. Through a line of impoverished trees, at the edge of the heaped detritus, was a series of sheds with corroding metal roofs. Grace and Lee stepped over a fallen barbed wire fence. Affixed to the falling structures were bright red tags, "Condemned Premises. Unfit for human habitation. Keep Out!"

Stretched across the shack windows was chicken wire glass, each small hexagon shattered, leaving jagged edges and shards of glass in the frames. Grace imagined all the piercing and cutting injuries that might occur if a living organism tangled with the disastrous huts, not to mention the rusty barbed wire perimeter and land mine of scrapped metal.

"I lived here before Aunt Ida took me in."

Grace swallowed. Lee was showing her a part of himself, one he kept hidden.

"With your parents?"

"Dad left us when I was in second grade. Mom and I couch-surfed for a while, then moved here with one of her boyfriends. It wasn't this bad then, and we made it work. One day, Mom left with him–nothing unusual. I was ten and used to being alone. But this time, they didn't come back. A friend of moms called child protective services when she realized they weren't returning.

"A caseworker came. I knew I was in trouble when the lady started snapping pictures and shaking her head. When she turned her back, I threw a sheet over Mom's drug paraphernalia. She told me she had to remove me from the deplorable conditions. I was distraught, begging her to let me stay, and I lied to her, telling her my mom was getting us a new apartment. I wouldn't go with her. She had to call a police officer to get me in the car."

Grace climbed into the truck. Lee turned on the ignition. "I spent a month in foster care until they vetted Aunt Ida. And the rest, well, is my history."

He navigated the dirt road, leaving the scene of his abandonment in the dust.

The weight of his disclosure settled in Grace's bones. This explained a lot about Lee when he was an adolescent. Cockiness was a way to compensate for feelings of dismissal, not only by one parent but by two. There was no comparison between her father walking out on them and what Lee had gone through. At least her father was still intermittently in her life and had remained there until he died. Who did Lee have?

"Did your mom ever come back?"

"Aunt Ida reported her as missing. The police didn't take it seriously. My parents had a history of addiction and minor skirmishes with the law. Investigating Mom's disappearance wasn't a top priority. To this day, I don't know if she's dead or alive. Once a month, I stop by the station to see if they have any updates. I know they are sick of me, but my visits may spur them to resolve the case."

"And your dad?"

"Aunt Ida asked if she should try to find him and let him know the situation. I told her not to. For the first time, I had a reliable rhythm to my life. Aunt Ida worked tirelessly to support us. She spent her free time tutoring me, helping me catch up in school, and encouraging my participation in sports. She was at every baseball and football game I played. Aunt Ida was my biggest fan and believed in me, even when doubt crowded in."

Ally would be ten next year, and Grace tried to visualize her daughter living the way Lee had. "You cooked for yourself, did laundry?"

He delivered a small chortle. "That would have been a luxury. This compound is off the grid. We didn't have electricity."

Life without running water, lights, refrigeration, and modern appliances was difficult to imagine. "How did you get by?"

"Our fridge was a moldy cooler that was never cool. We had an outdoor fire pit for cooking, primarily canned goods. Those never spoil. We used blankets and newspapers in the winter to insulate the shed's windows. When the hovel was a furnace in the summer, I'd haul a mattress outdoors and sleep with a sheet over me so the bugs wouldn't eat me alive. Behind the complex is an outhouse. The junked cars and tires were my playground."

Grace didn't have the words to respond. As they drove, she surveyed the shifting landscape, digesting this information while visualizing Lee's life as a ten-year-old.

"Didn't they miss you at school? I can't imagine a week going by without anyone reporting you absent and checking in on you."

He gripped the steering wheel, looking straight ahead. "After Dad left, Mom 'homeschooled' me. I hadn't been in a classroom for two years."

Chapter 47

No Call, No Show

A series of staccato kicks deep in her womb
brought Dallas reeling back. In an adrenaline fueled
superhuman response, anger replaced surrender, which
supplanted fear. *Oh no, you don't. You monolithic
monster, you don't get to be the one to take away my
chance at being the world's worst mother.* Dallas
kicked him furiously between the legs. His hands went
slack as he bent in pain. She vomited, her stomach
purging its partially digested contents all over his pants,
then ran away.

****

"Are you sure I can't call anyone for you? Your
husband, a family member, a friend?"

"No." Dallas didn't mean to sound ungrateful. The
victim's advocate was only doing her job. The police
had taken her report, including a detailed description of
the assailant. They'd taken pictures of her neck,
swabbed underneath her fingernails for DNA, and
offered to drive her to the emergency room. Dallas
adamantly refused. Even though there weren't any
cameras where the attack occurred, they planned to
review the area's surveillance footage and call her if
they found anything.

In the frenzy following her assault, Dallas missed

her pre-natal check-up. Her absence would go in her chart as– 'No Call, No Show.' In other words, *irresponsible*, another black mark on her mother of the year record. She'd missed her eyes-closed weigh-in, the measurement of her abdomen, and the reassuring galloping of her son's heartbeat. But she didn't need a doppler to know. Her son was alive and fighting. He'd furiously jolted her when she most needed it, and she responded. Already, they were a kick-ass superhero team, Ballcrusher, and Spawn. My son, my son, she repeated, a mantra, unable to move her hands from her center. And beneath the curve of her palm, she felt a subtle turn of his body. Only then, in the solitude of her parked car, did she allow herself to cry.

****

"Not much further. Are you hanging in there?" As they ascended another rugged trail, Lee offered her a hand, the flash of scar tissue tight in his palm, pulled the surrounding skin.

Grace scrambled over a fallen tree. "Even in the heart of winter, these trails are magnificent."

"If you think this is nice, I'll have to get you up here in the spring, summer, and fall."

"What a perfect way to decompress after a crazy shift, with a swim or hike."

"Speaking of insane days, Grace, you may have saved Lois' life. With an ejection fraction of seventeen percent, she was one shovel full of dirt away from an acute cardiac event. And you know how she loves to garden."

"It wasn't a big deal. The signs were hard to ignore. You would have picked up on them, too."

"But I didn't."

"You were busy all day. You didn't have time."

"So were you, Grace. You ran as much as I did, yet you didn't miss a beat. And your gentle persuasion to get her to have a physical made all the difference."

Grace hid behind a sheath of hair, embarrassed.

Lee stopped her, pushing the strand behind her ear. "How did you get this inaccurate, distorted picture of yourself? I wish you could see how truly amazing you are."

"The way you see me is all wrong. But even if my image is a skewed Picasso, what can I do about it? The things I learned from my dad, past relationships, ex-husband, and how I failed others along the way created that snapshot."

"It seems you've also done a paint-by-number job on that portrayal, filling in the empty spots with self-doubt and depreciation."

"Maybe I did. The reality is–you carry that snapshot with you. No matter how far you get, it is always in your back pocket, impacting future interactions. There's nothing a person can do about that."

"Oh yes, there is." Lee stepped closer.

"Tell me."

With a swift motion known only to magicians performing a sleight of hand, he reached behind her, slipped his hand into her back jean pocket, and flashed before her an imaginary card, a self-portrait. "You can tear the damn thing up." He flung the ripped pieces into the air.

Grace swallowed hard. Nothing could be that easy, could it?

"Come on. We're close." Lee veered off the beaten

path and led Grace to a bluff.

She stepped onto the limestone outcropping and caught her breath. The vista undulated and stretched to a far horizon where winter's sinking sun shattered rays of pink and gold into the deepening blue. Cutting through the panorama, ablaze with the sky's reflection, was the river she had swum in last evening. Breathtaking.

From behind, Lee wrapped his arms around her. For a glorious minute, as the sun retreated below the horizon, the complex world fell away. She leaned back into his embrace and inhaled. Sharp, frosty air assaulted her lungs. In his arms, she was warm. For the first time since her father's death, since Andrew's abandonment, since the Gizmo Affair started, she was at peace.

They stayed until the ridges, gorges, and trees disappeared, and all that was left was an immense and brilliant star-saturated sky.

****

Inside the shower, the water pounded her back, almost scalding. Yet Dallas could not stop shivering. The magnitude of the close call hit her in turns. What if she had died? What if a temporary lack of oxygen had killed or injured her son? What if the monster tried again? She slid down to the tiled floor, arms protectively shielding her swollen abdomen, and rocked back and forth. She stayed until the shaking stopped, then stood resolved–she must not let herself fall apart.

After donning her favorite fleece robe, Dallas padded into the kitchen. Bryce turned to face her, a spatula in one hand, moisture in his eyes. Dallas reflexively touched her tender neck.

"I almost lost you both," he said.

Thin lines darted from the outer corners of his worried eyes. Bryce looked much older than he had on their wedding day. Had living with her caused him to age? She went to him and, using the sleeve of her robe, touched his cheek, absorbing the tears. "But you didn't. We're still here. This little man is ready for his first mixed martial arts tournament...feel."

Bryce put down the spatula and slipped a hand through the opening of her robe, a smile wider than a structural beam spreading. "Whoa, that's some serious kicking going on." He kneeled, fingers grazing his wife's taut, stretched-to-the-limit skin. "My son, you're working up quite an appetite in there. I scrambled eggs for your mom. There's also toast and a fruit cup if you prefer."

My son. Dallas sat on the couch with her aching legs propped and ate the meal Bryce had prepared.

Bryce cleaned the kitchen, started the dishwasher, and left a message on her obstetrician's answering machine, explaining why Dallas missed her appointment. He was there when she needed him, holding her and comforting her. Equally important, he recognized when to give her space. He didn't push.

Over the years, her husband had granted Dallas a landscape of unconditional acceptance. Patiently and without pressure, he let her set the boundaries and pace of their relationship. Of course, she was oblivious to this at first, but now, with the insight she gained from Dr. Kay, she could see. Loving Bryce was like sitting in your favorite spot on the couch–you didn't want to sit anywhere else in the room. It didn't feel right. When someone else sat there, you felt out of sorts. The give and curves were made just for you. When you slipped into the folds, it was always with a familiar satisfaction and release–I am home. Steady and sure with a cadence of comfort–that was what Bryce gave. Was this quiet love enough?

****

Dallas called Grace. When it went straight to voicemail, she hung up. Her sister would be home in a handful of days. They would figure everything out then. As Dallas' exhausted body slipped into sleep, she thought of her sister and the pale pink negligee. *I hope you have the chance to use it, my sister. You deserve happiness.*

Chapter 48

Free Range Eggs

Grace slipped into her off-the-shoulder dress in the muted light of Lee's bedroom. She smoothed the bodice and soft material around the natural waistline. She'd been going for simple elegance, but was this over-the-top? Thank goodness she hadn't given in to Dallas' suggestion of a side-zipping, form-accentuating scuba dress. "It's a fuck-me dress," Dallas unapologetically said as she held up the shiny slip of fabric. "Come on, sister. Surely, you've heard of those? A dress a man can take off with one fluid, frenzied, I cannot wait for another second to ravish you, zip." Grace never had.

The house had no mirrors. Consequently, she applied clear lip gloss by feel and brushed her shower-damp hair, forming a loose French braid that hung down her back.

Grace stepped into the kitchen. Lee, wearing khaki pants and a button-down shirt that strained at his broad shoulders, peered woefully into a virtually empty refrigerator, muttering, "Well, I certainly didn't think this part through. No Lois, no food."

Grace moved by his side. "I'm sure we'll come up with something." He stared at her intensely and swallowed. Had any man looked at her this way before? Even on her wedding day, as she walked down the aisle

249

in Vegas in a wedding gown, Andrew hadn't regarded her as if she was the only woman on the planet.

"You're stunning, Grace," Lee said.

Embarrassed, she gently hip-checked him. "Awe shucks, Doc. You clean up nicely, too. Now, let's see what we can whip up for dinner."

"All we have is free-range eggs, given to me by Mr. Agilar instead of payment for stitching up his son and one of Lois' leftover sandwiches." He shrugged apologetically.

"Alrighty then, I'll make the omelet, and you pan-fry the sandwich." Grace searched through the compact kitchen, grabbing what she needed.

A fire danced in the wood burner, sending shafts of orange and yellow across the room, across his visage. The small kitchen table, covered with a bed sheet, had an evergreen shoot centerpiece. And they ate, their legs tangling beneath it.

****

"I feel like an adolescent again," Grace said with a smile as Lee wrapped his arms around her waist and nuzzled her neck. She leaned back into him, a soapy dish in her hand.

"I don't remember cooking or washing the dishes together when we were in high school. Still, you're right. That seems ages ago," Lee said.

A single finger skimmed, feather-soft, up Grace's arm, causing the hair on her arms to spring in its wake—sunflowers following an attentive sun.

He grinned. "The clinical term for that is piloerection. It's an involuntary contraction of the muscles at the hair follicles' base." Lee took a towel from the drawer and dried the dishes on the rack.

Grace tried to keep her face straight. "I'm well aware of the medical term describing goosebumps. If I were a dog, I'd be sporting raised hackles."

He emitted a chortle. "Merely a sympathetic nervous system response. But the question is, will you fight me, Grace, or take flight?"

It was her turn to laugh. "Fight you, never. Still, there's another cause for goosebumps."

He stepped in front of her, taking the last dish from her hands and drying it, his eyes never leaving hers. "Tell me, Nurse Holden, what else stimulates piloerection."

"Arousal." She took a sharp intake of breath. "Caused by fear or excitement."

"And with you? Grace, what is it, apprehension or anticipation?"

"A little bit of both." There it was, her truth. He didn't mitigate what she said or try to convince her that she had nothing to fear. He nodded, put the last dish away, put the kettle on the stove, and gently cupped her face, drawing her close. His lips covered hers with purposeful care. With restrained intensity, the way you'd eat an exquisite strawberry dipped in the most decadent chocolate in the world, savoring the taste because you might never get another, he kissed her. Grace responded.

Kissing him was like medicine, something you appreciated would make you feel better, yet you also recognized that ingesting too much might be dangerous. To hell with medical advice and her internal warning system, the unimaginable sweetness of someone wanting you, kissing you, despite the hot mess of your life, was an alluring intoxicant, something she could not put down, at least until the tea kettle whistle intervened with its persistent shrillness and hot steam aimed directly at them.

Grace thought they were showing impressive adult restraint as she sat on the couch, her legs stretched across his lap, drinking hot beverages.

"Remember when I told you about Aunt Ida being clairvoyant?"

Grace took a sip of her cinnamon-steeped tea.

"I asked Aunt Ida about you, Graceland. You'd been over several times to work on projects and study. She'd seen us interact. I didn't tell her, but undoubtedly, she knew that I liked you." Lee put his empty coffee mug on the floor and rested his right hand, the one with the scar on its palm, against her ankle. "She told me, 'If you want her in your life, you must wait a long time.'"

Grace put her mug beside his and joked, "You waited for me?"

"No way. I was nineteen when we graduated, ready to take on the world. I forgot about you. I lived my life."

"Phew," Grace said, trying to ignore his fingers now playing with the hem of her dress. "That takes some pressure off."

"Somewhere along the way, through the grapevine, I heard you were married with children, living up north. Then, one day, I walk into a code, and there you are, on a man's bed, giving him chest compressions."

Grace slid closer to him. It was her turn; she undid the top button of his shirt and rested her palm there. "About that day…" She kissed him where her hand had been.

Lee's focus did not waver. He leaned down so close that she thought he would kiss her again. He whispered, "Is this what you want?"

Grace nodded.

"I should have asked you that the first time. Afterward, when you dumped me like a hot potato, I was sure you regretted getting together, that it was awful, that I was awful. I assumed that was why you didn't want anything to do with me. Despite my external bravado, I had insecurities. My biggest fear was that I had misread you or that you had changed your mind. What if I was too caught up in the moment to realize it? I never checked in. For that, I'm sorry."

"For the record, I initiated that encounter. You could chalk it up to the impulsivity of adolescence, blaming my underdeveloped executive brain. That, however, would be a lie. It was what I wanted." Grace remembered herself then, skin smooth and tight, the body of a young, consenting teen. "Be forewarned, though, I'm not sixteen anymore. I've had babies. There are stretch marks and–"

"Stop." He kissed her hard enough to overwhelm protests. "I'm here for the grown-up Grace, the mother of three daughters, the woman who talks to patients even though they cannot hear, the one who keeps–"

"Stop." She took his hand, pulled him up from the couch, and wrapped her arms around his neck. "This, you, are what I want," she said, her words soft against his lips.

****

During the night, tangled in blankets, sheets, and each other, Grace took Lee's palm and ran her fingers over the thickened scar tissue.

"When I was three, I grabbed the coils of our oven. The door was open, heating our apartment."

"A blistering burn like that must have hurt like crazy."

"I don't remember anything. Much of my early childhood is dark and all dried up."

Grace kissed his palm. Remembered or not, the scar was a vestige of extreme pain.

"I'm so sorry." Her voice broke in a way she did not expect.

Lee folded Grace into him, muscular arms and legs, a comforting weighted blanket pressing against her.

"Lee," she murmured.

"Hmm."

"I keep thinking of you living in a compound off the grid. It's hard to fathom that the most prosperous country in the world still has people without electricity."

"Around sixty thousand people in America lack access. Worldwide, it's worse." His voice drifted. "An estimated thirteen percent of the world's population still lives without this basic necessity."

Grace pondered the magnitude and the impact of this singular fact. She spoke quietly, sorting thoughts, unsure if Lee was still awake. "If you can't turn on a tap for water, you must haul it from somewhere. What if that source was miles away or contaminated? Without power, you wouldn't have a functioning toilet, and there'd be no way to preserve food, no heat source for warmth, or meal preparation. You'd have to gather wood, or even dung to burn. And what about communication? Staying connected with friends and family is impossible without internet or cell phone connections, but you need a way to charge these devices, or they're useless. I suppose you could write letters, but that wouldn't work in the case of an emergency. Families living without electricity would exhaust their reserves quickly after struggling to get the essentials for existence. Nothing would be left. Each day would be a monumental slog to survive."

In the darkness of his bedroom, deep in the interior of an earth berm, Lee's respirations slowed to an even rhythmic cadence.

"Lee?"

His relaxed arms cradled her. He did not answer.

As his chest rose and fell against her back, Grace followed the progression of all she had learned since being introduced to Gizmo. Finally, she let her expanding awareness, a higher consciousness, intertwine with this information. What makes the most sense?

Grace heard her father as she had the last time he had the strength to venture outdoors. 'I found a way to make things right with the earth while helping humanity.' His thin voice was steady, his blue eyes luminous. With distilled clarity, Grace understood.

"Dad?" she whispered into absolute blackness, so encompassing she might have been lying on the edge of a cliff. "Dad, I figured it out. I know what to do."

Chapter 49

The Morning After

Lee engaged his parking brake and was about to turn off the ignition when he stopped. "Shoot, I left the charts on the counter."

"Don't blame me for your frontal lobe not functioning." Grace affectionately traced the contours of his eyebrows. "But I'm glad everything else was."

He laughed appreciatively, kissed her forehead, and mused, "Good gravy. What delightful trouble I've found. Are you coming with me?"

"No thanks, I'll stay, stock the rooms, call my family, and catch up before our first client arrives. We've still got thirty minutes."

"You know the drill: Get the patient ready, take vitals, and do an assessment. I should be back by nine-twenty. If they can't wait, have them reschedule."

He handed her the keys and winked. "I'll miss you."

"Good, that was my fiendish plan all along."

Grace closed the clinic door behind her. She turned on her cell, a missed call from Dallas and her mom—no voicemail messages. Something had to be wrong.

Then a ping, a text from her sister sent seconds ago–*Ignore the missed call. Baby and I are well*–

Grace shot her a hug emoji back.

Ping, from Dallas —*give me the dirt*—

Ping, from Dallas —*did you HU?*—

When Grace realized what HU meant, she brayed.

Ping, from Dallas —*don't ghost me, sister*—

Ping, from Dallas, again —*details!*—

Everything had to be okay if Dallas was pestering her.

Grace responded —*TTYL, G2G*—

Figure that out, Dallas.

While she stocked the rooms, cleaned the surfaces, and ensured the clinic was ready for their patients, she put her daughters on speakerphone. She listened to the music of their escalating voices, interlaced, telling stories about the snowman they built, the hot chocolate they were drinking, last night's dreams, the from-scratch waffles Momma Sabrina made them for breakfast, and the plans they had that afternoon for ice skating and shopping.

"All right, guys, it's time to call Grandma Mary. I'll talk to you again around five o'clock-six your time. Be good, and have fun. Love you!"

"Bye! Love you, Mommy! See you soon."

****

The stillness of the clinic shattered.

Someone was lying on their horn-heavy, hard, and unrelenting.

"Mom, something is going on. I'm glad Dallas and her baby are doing well, but I gotta go." Grace threw her phone on the reception desk and flung open the door.

The blaring stopped. Sue Ann, pressed against the side of an old station wagon, slid to the ground. She was on her elbows and knees, her stomach skimming the earth, rocking back and forth. Her face was a contortion of pain.

"No!" Grace didn't mean for her voice to sound hysterical.

Sue Ann looked up from her contraction. Grace continued. "We're not equipped for delivery, let alone a complicated one. Ian, get her to the hospital now!" Even as the words left her mouth, Grace knew the demand was unreasonable–worse than delivering a baby in an ill-equipped clinic would be a breech delivery in a car, with no skilled medical personnel around.

"I called the ambulance," Ian said. He was by Sue Ann's side, helping her navigate the clinic's steps. "They said they'd meet us here."

Another contraction overwhelmed Sue Ann. She bent over, her feet apart. She hugged her belly and moaned, panic on her young face. Grace glanced at her watch. They were less than three minutes apart.

"I have to go to the bathroom," Sue Ann keened, gasping for air.

"Look at me." Grace tilted Sue Ann's head up so she was looking her in the eyes. She smoothed her hair off her face. "You can do this. Follow my breathing, Hee-hee-hoo. Nice and light, Hee-hee-hoo. Good, just like that. I'm going to touch your abdomen to see how strong the contractions are. Keep breathing–hee-hee-hoo." Grace lifted Sue Ann's thick flannel shirt and palpated her uterus, firm like the frontal bone in a forehead. She breathed with Sue Ann until the contraction was over.

"The pressure isn't stopping. Get me to the toilet! I can't take this anymore!"

As Ian and Grace helped Sue Ann onto the exam table, her sweat pants pooling around her ankles, Grace beseeched the universe: *Please let the ambulance come now. Please let Lee make the trip at lightning speed,* for Sue Ann was in the throes of advanced labor, and her baby, breech presentation, and all was not going to wait.

Grace directed Ian to get behind Sue Ann and hold her upright.

Sue Ann shrieked–a primal, raw cry echoed through the empty clinic. Grace slid on her sterile gloves and bit the inside of her cheek to swallow her own scream.

****

It wasn't until Lee poked his head into the exam room, his mouth and eyes wide in surprise, when he took in the nascent infant suckling, an attentive mother and father's head bent over the sterile towel blanket, that Grace could finally let go.

"The ambulance is almost here." Her voice was taut. " They'll transfer them to the postpartum unit for further evaluation. Sue Ann's fundus is firm, with minimal postpartum bleeding. Baby's Apgar scores were eight and nine. She's six pounds, ten ounces, with an initial blood glucose of fifty. She's latching on without difficulty."

Grace rushed past Lee, pushing open the clinic doors, not making eye contact. "You're taking over," she said, her breath coming in sharp jags.

****

He found her leaning against the clinic's side. "I did a quick assessment of mom and baby. Everyone's doing well. Good job, Grace. I hate to think what might have happened had they delivered in route to the hospital."

"You abandoned me!" Her tremulous words, laced with anger and angst, were like a slap. He stepped back, but despite registering his shock, she continued. "You left me in a horrible situation. The baby's head or shoulders might have gotten stuck. Her umbilical cord could have prolapsed. What if the baby had died?" Against her will, the tears fell.

"But they didn't." He stepped closer, reaching for her. Grace moved back, out of reach. "Grace, I don't understand this reaction. What's going on?"

"You don't get it!"

"Explain then, please."

Grace slumped to the ground and hugged her knees. The blood of delivery splashed across her scrub pants and tennis shoes. "On the last day of my labor and delivery orientation, a woman who'd been in labor over thirty hours delivered a healthy ten-pound baby girl." She looked up. Lee was sitting cross-legged in front of her. He nodded.

"I was giving the infant her Vitamin K shot when the mother gasped. A smooth, pearly gray mass protruded from her cervix. Her uterus had turned entirely inside out, not a mere prolapse, but a full-fledged, complete uterine inversion. I hit the call light for help. All hell broke loose. Blood was gushing from her. It splattered the floor, the infant warmer, the walls. She was hemorrhaging. We weren't able to replace fluids fast enough.

"She went into hypovolemic shock. And now, a little girl is growing up without a mother because of me."

"Grace, that's not rational thinking. Even if you were standing with your hands right there, you couldn't prevent an inversion. You can't blame yourself for that."

"I can't? I had the knowledge base. She had prolonged labor, the umbilical cord was short, and the doctor told us he suspected a retained placental fragment. She presented as being stable, but I missed something. I should've been more attentive."

A distant siren nudged the morning stillness.

"I'm sure the resuscitation effort was exhaustive. You guys did everything possible. This is not your cross to bear. The United States still has the highest maternal mortality rate among developed nations."

"None of this makes me feel better. That mother is more than a statistic. You didn't see the joy on her face when she finally delivered her baby. She and her husband had been trying for years to conceive. They were ecstatic. They were supposed to have a lifetime together. Lee, I don't know how you cope when you lose a patient. Doesn't the loss send you into a spiral?"

Grace wasn't open to a response; she continued. "And this is why I stopped doing direct patient care. What was I thinking? Because this is a rural clinic, nothing horrible will happen. Things fall apart just when you think everything is going well."

The siren's crescendo grew in intensity.

"I'm sorry, Lee, I can't do this anymore. I can't help at the clinic, and whatever we have going on has to end. Last night was a mistake. You're better off without me, anyway. I'm a disaster. I certainly can't be what you need me to be. And I can't afford to become attached only to have you leave. I know you don't think you will, but they always do. Something inside me sends men running–a week, eight years, it doesn't matter. This must be my superpower. It's better this way."

The ambulance pulled into the grassy lot, lights and sirens unrelenting.

Grace rushed to meet the medics, calling over her shoulder. "I'm going with Sue Ann and the baby to the hospital. From there, I'll get a bus to Tulsa."

****

Grace sat beside Sue Ann's stretcher on the ambulance bench and watched Lee recede.

Out the back window, his figure grew smaller and smaller until he was gone. A tsunami of emotion followed in the moving vehicle's wake. What just happened? What had she done?

Chapter 50

Sea Change

Mary honked to signal her location across the street from the bus terminal. Grace disembarked, her rangy legs finding purchase. Spotting the car, Grace mustered a feeble wave. Her long dark hair fell like a curtain, hiding her expressions as she navigated the dispersing crowd.

"Thanks for picking me up," Grace mumbled, sliding into the passenger seat. She offered a perfunctory peck on Mary's cheek but did not meet her mother's eyes. Mary's heart sank. Where was the animated daughter she had lunch with a week ago? Gone was the confidence of a woman ready to ride a rolling wave into her future.

She had no luggage and was home days earlier than expected. Mary nodded, scrutinizing her daughter's profile before merging into traffic.

"Yeah, I've been crying. How do I keep finding new ways to wreck my life?"

Mary didn't offer platitudes. Watching when your children were in pain, granting them space to see their way through, was one of the complex parts of being a mother. Thus, Mary provided what she usually did: objective truth. "Grace, we often sabotage our lives because we're trying to protect ourselves in some twisted way. It's a form of self-preservation and an attempt to avoid confronting painful emotions."

The chortle was between a laugh and a sob.

Mary leveled a long, steady gaze at her daughter before raising a solitary eyebrow. "Just saying."

Grace changed the subject. "I got a text from Andrew. His dad is going in for emergency gallbladder surgery. I tried to call him from the bus, but it went straight to voicemail. Hopefully, the girls are doing okay. They adore their Grandpa Holden. His hospitalization will be scary for them."

Grace squared her shoulders. "Though my personal life is a disaster, I've figured out the Gizmo Affair. I talked to Dr. Brody on the bus, and we have a plan I know Dad would approve of."

"What a relief." The words escaped without thought. She hoped Grace didn't register them. "Tell me."

"What do you mean 'relief'? Mom, did something else happen?"

Mary wanted to wait until Dallas was able to tell Grace about the madman who tried to strangle her–until Grace saw for herself that Dallas was alive and kicking. Mary was highly suspicious that the man who attacked Dallas was the same one who confronted Grace in the parking garage. A copy of the sketch artist's rendition was in her purse.

"Let's just say Caligula isn't letting up. Dallas is waiting for us. She ordered carry-out. We'll talk about everything then. Fill me in. What's the plan?"

"Dr. Brody is leaving for a global conference on renewable energy tomorrow afternoon. I'm taking Gizmo to New York with him. I'll be back before the girls' winter break is over."

Mary shot her daughter a sideways look, unable to conceal her surprise.

"I know, crazy, right? Go big or go home. The organization is called WAGER–the World Alliance for Green Energy Resources. The Keynote speaker agreed to give Dr. Brody half an hour at the start of the conference. He's going to explain the inner workings of Dad's invention. Those thirty minutes will change the world. We'll give every representative a 3-D copy of Gizmo and the informational booklet with Dad's formulas. By tomorrow, the world will have access to affordable, accessible geothermal power."

There it was again, a focused determination in her daughter's eye. Mary smiled inwardly. Grace was going to be all right.

"Mom, this is the first step in eradicating extreme poverty, which is nearly impossible to escape without reliable, low-cost energy. Dr. Brody is working on a PowerPoint presentation. He wanted me to give it, but I'd surely mess up standing in front of all those people. Dad's invention will soon be part of the public domain, meaning it's not proprietary and is available to all. Every region worldwide will have access to geothermal energy at a fraction of the cost. For impoverished areas, non-profit and apolitical organizations have grants to help. This way, no company or government can become rich from Dad's invention. No jurisdiction or regime will have the power to hold another region hostage or deny anyone access."

"Amazing, Grace, this is exactly what your dad would have wanted. One of your father's favorite quotes was from Franklin D. Roosevelt: '*The test of our progress is not whether we add more to the abundance of those who have much. It is whether we provide enough for those who have too little.'"*

"I know we are doing the right thing, Mom. There's tons to do before I leave. I'm going to need help. But most importantly, we can't give Caligula any indication that the world will soon have access to this sea-changing information. Once in the public domain, they'll lose their power to profit from Dad's invention. They'll leave us alone, and Michael Walker's legacy will live on for hundreds of thousands of years or until our planet packs everything up and calls it quits."

"That's incred—"

"Sorry, Mom," Grace interrupted as she pulled the vibrating cell from her pocket. "It's Dallas…What's up, sister?"

Mary's hands clenched the steering wheel, her knuckles whitening under the strain. Dallas rarely resorted to calling, and her mind returned to the previous day's chaos. Dallas had been hysterical during their last conversation, her words frantic and breathless following the attack. Mary had to talk her down, urging her to hang up and call the police. Now Dallas was on the other end of the line with Grace, and Mary was afraid to know why.

She strained to pick up clues from her youngest daughter's staccato words, the pitch and rhythm of her voice, a Morse code she desperately sought to interpret.

"Listen, Dallas!" Grace was using her calm-down, I-mean-it- voice. The one she used with her daughters when they worked themselves into a frenzy over some perceived injustice.

"Lie down, elevate your legs. Hang up and call

911. Tell them you're thirty-six weeks pregnant and experienced a sharp, sudden abdominal pain accompanied by a gush of bright red blood. The ambulance will get to you before we can. Is there anyone available to come and be with you until they arrive? A neighbor, a friend?"

Grace listened intently. "No one? You can't be alone in this condition. What about that respiratory therapist who lives in your complex? What's his name? Yeah, that's right, Peter, I remember. Call 911, then call Peter. I'll call Bryce. We'll meet you at the hospital."

Mary flipped on her turn signal, cutting in front of a semi. The driver laid on his horn as she waved an apology out the window. "Sorry, mister. We have an emergency." She made a U-turn.

As she drove toward the hospital, she focused on the road, trying to ignore Grace's face, drained of color, and how her daughter's fingers shook as she found Bryce's contact information. Detached observation: what a fallacy. Her daughters believed she had command of every situation. However, when her daughters were in danger, Mary's characteristic fortitude shattered.

"Hey, Bryce. Dallas had some abdominal pain and is bleeding. She's on the way to the hospital to be evaluated. Meet us there. All right, I understand. Drive safely. We'll see you then."

Grace shoved her phone into her pocket. "Bryce is on-site, thirty miles away. But he's heading out. Mom, from what Dallas told me, she may have a placental abruption."

"What does that even mean? For her? For my grandson?"

"It's serious. The placenta detaches from the wall of the uterus before birth. It can be a partial or complete separation. If the bleeding stops and the baby is doing all right, they'll put her on bed rest and monitor them. On the other hand, if the tear is severe, if her bleeding doesn't stop and the baby isn't getting enough oxygen, they'll do an emergency C-section."

"Oh, Holy Hell." Mary swung the vehicle onto the Broken Arrow Expressway and pushed the accelerator to the floor.

Chapter 51

The Blood of Her Sister

Grace pushed a cup of coffee into her mother's hands and guided her onto an upholstered chair. "I'm going to meet the ambulance. I'll let you know when I hear anything."

Her mother nodded as her fingernails dug into the styrofoam. She appeared diminished, swallowed by the vast waiting room and fluorescent lights. Grace kneeled in front of her. "Dallas and her baby are going to be fine. She's a fighter and in excellent hands."

With those words, her mother shored herself, the tension still evident in the tremor of her hand. "I know she's scrappy. I'm just afraid. Oh, Grace, ignore me, go. Find Dallas, be with her."

Grace rushed toward the emergency room entrance. The image of her mother fighting for control unnerved her. Stoic Margaret Mead was level-headed, a detached anthropologist, an observer. When was the last time she'd seen her mother upset? Had Grace ever seen her cry? She held everything together the day her husband left them, staying strong for her daughters. Had her mother cried upon learning of his death or at the funeral? Grace was ashamed to admit that she was so absorbed in her pain, the loss of her father, and then the humiliating way Andrew dumped her that she hadn't taken a moment to check in with her mother. What kind of daughter was she? That had to change.

The paramedics raced in with Dallas on the stretcher. Blood saturated Dallas's fashionable sage leggings and pooled around her.

The lead technician yelled, "BP is 78/36, fetal heart tones dropping." A resident rushed forward and began squeezing the liter of IV fluid going into Dallas' vein as hard as possible. Grace understood what this meant. She moved aside to let the response team crowd in, working to stabilize Dallas while whisking mother and baby to the surgical suite.

Dallas's face was translucent against the sheet, her lips the color of her terrified blue eyes. Around Dallas' neck was an ominous purple-black bruise. Like a high tattooed collar, thick finger marks interlaced across her bleached flesh. Someone strangled Dallas. Is this what caused the abruption? No, the bruise was older; the coloration told Grace a partial story. A trauma site is initially red due to the bleeding of ruptured vessels spreading oxygen-rich blood under the skin. Dallas's injury was at least twenty-four hours old. Information was coming faster than Grace could assimilate.

Grace made eye contact with her sister as the team rushed by, and Dallas cried out, "Help me."

Grace ran to Dallas's side, helping push the gurney while hanging onto her sister's cold hand.

"You have to give blood! Please!!"

"Of course, Dallas, I'll do whatever's necessary."

"Not for me, for my baby!"

"Of course, of course! I'm a universal donor, but the hospital has emergency supplies ready to go, and Bryce will arrive before long in case your son's blood matches his–"

"No!" Dallas interrupted, squeezing her hand hard. Blood congealed underneath her manicured nails.

They reached the surgical suite. Grace wasn't wearing authorized scrubs. She didn't have the required shoe coverings, face mask, or surgical cap to continue. Besides, they'd be putting Dallas to sleep and doing a classical incision to get the baby out as quickly as possible. The anesthesiologist was prepping her equipment.

"Listen! Please." Dallas' lips were shaking, and her voice a murmur. Grace nodded and leaned in to hear. "Bryce might not be the father." Her respirations were shallow and quick. "Please, I can't let him find out this way. I must be the one to tell him. If my son needs blood, donate."

The information was a gut punch. "Of course, Dallas. I'll donate if necessary." This wasn't the time for questions. "I love you, sister."

The steel surgical doors started closing. Someone yelled, "Her pressure's dropping again!" Another voice shouted, "I need suction!" The last image she saw before the hatchway clamped shut was the anesthesiologist sliding a tube down Dallas' bruised throat.

Grace slid to the hallway floor numb, her mind in the surgical room with her sister. Weighing on her shoulders was the gravity of the situation–what she failed to tell her mother–another cold truth: Placental abruption can result in a stillbirth and death of the mother. Please don't let my sister and nephew be another statistic. She implored the universe. Would this nightmare of a day ever end? Grace was running on fumes.

Compounding the shock of the abruption were Dallas' words. They reverberated like a small earthquake. *Bryce might not be the father.* When Dallas found Grace holding the unused fertility medication, her sister's face belied confusion and shame as if caught with her hand in the proverbial cookie jar. And she'd been evasive when Grace broached the subject. Did this subterfuge involve Dallas' long-time 'friend,' the respiratory therapist? Or had Dallas resumed her pre-marriage pattern of sleeping around? *Oh, sis, what have you gotten yourself into?*

Grace took a deep breath and shook her head. None of this mattered. What was important was the well-being of her sister and her nephew. Grace scrambled to her feet on autopilot. She knew what to do. Get going, keep moving. That's what she'd always done in a crisis: figure out what needed to happen and just do it. She took one step, another, then stopped.

At the end of the hall stood the respiratory therapist, Peter, the man who had rubbed sunscreen onto her sister at the pool, the man who worried when he hadn't seen her in a while, the one who waited by her side until the ambulance arrived.

He stood alone, his face ashen and stunned, the blood of her sister caked on his hands.

Chapter 52

What Kind of Mother Are You?

Grace's blood pulsed through the clear plastic tubing down into the receptacle below.

"Oh, for goodness' sake." She tried to ignore the vibration of her cell as she clenched and released her fist, hoping to speed up the donation process. Her phone was in her jacket, stashed underneath the stretcher, out of reach.

During the emergency cesarean section, Dallas received two units of blood. If her nephew required some, then Grace's donation would be ready. Several hours had elapsed since the birth. Dallas had difficulty recuperating from anesthesia and spent longer than usual in recovery. Then, there was the matter of stabilizing her baby. The last Grace heard from Bryce was that Dallas and the baby were finally together on the postpartum floor. Grace was anxious to see her sister, but Bryce was with them. How was this going to play out?

The cell shook. Who was calling? Her mom and sister were here. She'd spoken to the girls at the clinic that morning. Andrew hadn't gotten in touch with her since he told her about his dad. He hadn't sent a text with an update. Hopefully, his dad was through surgery and doing well. Maybe he was ringing with an update.

After seeing Dallas, she would call and let the girls know they had a new cousin.

"You're all done." The medical assistant put a cotton swab over Grace's line and expertly pulled the catheter from her vein while applying pressure. "You know the ropes. After your vitals, have something to eat and drink, and make sure you're not lightheaded before heading out."

"Sure, thanks, Greg." Grace grabbed her jacket and headed over to the snack table. Her phone buzzed again; she pulled it from her pocket–Andrew.

"Hello?"

"Where the hell have you been? I've been trying to reach you for hours! What kind of mother are you, anyway? Being out of reach? I had to call Mary and give her the details." He was furious. Her life had inconvenienced him.

"Sorry, Andrew, it's been–"

"Forget it. I don't want to hear excuses. Look, father's operation had complications. He's in the surgical intensive care unit, and the girls are on their way back to you. Your mom has the flight information. Their plane gets in at nine p.m., Central time."

"Andrew, that's in thirty minutes. I can't–"

"Well, you have to."

"A lot's going on, Andrew…you were supposed to have them another four days."

"What can I say? We didn't plan for this emergency, and right now, they are too much for anyone." His voice turned patronizing, "You wanted primary custody and got it, so deal with it. Figure this out, Grace." He hung up.

Grace bypassed the nourishment center and headed

straight for her mother.

Being angry wouldn't change the situation.

"Mom, can I borrow your car? After I pick up the girls, we'll return here."

"It's all right, Grace. I'll get them." Her mother swung her satchel over her shoulder and grabbed her keys. "You haven't seen Dallas or the baby yet. And if she needs medical advice, it's you she'll need. Give her my love and tell her I'll be in to visit first thing in the morning."

"Will you keep the girls overnight?"

"They'll be more comfortable in their own beds. We'll head to the trailer once we collect Tinkerbell at my house. I swear the girls missed her more than me, which is completely understandable." She smiled fondly. "She's one naughty, adorable kitten. Everyone'll be fast asleep when you get home. We'll talk then."

"God, Mom, what a day this has been." Her mother didn't know the half of it.

Her mother's touch was light. "Considering everything–we have plenty to be grateful for."

Grace hugged her mother with abandon. "Thanks for picking me up at the bus station, being here, getting the girls. I don't know how I'd do life without you."

"Oh, Grace, you'd do just fine. Get going, see Dallas, and I'll retrieve our darling lambs. See you in a few hours."

****

Grace stood by her sister's hospital room, knocked, and waited until Dallas called, "Come in."

Seated in a chair next to the bed was Bryce. He stood, acknowledging Grace's presence, the

275

consummate gentleman. Grace hugged her brother-in-law before placing the bouquet of gift shop flowers on Dallas' bedside table. The helium balloon bobbed a friendly hello.

"Now that reinforcements are here, I think I'll head out," Bryce said, pulling on his Carhartt work jacket. "I'll bring your bag in the morning. Is there anything else you need?"

Dallas shook her head, pallid against the linen. Another unit of blood dripped into her vein. Bryce leaned over, kissed Dallas, and gently grazed the back of the nursing baby's downy head. "If you think of anything, text me."

He passed by Grace, his face tired, drained, his soft grey eyes rimmed red. Before closing the door, he looked again at Mother and baby. "I love you, Dallas."

He was gone before Dallas could respond.

Grace slid into the bed beside her sister and put an arm around her. "Oh, Dallas, He's beautiful."

"You don't care that he shares a name with your son? With Dad?"

"Of course not. My son's middle name is now your son's first name, forever linked to Dad. It's an honor. Welcome to the world, Michael Mark Walker."

"So, spill the beans. Where does Mark come from? Is it from Bryce's family or Peter's middle name?"

Dallas raised her eyebrows. "You figured out who the other daddy candidate is."

"You know me, connecting the proverbial dots."

Dallas grazed her fingers over her son's petal-soft skin, then smiled mischievously. "In the spirit of Dad's tradition of naming us after the place of conception, I nicknamed him Mark."

"What? The Farmer's Market–The Marksmen Shooting Range? Oh, I know, you were vacationing in Marks, Michigan."

"Ha, excellent guesses but not quite right–Question Mark."

Grace laughed with a lightness of being. Trust her sister to come up with something ridiculous yet fitting. "I love it."

"Me too. That's why it's his middle name."

"So we'll call him M & M." Grace bent to kiss him. "Delicious."

"Mikey, for now. At least until he's old enough to tell me he hates the nickname."

Mikey nursed; an encompassing stillness fell around them.

Dallas punctured the quiet. "I've treated Bryce like shit. False advertising, you might call it. I acted like I wanted a secure, stable relationship and wanted to connect on a deeper level, but little did I know I was incapable of such a thing. Once we were married, I flip-flopped. Emotionally, I disengaged. I became unreliable and unavailable while blaming him. I focused on his flaws and criticized his imperfections. I picked fights and channeled my energy outside of our relationship. I flirted with other men and had one affair. I kept secrets. I sent him mixed messages, 'I want you, but go away, don't get too close.' I equated intimacy with being suffocated, controlled, and vulnerable.

"Consequently, everything I did made him feel unseen, unheard, and unimportant. The miracle of this all, Grace, is that he says he still loves *me*–the complicated, messed up whole. I told him everything. Bryce says he's all in. We're a family. He'd rather not know who the biological father is. He's ready to be a dad. He would even go to see a counselor with me. Whatever it takes, he says. But ultimately, he'll support me in whatever I decide."

Grace didn't respond. Dallas had more to say.

"Peter says if he's the dad, he'll be financially responsible. A baby wasn't in his plans, but he will not turn his back on us if Mikey is his." Dallas paused. "He's not a bad guy, Grace."

"I never said he was." Grace took stock of her sister and nephew, who had fallen asleep, sated. "What are you going to do?"

"I don't know yet. Should I stay with Bryce and never know who the biological dad is? Should I get the DNA test? Maybe raise him as a single mom with two father figures in his life? A spare one? For all the times Dad wasn't able to attend one of our events because he was busy, we could've used an extra one to fill in the gaps."

Grace laughed softly. "No kidding."

"I want to do the right thing for Mikey and me. I don't want to rush into a decision. But no one is pressuring me. I need time and perspective and want to discuss things with Dr. Kay."

"Dr. Kay?"

"Oh, yeah, something else I failed to tell you besides I had an affair with Peter, and I don't know who the father of my baby is–I'm seeing a therapist. She helped me see that I have an avoidant attachment style. And you, my sister, have an anxious attachment style."

"You talked about *me* with your therapist?"

"We were discussing what happens to little girls with daddy-sized holes in their hearts."

Little girls with daddy complexes–Grace suddenly wanted to be home in her double-wide with her daughters. But they were safe with her mother and, more than likely, fast asleep. She would be with them soon enough.

Dallas traced the contours of her son's face. "Courtesy of Dad, I learned that men I'm close to can't be trusted. Rather than letting anyone in, giving them the power to hurt me, I engage in distancing behaviors to avoid true intimacy. News flash–because you have sex with someone doesn't mean you're in an intimate relationship."

Grace's laugh was superficial. "Good to know." She swallowed hard.

Last night with Lee was not a casual one. It was a communion of experience built upon deep, playful affection and trust. It went beyond a meaningless hook-up. And what had Grace done? She betrayed Lee's faith in her. She hadn't changed at all since high school. She assumed he'd be like her father, like Andrew, and tossed him aside. By expecting the worst in him because she didn't value herself, she felt justified in ending something before it began. Maybe Dallas' therapist was onto something.

Dallas was talking again. Grace focused on her sister, who was staring at her in earnest. "No matter what, I think we'll be good."

"You got that right. You and Mikey are going to be fine. What a natural mother you are. Your son is fortunate to have you."

Grace gently traced the deep purple ring around her sister's neck. "What happened?"

Dallas blinked away tears. Tiny magenta pinpoints

279

dotted the whites of her eyes; they splashed across her milk-white face, clinging to her ears and peeking from her scalp. *Petechiae*–Grace rolled the cold, clinical term in her mouth, fighting the anger and ferocious need to protect. Someone constricted her sister's neck with such force that the tiny blood vessels in her face exploded under the pressure. When her voice was silenced, her body responded with a ruptured scream.

Dallas adjusted the blanket covering her infant. "Everyone's safe. The police have his description and are searching for him. The day's been overwhelming. We'll talk more later."

"Of course." Grace gingerly climbed out of the bed and dimmed the bedside light.

She walked to the window. Sleet pelted against the glass–tap, tap, tap. Across town, in a Tulsa high school, where every room was dark save one, hundreds of 3-D Gizmo replicas were in production courtesy of a grant from the World Alliance for Green Energy Resources organization. Ronnie was pulling an all-nighter. She promised that she, Maya, and the shop teacher, Mr. Mills, fueled with coffee and donuts, wouldn't stop until every representative at the global conference had a working model in their conference swag bag. An information link would be available online. For regions without internet access, Dr. Brody printed and collated formula booklets. After Dr. Brody's presentation, WAGER planned to set up field response teams to help underserved areas learn how to implant and maintain the geothermal network. By tomorrow night, the world will have access to Michael Walker's invention–a reliable, affordable energy source.

The wind picked up in intensity. Thank goodness

her children's plane had landed before the front moved in. Grace shuddered, thinking about the rapid accumulation of glazed ice on airplane wings.

One of her guilty pleasures when on bedrest while pregnant with Ally was watching Airline Disasters– she'd ingested one too many episodes. Sheets of ice = increased weight = decreased lift = disruption of airflow over the wings and tail = increased drag = epic disaster. One installment featured a domestic passenger flight from Indianapolis to Chicago, a mere 185 miles. The experienced pilot was in a holding pattern due to adverse weather in Chicago when he encountered unavoidable freezing rain. Once cleared to land, the ice accumulation rendered the craft uncontrollable; it pitched, rolled, yawed, and crashed. The high-speed impact killed everyone aboard. Good gravy, why did her mind take her into these dark places? Everyone she loved was safe.

Her mom texted Grace once the kids landed and again after they collected Tinkerbell —*Life is back to normal, girls fighting over who gets to hold the cat carrier on their lap*— Her third and final message was to let her know they were safely at the double-wide.

Grace accessed her Street Gondola app. "My ride will be here in ten minutes. You need rest. Time for me to head home."

"To your girls," Dallas sighed. "My adorable nieces. Do you know, I never wanted children until I held Ally? She was the one who started to chisel at my hardened–keep everyone out–shell. Then, when I met Amanda, I told Bryce I was ready. Ora only reinforced my decision. Conceiving took forever. I was convinced nature was telling me pregnancy was a bad idea–that I shouldn't be a mom.

"Then it happened. Every day for the past eight months, I questioned my decision, wondering what I'd gotten myself into. But now..." She kissed her son's wrinkled raccoon fist that worked its way out of the swaddling. "Now, I cannot imagine a world without Mikey. And he's barely six hours old."

"Children change everything." Grace understood the overarching enormity of unconditional love. She'd do anything–work around the clock, realign the stars, stop the earth's gravitational pull for them. And in the simple day-to-day operations, they altered how she saw the minutia of the world, noting unexpected treasures and hidden dangers. Yes, children change everything– how you hear a cricket singing or see an ice storm descending.

Grace adjusted the pillows behind Dallas' head and filled her water pitcher. She closed the blinds against the winter storm. "Sweet dreams, my loves. I'll swing by before heading to the airport."

Dallas sleepily grinned. "Hey, did you know nursing burns five hundred extra calories daily? It's a win-win."

"Yes, but pregnancy and breastfeeding also ravage your breasts. Your girls will never be the same."

"Who cares about that? I just want to make sure Mikey is getting enough."

"Sounds like something a good mom would say." Grace gently closed the door, leaving her sister adorning the newest man in her life with butterfly kisses.

Chapter 53

Herding Cats

Ally held the scraggly cat underneath her front paws, her lean body stretching downward like pulled taffy. "Grandma Mary, what happened to Tinkerbell's collar?" Tinkerbell blinked golden eyes at her as if to say, yes, remind me again why I'm naked.

"Naughty Kitty was sitting nice and snug on my lap in the gazebo when she decided to chase a songbird. I grabbed her by the collar, but the little escape artist slipped away. The collar's still at my house. We'll retrieve it tomorrow."

"That's okay. We have a new, fancier one, anyway." Ally raced to the girls' bedroom with Tinkerbell in tow, where shrieks ensued.

"You got to hold Tinker first. It's my turn." Ora came flying into her grandma's arms, tears and outrage splotched on her cherry-red face. "Grandma, it's my turn! Make her give me Tinkerbell."

Amanda stood with arms crossed against her chest, implying but not saying, '*What about me? When do I get my turn?*'

Her granddaughters were exhausted and off-kilter, picking fights and being cantankerous. Their grandpa was in critical care, and their father sent them packing days before they were due to leave, summarily dismissing them because they were a handful. The day was challenging for all the Walker-Holden girls. If only she could get her granddaughters into a bubble bath, flannel pajamas, read them a story, and tuck them into bed, dawn's forgiving light would gentle their losses.

Mary pushed back Ora's matted blonde hair and kissed her forehead. "One more minute, then it will be your turn. Amanda, you're after Ora."

Amanda's lower lip quivered. Mary understood what her middle granddaughter couldn't say aloud: *I'm the next oldest. What about me? Why do I always have to go last?* And if it had been any other day, if tension and emotions weren't already stretched taut like a fishing line caught in the teeth of a shark, she might have given voice to her quiet granddaughter, the pacifier.

Ora furiously stomped, clipping the side of her grandmother's stockinged foot. *Ouch, for such a pint-sized girl, you have one mean wallop.*

"It's not fair! I want Tinker now," Ora wailed. "Ally's so greedy. She always gets her way!"

Ally clutched the cat tighter. "Grandma said, one more minute."

Ora raced to the back door. "I want my mommy! I'm going down the path to be with her."

"Ora!" Mary called, trying to make her voice sound harsh to stop her. "Ora, it's a mess outdoors and getting dangerous. Ice can bring down branches and power lines. Your mom's not on the path. She's at the hospital and will be here soon. I promise."

"You don't understand anything, Grandma! It doesn't matter where she is–she'll meet me in her heart."

Pushed by a little girl's determination, abetted by a ferocious wind, the back screen door slammed open, knocking the songbird wall clock off its hook. Ora flew into the night. The newly adorned feline, wearing a bejeweled choker, streaked behind her. Amanda, suddenly afraid for her baby sister and cat, followed.

"Come back!" Ally keened, her sturdy legs hauling bottom after them.

"Oh, holy hell," Mary threw her arms in the air, shoved on Grace's slippers, which were four sizes too big, and rapidly pursued. It was like trying to herd cats.

Chapter 54

The Eye of the Storm

"Sleet likely to put out an eye." The man hunched behind the wheel didn't even turn around to greet her, let alone open the door for her, and Grace didn't blame him. Her skin stung where the sharp shards hit her exposed flesh. Her app sent a picture of her driver–Vern Vulpine. His pointy bat-like ears were the only identifying feature she could discern from the back seat. It was enough.

"Thanks for coming out in these conditions. Hope the roads weren't bad." She offered casual conversation—a loud harrumph issued from the front seat. Sharp elbows rose, a deflecting shield. Fine by her. She didn't have the bandwidth for aimless chatter anyway. He turned the heater on full blast. Grace huddled close to the door, pressing her cheek against the cold window, and texted her mother —*On my way home*—

Despite overwhelming physical exhaustion, the day's stress left her brain hard-wired and racing. She mentally listed what she needed to do before departure. Her mom agreed to watch the girls and Tinkerbell.

She'd have to use a gym bag or backpack. Her fashionable carry-on suitcase was still at Lee's.

Thinking of him caused her stomach to lurch. How had she messed that up so badly? What had she done? He'd opened himself to her. He'd revealed intimate parts of his story with *her*. He shared his home and his bed. She told him she wanted him; she acted upon that, and he, in turn, had trusted her. Then she threw him to the curb. Again, she violated his trust, all because she developed a dysfunctional, "anxious attachment style." Who heard of such a thing? She hadn't.

When Dallas got up to use the hospital bathroom, Grace opened her cell, whispering conspiratorially to her nephew, "Let's see what Doctor Google has to say about your Auntie's bonding behavior." *Those with anxious attachment styles struggle to feel secure in their relationships. While they long to feel close to their partners, the need, driven by fear of abandonment and low self-esteem, is delineated by concern that their partners will not reciprocate their desire for intimacy. A lot of energy and time is spent trying to be what you think the other person wants.*

A need to feel safe, fueled by the fear of desertion and low self-esteem–trying to be what you think the other person wants, not what you truly are. *Oh God*, Grace groaned.

Vern Vulpine slouched lower in his seat.

Grace met his gaze in the rearview mirror. The outer canthus of his eyes were elongated. *It's been a long day for me, too, lady*. He blinked once and looked away.

Grace mentally charted the course of her relationships and mapped the turning points. When the looming prospect of loss became compounded by desperation, her partners fled. Once established, that pattern did nothing but intensify. Her attempt to morph into what she imagined her partner wanted caused her to lose pieces of herself.

As a child, I couldn't protect myself from feeling rejected and betrayed. But I can refuse to let the pain of loss define who I am as an adult. Look at Lee. Scars cover his ankles and hands, from hot oven coils to stray pieces of steel and broken glass. Yet he hasn't allowed injury or his parents' absence to derail him. He persevered, and he probably has the healthiest of all attachment styles.

He accepted Grace entirely, flaws and all, and never intimated she wasn't enough. Never once had he made her feel judged and inadequate. Nor did he suggest that she would be more appealing if she dressed differently or acted more refined. She had been the one to project her fears on him and to assume that he was a player, a jet-setting doctor incapable of rooted connection. The joke was on her.

Knock, Knock.

Who's there?

Shore.

Shore who?

Shore hope you like bad jokes.

Navigating the curving country road was challenging in the best of conditions. Grace, absorbed in thought, didn't think to warn Vern of the sharp turn half a mile from her home, which had caused a motorist to slam into the warning sign last month, sending his car and the metal pole flying into the ditch.

The caution sign was still a tangle of metal. Vern was paying close attention. Around the bend came a sedan, traveling too quickly for the conditions, its brights temporarily blinding them. The driver flashed his lights, and Vern tapped his brakes, sending the car into a skid. Vern's bent arms moved with measured precision, making minor adjustments in one direction, then the other until he regained control.

Grace sighed. Lee repeatedly offered insight, but she dismissed his observations, thinking he was overly generous and trying to make her feel better. Didn't he tell her, "I don't say what I don't mean?"

Her actions told a different story. They invalidated everything she told him, that she trusted and wanted him. On the way to the hospital that morning, Sue Ann had talked nonstop about how Grace had saved her and her baby's life and how she wanted to become a nurse because of what Grace had done for her. And because Grace was immersed in the terror of what might have happened, she didn't take the words to heart. She hadn't taken a moment to acknowledge what she had done in a crisis, how her instincts and training had kicked in when they mattered most.

The storm intensified. The precipitation froze when it hit the windows and roads, coating the external world with ice. Grace no longer saw her reflection in the glass.

And though visibility was nonexistent, Grace had a moment of clarity. The bedrock of her problems was self-confidence, stemming from the belief she was never enough. She wasn't secure in who she was. Yes, there were contributing factors, but this was her narrative to own and reconstruct. No one else could do this for her.

'Rip up the false portrait of yourself. Let it go.' Lee's voice whispered in her consciousness. He respected and valued her. He believed in her.

The defrost was on full blast, and the wipers, which were once wildly flapping, were stuck–the windshield was ice-caked.

"Flashers up ahead." Vern rolled down his window and peered into the darkness. "Looks like an accident. I'm turning around here."

Grace fumbled with her phone and transferred the money, giving Vern Vulpine a five-star review and generous tip before leaving the heated cab. He glanced at his cell and issued another low, rumbled growl, which sounded like something approximating approval. She stepped into the storm and put her head down against the pelting ice; less than a quarter of a mile to go.

She was almost home.

Chapter 55

His Promise

The dirt road was a ribbon of ice. Grace walked like a penguin, her toes slightly pointing out, taking small steps, both flappers to her side for balance. The flightless birds had perfected this way of navigating slippery conditions for millions of years. Why wouldn't it work for her? The last thing she needed was to fall and end up in the hospital, a floor above Dallas, with a broken appendage.

As she inched her way forward, the ice began coating her hair, jacket, and eyelashes. *The accident must be in front of our house.* Registering only one police car gave her solace. If the crash caused severe injuries, there would have been more response vehicles on the scene. The flashing lights grew, disorienting in their intensity.

The cruiser was not in front of her house but in the driveway parked behind her mother's car. What in the world? Grace had a cognitive disconnect. Her mom's last text had been when they'd safely arrived. Everyone she loved was accounted for. She moved slowly through the strikes of red, blue, and white, hurling eerie strobes into the sleet-laden night.

Grace pushed open the door to her home, her heartbeat pulsing in her neck.

Her mother was in the kitchen, talking to a short, heavy-set officer who scribbled in a notebook. They looked up when she entered.

"MOMMY!" Ora flew into her arms. Ally hurled herself from the couch, grabbing Grace by the waist and holding on as if her life depended on it.

"We can't find Amanda," Ora wailed.

"What?" Grace moved Ora to her hip, keeping one arm around her while putting her other arm around a sobbing Ally.

"I went down the path to be with you." Ora's words came in crying jags. "Tinkerbell followed me."

Grace's mother interjected. "Amanda followed Ora. Then Ally. Of course, I was right on their heels." She gulped. "I gathered them up, but once they realized Tinkerbell was missing, they scattered in all directions, looking for her. Even though the storm was bad, the girls wouldn't come in."

"We couldn't let Tinker stay outside–what if she freezes to death?" Ora was defiant through her tears. "Now they're both gone."

"When I convinced Ora and Ally to come in, we called for Amanda to join us. It wasn't more than a few minutes, Grace. We searched high and low for her. I realized we needed help and called the police. This gentleman is Officer Oso."

Officer Oso shook Grace's hand. "My name is Randy." The hair on his knuckles was coarse on her fingers. "The more eyes we have looking for a lost little girl, the better."

"I don't understand…" Grace was trying to put the pieces together. Her children roamed their acreage like wolf pups. "Amanda knows this area like the back of her hand. Even with the storm, I don't see how she became disoriented."

"She can't be far." Her mother's words lacked conviction.

Grace's mind raced. Amanda wasn't home because something happened to her. *I don't remember seeing anything on the road. But then, my thoughts were preoccupied, and I wasn't paying close attention. Oh God, what about the river? With all the precipitation this month, it's moving briskly. What if she tripped and hit her head on a rock? What if she drowned?* Grace took a deep breath through her nose and out through her mouth. She could taste the adrenaline coursing through her body.

On the floor, partially hidden under the couch, was one of Amanda's favorite butterfly barrettes. She visualized Amanda, the hair clasp sparkling purple against the waterfall of her russet hair. A rescue mission for a stuffed animal at bedtime was something she was used to, but one for her daughter? Once the policeman left, Grace would begin her fevered pursuit. She would search to hell and back. No stone would be left unturned, no river left unforged. She would dismantle the world piece by piece until she found her. She would not stop until Amanda was secure in her arms.

"Ladies," the officer said, nodding at Grace and her mother as he closed his notebook, "I have a school picture of Amanda and a description of her clothes. I'll get this information into our system. I'm sure we'll find her in no time." His bulging eyes pointedly stared at Ora and Ally.

"Now, girls. Before I go, is there anything else you remember? Even the smallest detail might be important.

You were looking for your cat, right? Did Amanda say anything that might indicate where she was going or what her state of mind was?"

"She was talking to the Sandman," Ally piped up.

"Who?" All eyes were riveted on Ally.

"The Sandman was going to help Amanda find Tinkerbell. He said there was a tracking chip in her new collar, and he had the app on his phone to find her. He told Amanda that Tinker didn't know him and would run away if he tried to catch her. But if Amanda went with him, Tinker would come to her. He said they'd be right back and not to tell anyone because they wouldn't be gone long. He's working on a surprise for you, Mommy."

"Ally!" Ora tugged on her sister's arm. "We weren't supposed to say anything about the surprise. You ruined everything."

Sonic booms went off in Grace's head as she sat her girls side by side on the couch and kneeled before them. She struggled to keep her voice steady. "Who is the Sandman?"

"Mom, you know him. He looks like the Sandman at the fairgrounds," Ora said.

"You mean the statue of the Golden Driller?" the officer asked as if making a mental note.

Ally nodded her head. "He's not a stranger. He's a friend of the family. He told us he knows you, Mommy, and has a surprise for you."

"You've seen him before?" Grace tried to control the shock waves reverberating in her bones.

"He met us after school one day. He knew all about Tinkerbell and gave us the new collar for her. I kept it in my sock drawer because she already had one."

"Why didn't you tell me?"

"Because of the surprise, we didn't want to ruin it for you." Ally was in tears again. Ora snuggled into her side, sucking her thumb, a habit she'd given up years ago.

The officer reopened his notebook and was furiously taking notes. "Where did you see them talking together?"

"At the end of the driveway," Ally said.

"And did you see what kind of vehicle he was driving?"

"No, he told Amanda his car wasn't far."

"On my way home, about half a mile out, a sedan flying at a breakneck speed almost sideswiped us. The lights were blinding, and I didn't see the exact color or make."

"That's useful information, Grace. Good. Girls, can you describe him for me?"

Grace's mother dumped her purse on the kitchen counter and retrieved a folded paper. She showed it to Ally and Ora.

"That's him!" they cried.

Mary collapsed into the kitchen chair, her limbs akimbo as if she'd vaulted over a high jump. "This is the sketch artist's rendition of Dallas' attacker." Her hands shook, dropping the paper to the floor.

Grace's world spiraled. The man who accosted her in the garage stared with menacing eyes–*I warned you, you'd regret not working with us.*

This man, a representative of Caligula, was the one who strangled Dallas, leaving her neck blackened and mangled. The same person unknowingly inserted himself into her daughter's trust–The Sandman. He'd made good on his promise, and he had Amanda.

Chapter 56

The Weight of Love

Grace ran through the undergrowth, screeching at the top of her lungs, "Amanda! Amanda!"

Long and full of anguish, her daughter's name echoed through the grove until swallowed by the steel-gray sky.

Officer Oso tried to hold her back, telling her that desperate searching would not be helpful in these circumstances. An Amber Alert was issued. The police department had notified the FBI's Child Abduction Rapid Deployment Team. She needed to remain home and wait for a call, which they were sure would come. The situation was grave–all emergency response vehicles were on high alert. In the immediate vicinity, checkpoints were stopping and searching vehicles. They had a photo of Amanda and her alleged kidnapper.

Grace refused to listen to Officer Oso. Sitting still and waiting was not an option. Her mom would stay with Ally and Ora and call immediately if any information about Amanda came through. Grace had her phone. If the Sandman contacted her, she'd let the police know–unless he demanded that to ensure Amanda's safety, she come with Gizmo alone. She didn't tell them this. She would do anything to have her daughter back. Anything. Her father would understand.

Sleet, pushed by a cyclone-strength force, caused the branches of ice-caked trees to scream–a banshee's wail. The police set up roadblocks, but what if the Sandman lied? What if he hadn't taken her in a car and instead had spirited her to a holding place? A spot not too far away, so when he made his demand, Gizmo for Amanda, he'd be close and able to slip in undetected. In rural Oklahoma, the land could swallow you whole. Finding Amanda, considering the circumstances, was a long shot but one Grace had to take.

Focus on clues, on finding her, do not dwell on how scared she is, how she must be crying for you–you have one job to do–find her!

Amanda's abduction wound around her, the weight of love, a python constricting her chest. Soon, she would not be able to breathe.

Grace only wanted to speak with one person. She hit his number.

It went straight to voicemail.

"Lee…Amanda's missing, abducted…I'm afraid and searching for her, hoping to find something. She must be terrified." Her words came in a panicked tumble. "What if he's hurting her? Oh, God, I can't even think of that…and this is all because of me…I'm sorry, Lee, for dumping on you, for dumping you. Again. Ignore this message. I had no right to call. I know you are out of range and won't get this until you're at the clinic. Please delete it and forget what I said. I'm sorry, Lee, truly I am–for everything."

Trees creaked and swayed. Barren, gnarly branches buffeted by the frigid air reached into the night, cracking like skeleton fingers until they fell under the burden of accumulation. Grace continued following the river, a dogged bloodhound searching for a scent.

The enormity of what was happening hit her as she navigated the treacherous terrain. Look at what danger her decisions put her family in. The Sandman, an agent of the oil and gas company, abducted her daughter, and she would hand over Gizmo in exchange for her safety. Caligula won. The corporation that pressured her father into using toxic fracking fluids, which led to his cancer, would now own, control, and profit from his legacy. Why did her father think she was the one who would figure everything out? Why did she have the audacity to believe she could fulfill his dying wish and keep everyone she loved safe?

Twisting superficial roots of river birch and swamp privet created a labyrinth beneath her feet. Grace pushed through.

One moment, her feet were grounded; the next, her body hurtled forward, slamming into the unforgiving earth and a jagged boulder. Her left wrist, trying to break her fall, popped as a sharp jolt of pain ripped through her. Her palms and knees, sliced open by rock shards, bled. *How am I going to see my way through this endless night?* Grace bowed her head with the weight of crushing desperation. She tucked her body against the ground and rocked, letting the waves of despair and anguish move her through a landscape of defeat. All was dark and lost.

And though she was alone, Grace felt the pressure of a small hand slip through hers. *"Mommy, I'm afraid."*

Grace scrambled to her feet–*Amanda?* The fleeting image of her middle child's upturned face, light freckles scattered across milky skin, centered her. "Be brave, my little one."

Be brave. Grace stared at her silent cell, a crack on its face, impotent in her hand. Why hadn't the Sandman called? What he wanted was uncontestable: Gizmo. And he had the perfect bargaining chip: her daughter. Why was he playing this cat-and-mouse game? To instill terror? To twist the knife deeper before removing it and plunging it into her again.

During her nursing prerequisites, Grace studied the phenomenon of learned helplessness, whereby a person believes they cannot control or change situations. Consequently, they do not even try. *Oh no, you don't, Sandman–Caligula, you don't get to have that kind of power over me and my family. There has to be a way out of this.*

Think, Grace, dig deep, tap those reserves, and focus on what you can control. Her mind raced over the encounters with the Sandman and Caligula, searching. And there it was, seemingly insignificant, flitting on the edge of experience, no larger than a moth, a slip of paper stuck under her windshield wiper, a wafer-thin business card in her purse. The Sandman and Caligula CEO, Mr. Renny Richeza, had left their calling cards.

The ball was in her court, and she'd be damned if she'd let it go without an all-out, balls-to-the-wall fight.

Chapter 57

A Constellation of Glass

The sleet slowed, but the creek was still a swiftly moving river of mud and broken parts of the night. Branches and wind-swept detritus churned in the water with projectile force. Though soaked and chilled to her core, exhausted and depleted, Grace ran. The iced earth crunched beneath her feet, a constellation of broken glass.

She shoved open the trailer's back door. Heads bent over a large area map on her kitchen table–her mother, Officer Oso, and Lee.

Lee!

She couldn't have stopped herself if she had tried. Grace flew into his arms, crumbling against his chest like an armful of clothes.

Grace didn't feel her body shaking until his strong arms wrapped around her, absorbing the vibrations. He held her and whispered, "I was checking up on Lois and Sue Ann at the hospital when I got your message. I drove straight here. Doc Jenner is covering me at the clinic for a few days." He smoothed the wet hair from her face. "I'm here to help, Grace. In any way I can."

Nodding, she swallowed and hurried to her room, returning with two business cards. "I'm calling the Sandman first, and if that doesn't work, the CEO of

Caligula. This ends here and now."

Officer Oso stepped forward, running a hand over his slicked-back hair. "We've got a hostage negotiator on standby. She's trained to diffuse dangerous situations. Don't call anyone until she's here. Doing this might increase the risk to Amanda."

"Every second we wait is another moment Amanda's in danger. I'm calling."

"Then put him on speaker. That way, I can record the call. I'll write down any additional questions on my notepad and flash them to you."

"With all due respect, Officer Oso, he'll ask me if the police are listening, and I can't risk him finding out. What if someone coughs or sneezes, and he knows I've been deceptive? I'll record the call in my room."

Grace's fingers, beginning to thaw, shook as she punched in the Sandman's number.

"I know you have Amanda! Put her on the phone."

"Your father's invention in exchange for your daughter." His voice was deep and menacing.

"Tell me where and when."

"No police."

"I promise, no police. Let me talk to her. I need to know she is safe."

"Not part of the deal. Listen, Grace, this is simple—if you want your daughter alive, bring me what I want."

"Okay, okay–I'm listening."

The bedroom door flew open, slamming the wall behind it. Particles of silica dust fell from the doorknob-sized hole in the drywall. In a headlong rush, all one hundred pounds of her mother hurled toward Grace, knocking the phone from her hand. Her mother grabbed the cell from the floor and hung up.

"Mom! What the hell?"

Her mother was jumping, her vertical prowess approximating that of a Jack Russel Terrier. "Gracie, they found Amanda! The news came over Officer Oso's scanner. He's in the cruiser, ready to take you to the hospital to see her."

Grace broke into tears of relief. She picked up her mother and swung her in a circle. Ally and Ora bounced on her bed, clapping and squealing.

****

Officer Osa waited for Grace to buckle up before driving off. "They found her by the Canyons at Blackjack Ridge."

"The golf course?"

"Yup, she walked out of the woods, clutching a cat to her chest, telling the checkpoint officers that she wanted to go home."

"Oh, my goodness. How is she-physically, did he-?" Grace couldn't bring herself to ask.

"Amanda won't let anyone touch her, and she's refusing to talk until you get there. According to the emergency doctor, though, she's alert and oriented and shows no outward signs of distress. I gather she put up one hell of a stink when the ambulance pulled up to the emergency entrance." He chuckled, low and rumbling. "When they tried to pry the cat from her hands, telling her pets aren't allowed, she screamed bloody murder and told them she didn't need a stinking hospital and would walk home."

She'd expect this fiery behavior from Ora, even an independent Ally, but from the family peacemaker? Amanda valued harmony and order, even if this cooperation meant giving up on something she wanted. Grace shook her head in disbelief before asking, "What happened to the cat?"

"That's the thing. No one could talk your daughter down. My guess is the creature's still in her arms."

Chapter 58

Ducks in a row

The policeman stationed by Amanda's room stopped Grace before she entered. "They have a person of interest in custody who matches the sketch."

"Oh, thank goodness! I'll tell Amanda. She'll be relieved."

"I still need to get your daughter's statement." His voice was gruff, but his tired eyes were kind.

"Can you give us a few minutes alone, please?"

He nodded and stepped aside. "When she's ready, I'll be here."

Amanda was huddled on the stretcher, quietly stroking a spent Tinkerbell, sleeping soundly in her lap. Her hair had broken free from its moorings and was a tangled riot around her waxen face. When Grace climbed beside her and collected her daughter, cat and all, in her arms, they both began to cry.

"He said he would track Tinker on his phone and help us find her."

"I know, sweetheart, I know." Grace kissed her forehead. Amanda's skin was cold, with lavender smears, the shape of half moons, beneath her eyes.

"He lied to me, Mommy. I knew she was never lost when Tinkerbell started meowing in the trunk. He stole her! I pretended to hear her meowing outside. 'Please,

Mister, my kitty is crying. Stop! You promised me you'd help find her.' I started kicking the seat, yelling, and throwing a full-fledged Ora tantrum. The Sandman wanted me to shut up and behave, but I didn't. He pulled off the road.

"'What do you know,'" Amanda said, trying to imitate the baritone timbre of her abductor's voice.

Grace's heart was whole; her daughter was alive, intact, and telling her story!

Amanda continued. "Then he studied his phone and said, 'You're right. My app tells me your cat is near the car. Good ears. Let's find her, and I'll drive you both home.' He coughed hard. He tried to fool me, but I heard him pop the trunk. He was so busy with his phone and his key fob that he didn't see me scramble behind him. I grabbed Tinkerbell and ran into the woods. First, I removed her tracking collar and threw it as far as possible. You should have seen him screaming at me. He was furious! 'You're going to regret this, Missy! I'll get your mommy, sisters, and grandma. Then you won't have anyone left.' But he's a liar. I didn't fall for that."

"Did he follow you?"

"He did, but he was slow." Her grin was quick and mischievous. "I'm like a rabbit, speedy and small, and I can hide. The last thing he yelled was that he would run over Tinkerbell and me with his car! I wasn't going to let that happen."

Grace caressed the top of her head.

"I was afraid. We were lost. But I went to the end of the path in my heart. I knew you'd be there and would be looking for me. I thought I heard you calling me, Mommy, telling me to be brave, so I was. I followed the tree line, ducking down and hiding when a car passed. I walked forever until I saw a policeman talking to the driver of a car. I didn't see the Sandman but hurried in case he was near."

Grace stretched out her legs and leaned back against the headrest.

The hospital door opened, and Amanda tensed.

"It's all right, sweetheart. They got the man who took you, and the police officer will not let anyone who isn't safe through those doors. Amanda, I'd like to introduce you to my friend and co-worker, Jill. She's the one who did such an amazing job stitching up Ora when she fell from the fairy tower."

Jill carried a milk carton and a glob of a meat-like substance on a plastic plate that Grace would have been hard-pressed to name.

"Rumor has is that we have one hungry kitty in here." She tore open the top of the carton and placed the milk on the floor next to the meat.

Tinkerbell sprang into the air, arching silently from Amanda's lap to investigate the offerings. Without hesitation, she tucked into the food, a deep purr emanating from within.

"Amanda, before we can go home, someone from the hospital has to do a physical, and ask you a few questions. My friend Jill is a physician's assistant and a mommy like me. Would it be all right if she checked you out? I'll stay with you the whole time."

Amanda nodded.

"And when Jill finishes, the policeman wants to talk to you. Tell him what happened, just like you told me."

"Okay, as long as you're here."

"I'm not going anywhere."

Amanda snuggled beside her mother and extended her slim, Lycra-clad limbs alongside Grace's. She poked her petal pink index finger through the ripped fabric of her mother's scrubs and touched Grace's blood-caked knees, then pointed to her leggings torn at the same place. "Mommy, we're twins."

"Two peas in a pod."

Amanda put her hand on Grace's thigh and counted their lined-up legs. "One, two, three, four. Mommy, Ally, Me, Ora. The Holden girls, four ducks in a row."

Chapter 59

Flight

"I forgot to tell you," Lee said as he strode down the polished corridor of the Tulsa International Airport with Grace by his side, "Sue Ann named her daughter after you."

Grace shot him a sideways glance but didn't break her stride.

Lee continued. "She also named the baby after me."

Grace stopped and raised an eyebrow. "What?"

"Grace-Lee, spelled Gracely."

"Oh, dear God, that poor child has no chance."

He joined her in laughter.

Grace checked her cell one last time. The departure was on time, and the security checkpoint line was manageable. She had a few minutes to spare.

She touched his arm. "Thanks for offering my motley crew, including cat and mother, a place to crash at your apartment. But I think they'll be okay staying at my mom's until I get back. The FBI is trying to find the links between the Sandman and Caligula. Once they have the necessary evidence, they can arrest everyone involved."

"My offer stands if anything changes. I'll be at the clinic for another week."

"That shouldn't be necessary. By the end of today, the world will have access to Dad's discovery. We just have to ensure that the Gizmo replicas make it safely to their destination and that Caligula doesn't get hold of one before he becomes part of the public domain."

"Speaking of Gizmo's offspring, here you go," Lee said, giving her a quick wink and handing Grace her duffle bag.

Grace shifted under the weight of the bright red canvas. "Thanks, also, for driving me to the airport."

"Is that all?" His evergreen eyes were steady.

"Thanks for being here for me. For being my rock."

"Your rock?" He smiled. "Do you mean solid and strong, or a non-sentient lump content with its station in life?"

She gently pushed a palm against his chest. "More like a boulder I keep stubbing my toes on but somehow can't seem to move because of his sheer obstinance."

Lee's laugh exploded. With a hand running through his hair, he stared down at Grace with an intensity that made her pull in a jagged breath.

That look hit her hard.

"I'm sorry, Lee. Taking my insecurities out on you wasn't fair."

"Ah, well, you see, we rocks are tough. It takes more than that to get us to crack."

She had to tell him her truth, even if this meant letting him and his friendship go. Grace was sure about one thing: she didn't want to hurt someone who had come to mean so much to her. She put a hand on his cheek. "I have tons to work on personally, as evidenced by how I botched things with you. My daughters will always be a priority. I don't want to lead you on."

"You assume rocks can be led. I'm where I want to be, with no demands or expectations."

Lee took her hands in his. "Don't get me wrong, I want a long-term relationship. And I want it to be with you. But for now, having you in my life as a co-worker and friend is enough. Look at you, Grace. What you are doing is incredible. You honored your promise to your father. You are almost there. Caligula flung obstacles at you left and right. They did unthinkable things, and despite the odds, you kept dodging whatever they threw. You persevered. You're a warrior. You don't let anything get in your way when you care about something. And it's not only the big things, Grace. It's the small gestures that make a difference. Good things don't get lost. You care more than anyone I've ever met. Are you aware of what most people would give to have someone like that in their lives?"

Grace curled her fingers around the collar of his jacket and drew him closer. "No demands or expectations?"

"That's what you took away?" His eyes belied the truth; they danced, reflecting the holiday lights strewn along the concourse.

"You undo me, Lee Leland. Here I was, moving through life, thinking there would always be another chance—one more day with my father, one more dance with my spouse, one more 'I love you, Mommy' from my daughters. But with all that's happened, I know that might not be true." Grace slid her arms around him.

"Each moment is a separate constellation. And I'm not about to waste this one." She gave him a kiss he would remember, kissing him as if they were alone, an

311

intimate and profound exchange, sweet yet yearning, exploring a convergence of history and possibility.

"On that note," —she wiped her forehead as if in a swoon— "I better get going. Dr. Brody took an earlier flight with his set of Gizmo knockoffs."

"In case one of your carry-ons gets lost."

"Or stolen."

"The finish line is so close."

"I'll leave a voicemail message after the presentation. Maybe we can talk in the morning when you get to the clinic before your first patient."

His smile was warmer than bread fresh out of the oven. "I think that can be arranged. Now go get 'em, Grace."

****

Every seat was taken. The steward urged harried passengers to transfer carry-ons into the checked baggage hold.

Grace resolutely refused.

She and her bag needed to arrive together. She had one job: never lose sight of her carry-on. And Grace did that for the non-stop three-hour and fourteen-minute flight from Tulsa to New York City.

At first, the canvas was stuffed beneath her seat, her fingertips grazing the fabric when her hand dangled to the side. But the flight attendant said the bulk extended into the aisle, representing a trip hazard. Thus, he took the bag to an overhead bin three seats ahead of her. He shoved the lopsided duffle between a navy blue and a white softshell valise, and at the last minute, he deposited a slim beige pouch in front of her bag. Grace watched him pull the door down, the flash of red fabric blinking; I *am here*, right before it shut. She didn't get up to use the bathroom; she didn't glance at the flight magazine or scroll through the movie offerings. She didn't accept the soft drink or chips when the cart wheeled by. Her cell was off and in her pocket. Her focus was vigilant, a spider guarding its dinner.

When the plane came to a complete stop, and the fasten your seat belt light turned off, the cabin erupted with activity. Around her, people stood and started pushing their way into the aisle. Claustrophobia, arthritic legs, racing to make a connection, seeing loved ones after an absence, a full bladder pressing down, there were countless reasons for this behavior; *we all want to get off people*.

Amidst the chaos, she kept alert, her eyes never wavering. Bins opened, hands and bodies flashed before their open cubicles in a disorganized fashion, flight blankets were discarded, coats donned, cell phones rang, babies cried.

When she got to the overhead compartment, her bright red duffle, impossible to miss, was gone.

She reviewed the details in the taxi to the convention center. How had it happened? Of course, flying under a pseudonym wasn't possible. Anonymity of flight was long gone. While the manifest was supposed to be confidential, Grace did not doubt that people with power and connections had ways of accessing this data. Somehow, Caligula determined she was flying to New York, and somehow, they managed to nab her bag. Thank goodness for contingency plans.

****

The Javits Convention Center was overwhelming in its scope, looming large on an entire city block. Grace's taxi driver effusively pointed to some of the predominant features as she navigated the bumper-to-bumper congestion. "Not only does the Center have the biggest solar panel installation in the city, but it also has an etched glass exterior, which greatly diminishes bird collisions."

"I can't think of a better venue for a green-energy conference," the driver said, her enthusiasm infectious. "This place is a beacon for sustainability. In addition to the bird-friendly structure, the six-acre rooftop is green. It absorbs over seven million gallons of rainwater annually, sports a food forest, has honeybee hives, a farm with over twenty different crops, a hydroponic greenhouse, and a compost system. On that note, here's your entrance. Hope the convention goes well."

Dr. Brody found her in the crowded foyer. "Grace!"

She slung the visitor pass over her head as he ushered her into a private seminar room.

"I'm delighted you made it!" His silver hair was recently cut, and his three-piece suit looked hot off the dry cleaning press. "And your bag?"

Grace scanned the room. No one else was there. "Gone, stolen. I had my eyes on it for the entire trip. I don't understand how this happened. What about you? Please don't tell me they got your cache of Gizmo byproducts, too?"

He shook his head. Incredulity shone in his glinting eyes. "Alas, they did."

Grace and Dr. Brody surveyed each other, stunned. Both bags were gone? Then they burst out laughing.

Thank goodness for contingency plans.

Chapter 60

Spiral of Possibility

Amanda's hospital discharge seemed a lifetime ago to Grace, even though it had happened just that morning. Her mother, Ally, and Ora met Grace and Amanda in the hospital lobby. But the spirit of Grace's father was also there, in the hopeful morning rays of a project near completion, in the musical spiral of possibility. Parts of Michael Walker's DNA found expression in the blue of Ora's eyes, in the way Ally commanded attention, in Amanda's negotiating skills and nimble intellect. He was present in visible and invisible ways around them and in them all.

Upon seeing her sisters and Grandma, Amanda broke into a smile that lit her face from within. She gently transferred Tinkerbell to Ora's arms. "You can have her. I've had enough holding for a while."

Ora snuggled her face into the cat's matted fur.

Tinker purred.

Ally did not protest.

Mary drove. Grace kept looking in the back, where her children happily sat beside each other, not fighting. "One last stop before you guys go to Grandma's. Gizmo's babies are ready to be picked up."

"Gizmo babies!" Her daughters' enthusiasm hugged her center like lustrous pearls. They clamored as they followed Maya through the halls of the high school to the 3-D reproduction room. "His babies are adorable. Can we have one?"

Grace, Ronnie, and Mr. Mills carefully packed two newly purchased, nondescript beige suitcases with accurate replicas. Amanda, Ora, Ally, and Maya played with the production scrap. With superglue, markers, pipe cleaners, and glitter, they created all sorts of Gizmo by-products, each more elaborate and fanciful than the other. They threw these into Grace's bright red duffle and Dr. Brody's twenty-two by fourteen-inch carry-on suitcase on wheels.

Dr. Brody and Grace had no idea how Caligula would steal their bags off the packed flights. Still, they were confident the Oil Company would try. Red flags must have gone off like fireworks when Caligula realized they were heading to New York City on different flights on the day the Global Conference for Renewable Energy started.

Grace hadn't come this far only to catastrophically crash before the finish line. So, their contingency reaction plan morphed into the prime directive. The goal was to prevent Caligula from securing any accurate representation of Gizmo before the conference started.

****

Dr. Holly Hawthorne got off the first leg of her trip in Tulsa, and, as is often the case, she ran to the bathroom. From the stall, she sent a text. Holly had two hours before her next flight to New York and planned to meet a family friend for a quick bite to eat at a nearby diner.

They talked and caught up, laughing and

exchanging stories with the ease of long-time familiarity. Never mind the fact they'd never laid eyes on each other before. Mary Walker, coincidently, had a beige valise identical to Holly's. After the quick meal, they exchanged hugs, and Dr. Holly Hawthorne walked off with the bag that Mary brought with her. The content caused no alarm as it slid through security, and Dr. Hawthorne proceeded unfettered to New York City with a valise full of authentic Gizmo replicas. Mary returned to her car with a suitcase full of thrift store clothes.

One hour later, Mary Walker, with a second bag full of accurate Gizmo prototypes, shared a meal with Holly's husband at a different restaurant. They were family acquaintances catching up. And, what do you know? Once again, the indistinguishable suitcases were switched.

****

Dr. Brody touched Grace's shoulder. "It's showtime. A front-row seat is reserved for you." He accompanied her to the auditorium. Dr. Brody spritely ascended the wooden steps. A heartbeat later, their cell phones simultaneously reverberated with a text message —*DO NOT PROCEED WITH PRESENTATION! THE AUDITORIUM IS RIGGED WITH EXPLOSIVES*—

Grace locked eyes with Dr. Brody. He was stunned. Grace surveyed her surroundings. Explosives here? This had to be a cruel, sick joke. But there, next to the podium, was her bright red duffel, and next to it rested Dr. Brody's circumspect carry-on, a particularly glittery Gizmo by-product, sitting on top of the case.

It was a message. Caligula had been duped, but they were not giving up. The Oil Company was upping the ante. Were Grace and Dr. Brody's carry-ons still full of Gizmo knock-offs, or were they housing bombs? It was a chance Grace would not take.

Chapter 61

First Snow

Sleet does not count. The National Oceanic and Atmospheric Association had strict criteria. The difference between freezing rain and snow was definable. Following the precedent of the first magical one they shared, Michael and Mary Walker adhered to that definition when they celebrated their first snowfall every year. For Michael, it would be with a neat finger of scotch. At first, this was Johnnie Walker's Black Label, an inexpensive blend of grains that promised— the best was yet to come. Mary did not doubt that Michael had finally tasted his dream–Balvenie's 21-year Portwood–top-shelf single-malt scotch before he died. For Mary, her drink of choice was a five-ounce pour of Malbec and, when she was pregnant, a mug of ginger-peach herbal tea. They would raise their glasses as the snow fell, toast each other, remembering and looking forward simultaneously.

Freezing rain choked the atmosphere the day Mikey entered the world, and Dallas almost became a statistic–the night Caligula kidnapped Amanda, the night her oldest daughter lost all hope and then found it with Amanda's return. Nothing was remotely magical about that time. Sleet did not count.

What a difference twenty-four hours can make. Her

daughters and grandchildren were safe. The flakes began to fall in the early afternoon after Mary shared a tomato and toasted cheese lunch with her granddaughters. The forecast called for three inches, enough for the girls to create feathery snow angels and have snowball fights.

Ally, Amanda, and Ora were making "Happy Birthday" cards for their newborn cousin when Mary took the draft of an article she was writing and curled on the couch, a comfy fleece across her knees. From her vantage point, she could edit while watching her grandchildren. Outdoors, full, lacey crystals spiraled in casual descent.

The flowers came in the late afternoon.

Shivering against the cold, Mary stepped onto her front porch while her granddaughters peered excitedly through the window. The florist handed Mary a spray of long-stemmed roses in a Waterford vase.

"First snowfall of the season, I'd say this counts. These Forever Young Roses are premium. Whoever sent you these is not messing around." The delivery person stomped their tennis shoes, a puff of flakes rising around bare ankles. Elevated above the arrangement, held firmly in place by a gilded fork, was an envelope with Michael's neat handwriting on the front: To Mary.

The elongated stems and flowers radiated an unapologetic glow, rendered more exquisite by snow-diffused light. Nature's poetry in its purest form, the bouquet embodied elegance and timeless allure.

Her granddaughters unrelentingly teased, "Grandma has a boyfriend! Wait till we tell Mommy and Auntie Dallas. Tell us who he is!" And while the rose petals sang a burning ballad, Grace's daughters crooned, "Grandma and her boyfriend sitting in a tree K-I-S-S-I-N-G. First comes love, then comes marriage, next comes mommy in the baby carriage." They shrieked with pleasure, spirited in their dance.

Life didn't get better than this.

****

Bombs! We've got to get everyone out of here. On autopilot, Grace called 911 while desperately surveying the full auditorium. The line was busy. Only in New York, she thought. Grace hung up. World delegates sat behind designated desks, putting on headphones and testing their translating equipment. Behind them, higher in the arena, sat other registered participants, avid environmentalists, and press members. Grace's stomach tensed as she scanned the crowd. How were they going to get everyone out safely? Near the top of the second level, surrounded by men in suits, stood Mr. Renny Richeza. He stared at her, waiting, watching her response to the text. Another message pinged —*Do not proceed with the presentation. The countdown is on. You have sixty minutes to deliver the original device. Await further instructions—*

Grace looked at Mr. Richeza. He pointed down at her, his hand a gun that he fired with his thumb. With a flourish, he turned and walked out of the exit. His entourage followed.

Sixty minutes? Anything could happen in that period. Grace didn't want to risk anyone getting injured or killed. The sanctity of life came before dreams. *I'm sorry, Dad. Your project will end, just as you didn't want, in the hands of a greedy corporation.* She didn't have a second to contemplate otherwise. Again, Grace tried calling 911 to report the bomb threat. She got through this time. Those around Grace processed her words, and fear ignited–a spark in a tinder box. "Bombs? Get out of here!"

Grace frantically sought out Dr. Brody. He was on the stage a minute ago. Now, he was gone. What happened to him? The convention center's evacuation protocol was in full swing. Loudspeakers and translation headphones provided detailed clearing instructions. Some attendees listened and briskly proceeded to the nearest exits, while others hysterically shouted and ran pell-mell, pushing anything and anyone over in their wake. In a city with far too much experience responding to disaster, masses spilled onto the sidewalks, looking dazed and confused even as bomb-sniffing dogs, experienced explosive ordinance teams, and first responders rushed in.

****

Grace slumped into a folding chair beside Holly in one of the NYCPD conference rooms, ignoring the dried substance on the seat. "Still no word from your dad?"

Around them pulsed the discordant rhythm of the police department. Grace had just finished a lengthy interrogation, signed her official statement, and turned over her phone to the FBI.

"One of the bomb-defusing technicians found his cell near the podium in the Javitz Center. Maybe he dropped it during the evacuation process."

"Or Caligula has him." The words came out in an unfiltered rush. "Oh, Holly, I feel terrible. What if they're using your dad for leverage to force us to comply? I never wanted anyone to get hurt. I–"

"Listen! Stop. My dad wanted to be part of this. You didn't force him into anything. And if, heaven forbid, something happens, he wouldn't have done anything differently. He believes in this project. I haven't seen him this animated in a long time."

"I've failed him and my dad. Caligula wins."

"Only if something goes wrong."

During Grace's interview, Caligula texted with instructions on where and when Gizmo should be delivered. Grace vociferously petitioned to be part of the operation, arguing that more lives would be risked if she didn't follow through. But the authorities found a decoy agent roughly matching Grace's description and had organized a sophisticated response. Grace turned everything over to the FBI, along with one of Gizmo's clones.

Grace sighed, defeated; they had been so close. "The whole sting may fall apart, and this will have been for nothing. Damn contingency plans, we didn't think this far ahead. If only I had offered to proofread your dad's presentation, I'd have a copy to give WAGER, who could forward it to the delegates before Caligula gets Gizmo."

"What did you say?" Holly's hazel eyes focused intently on Grace.

"The PowerPoint presentation. Your dad wanted to email me a copy, but I declined. I wanted to experience it firsthand. What was I thinking?"

"You were thinking like a daughter, anticipating the gestalt of your dad's invention. You and I are alike, always wanting dad's approval. You couldn't say no when your dad asked you to go on this crazy journey, and I couldn't refuse my father when he wanted to see if an average layman like me would understand his presentation." Holly scrolled through her phone. "Let me see. He sent two versions. But I have the final speech and slides here."

"You can give the presentation instead of your dad!" Grace jumped up, knocking over her chair.

"Grace, there is no way I understand the concepts like you do. And I sure as heck don't know how to operate Gizmo. If you read my dad's presentation, you'll be fine. You can use my tablet. Here you go." Holly's fingers flew across the keyboard. She handed Grace the screen; the PowerPoint document was ready to open.

"No, I can't do this. Please." But even as she said the words, Grace understood this was her Hail Mary. Disseminating the information before Caligula had it was their last chance to make her father's dreams come true. Once Gizmo was part of the public domain, Caligula would no longer have a claim. And even if Caligula went to court, WAGER assured her they had their attorneys lined up, ready for battle.

"I'll livestream your presentation on my YouTube channel. Desperate times, right? I'll ask the captain if we can broadcast from here." Holly's enthusiasm was contagious. Maybe they could still pull this off.

Grace cataloged the pieces that needed to fall into place. "I'll contact WAGER and let them know our plan. They can text or email the delegates the link. They have their conference swag bags, so it will all make sense when I get to Gizmo."

****

Grace walked to the podium of the police department's conference room. A few curious officers sat in the back.

"Ready?" Dr. Holly Hawthorne smiled conspiratorially as Grace put the tablet on the table so she could scroll through Dr. Brody's presentation.

Grace was tense. Was this possible? Fighting misfiring nerves, she adjusted the microphone height and then did a quick series of taps to ensure that everything was in working order.

Holly held up her cell phone, poised to capture the presentation on video. "I'll count down to one, and you'll be live. Three, two, one." A few WAGER representatives and a reporter slid in the partially ajar door.

Grace took a deep breath and opened the PowerPoint document.

"Michael Walker had a vision." Below the opening sentence was a picture of her father with the dates of his life span underneath. Of course, no one else could see this image, and it nearly undid her. *Dad.* Grace swallowed hard and struggled to regain her composure.

Holly gave her the thumbs-up sign. *Come on, Grace. You can power through. There will be time for tears later.* She found her footing: "Today, that dream will revolutionize the world. Listen closely and prepare to be amazed."

****

Mary waited until after dinner and the girls were asleep.

She waited until darkness descended and a carpet of snow blanketed the yard. Only after donning her wool hat, scarf, winter jacket, and boots and shoving the card into her coat pocket did she pour herself a glass of wine. She pulled a kitchen chair to the refrigerator and climbed onto it, reaching into the back of the upper cabinet where his Black Label scotch remained—not touched in twenty-two years since he walked out of their lives and stepped into his new one–leaving them forever changed.

The fairy lights her granddaughters insisted she install whimsically wound through the gazebo, illuminating the soft flakes as they fell, creating an illusion of being in a real-life snow globe.

"All right, Michael, I give in," Mary said, her breath white in the dark air. "I didn't invite you to sit with me in the gazebo all those years ago, but you are impossibly relentless, even in death."

She raised her glass skyward. "Here's to our first snow. Now, let's see what you have to say."

Mary held the poem for a long time, absorbing it.

Snow crystals sifted down through the fairy lights, full-bodied frozen tears. Contained within the *Forever Yours* acrostic verse was everything the roses symbolized: a story of devotion and admiration. Like the perfect petals, each letter held secrets of cherished memories, sincere confessions, and whispered yearnings, words from Michael immortalizing his enduring love.

Ultimately, the only man Mary ever loved had seen her and acknowledged what they shared.

There is peace in knowing you've left nothing unsaid.

Back in the house, Mary pulled off her boots, shrugged off her winter jacket, and sipped her ex-husband's scotch. The liquid exploded from her mouth. The detonated taste buds burned her like lighter fluid. She slammed the glass down. *Good gracious, how did you stand this stuff, Michael? Despite your questionable taste in alcoholic beverages, here's one last toast to you, my onetime husband. Here's to your enduring legacy, not only the one you offered the world but the priceless offering you gave me–through our daughters and grandchildren, a gift of spirited determination, and abiding love.*

The snow continued to fall.

Chapter 62

All My Strengths

When Grace began her presentation, she was unprepared for the impact of seeing her father on the screen before her. The photograph was taken after one of his successful core drills. He was young and full of vitality. Grace was overwhelmed. She'd felt his presence and talked to him since his death. This, however, was different. It represented a culmination.

Once she regained her composure, Grace read Dr. Brody's words clearly and calmly. Following the detailed explanations of how Michael Walker's brilliant mind yielded an exquisitely fashioned invention, simple in purpose and execution, the journey of discovery unfolded, and Grace found her rhythm. Her intensity increased as the audience realized what she was saying. *Dad, this is for you. Can you see what is happening?*

When Grace reached the final slide, another picture of her father appeared. She held up the tablet so that Holly could include the image. Michael Walker held the paperwork in one hand and Gizmo in the other, with a grin more expansive than the Mississippi River on his cancer-drawn face. The sparce audience erupted in wild applause. Though less than ideal, the presentation was successful. Her father's invention was accessible to all. The WAGER representatives, fully understanding the magnitude of what was in their conference swag boxes, were popping the tiny Gizmo replicas in and out of his sheath as if at a New Year party.

Holly hugged her fiercely. "You were terrific, Grace!"

"But what about Dr. Brody, your dad? Have you heard anything?"

Holly broke into a grin. "He lost his phone in the evacuation madness and was herded onto a bus that took him to a shelter outside of the detonation zone. He'll meet us at the fundraiser."

"That's still going on?" All Grace wanted to do was get home.

"Of course, the show must go on. Besides, Dad says tons of people want to meet you. He caught the last half of your presentation and said he couldn't have done it better. You're a rock star, Grace. Catch your breath. Our cab will be here in ten minutes."

Grace was desperate to reach her family, ensure their safety, and reassure them she was okay in case they saw the news. "Holly, can I borrow your phone? I'll meet you outside in a few minutes."

She found a cluttered corner near a muted television. The news broadcast was from the Javits Convention Center as the bomb squad diligently worked to defuse the explosive devices. A digital clock at the bottom of the screen kept track, down to the seconds, of the elapsed time they'd been working.

Grace left a voicemail message for Lee and checked in with Dallas and her mom. She spoke with each of her daughters. Everyone was well.

She palmed the phone and glanced at the news feed before heading outside. The scrolling ticker tape read:

BOMBS DEFUSED. NEIGHBORHOOD EVACUATION ORDER LIFTED. And then, the camera broke away from the news conference in front of the Javitz Center to a swarm of police cars, their lights flashing, outside a high-rise hotel where five men with designer suit coats, pulled over their heads, were being led in handcuffs into the waiting vehicles. PERSONS OF INTEREST DETAINED, the newsfeed read. And for a moment, Grace was sure she saw a tuft of Renny Richeza's dyed black hair rising above his ducked countenance.

****

The fundraising event went on forever. Between courses of food, speeches, and silent auction bidding, Grace mingled with foreign delegates who profusely thanked her for her father's contribution. The whole process would have been unbearable had it not been for Holly Hawthorne and Hiram Brody, who stayed by her side, keeping things light and deflecting more intense attention. Though the father-daughter duo petitioned for her to stay the night, have a leisurely breakfast together, and then attend the first organizational meeting to launch her father's project, Grace didn't want to spend any more time away from her loved ones, opting for an after three a.m. flight home.

****

The plane taxied down the tarmac to the end of the runway, wheeled around, and paused. Then, the jet accelerated, its engines roaring, and lifted ponderously into the winter air. From her economy cabin window, the night lights of New York tilted and dropped away.

After straightening from its curved accent, the aircraft climbed. As Grace leaned back against the

330

headrest and stared out the window at a star-saturated sky, memories of her father appeared, a visual slideshow of experiences. He was reaching for her hand as she crossed the street. A knowing gleam flashed in his blue eyes as he talked animatedly over grilled cheese sandwiches. Then, he was laughing uncontrollably at a ridiculous knock-knock joke she told. She felt his shoes underneath her stocking feet as they danced at his second wedding and the rush of adrenaline as he hoisted her in the air, placing her on his shoulders. *You are all my strengths and none of my failings. You've done it, my muse. Grace, I never had any doubt.*

Her father gave her the earth. He also delivered the heavens. Out of humble beginnings and a meteoric rise, her dad had streaked across the infinite sky of Grace's life with blinding brilliance. And as flawed as her father was, Grace understood that he had done his best. In his over-the-top, imperfect way, he had loved her and Dallas. Michael Walker didn't leave because she wasn't lovable, too loud, or not what he wanted. He simply kept moving, following his inner trajectory, leaving a contrail of phosphorescence in his wake.

Now, she was heading home, the plane banking in its measured descent. Small lakes, rivers, and roads emerged from the darkness as the sun peaked over the distant horizon, infusing the sky with color. Below, in the fading crystalline maze of Tulsa, was her family sleeping. To the east, in the wash of dawn, nestled in the foothills of the Ozarks, was an earth berm, a clinic, and a man. And a future as wide open as the Oklahoma sky, waiting.

Epilogue
Tonight, You Dance
Two Years Later

"I have an adventure planned. Will you come with me?" Grace asked over coffee in the hospital cafe. "This summer, before my final year of midwifery school starts, I have a break. The girls will be with Andrew."

Lee squeezed her hand. "You know the clinic always has a place for you. You don't have to ask."

"I was thinking of a new destination–if your passport is ready."

Grace understood Lee's definition of downtime and saw him wrestling with the getaway concept. Still, his curiosity was piqued, he played along. "And where will we be jet-setting this time, skiing the Swiss Alps, driving a race car in Monte Carlo, surfing in Bali? But more importantly, what should I pack? My party clothes, scuba gear, a motorcycle helmet?"

She had him.

****

The newly erected medical facility in rural Malawi made the Rolling Hills Clinic in Oklahoma look like a five-star hotel. Under a harsh sun, men, women, and children waited, in line, swatting away biting insects and flies. Some stood, others sat. Children clutched jars of urine for Bilharzia tests, a disease caused by parasitic worms. Grace and Lee treated residents for malaria, hepatitis, and respiratory diseases like tuberculosis. They'd seen the ravaging effects of malnutrition, cancer, and AIDS. Mothers cradled infants with little reserves in their skeletal bodies who had diarrhea, causing severe dehydration and sometimes death. It was hard not to be overwhelmed by the magnitude of need.

Despite the constant struggle for survival, people waited patiently—word spread to surrounding villages that a medical center had opened, one that would soon have electricity.

The clinic, where kerosene lamps now flickered, was sweltering and crowded. Grace crossed the dirt floor, gingerly stepping over outstretched legs, woven baskets, and sleeping children; she slipped into the curtained area separating men from women. Asante, newly certified by the Nurses and Midwife Council of Malawi, measured a woman's pregnant belly. She smiled at Grace from beneath her bright orange headscarf. "Did the village leaders approve the birthing hut?"

Before responding, Grace helped the pregnant woman stand on the scale. She recorded the measurements in the patient's chart. "The village leadership unanimously agreed that after powering the central well and after the school is built, construction will start on a birthing house."

"Imagine," Asante said to the pregnant woman, her flawless brown skin glistening in the dim lantern light, "soon, we will have a place where you can labor in peace and recover without putting in a full day's work. You won't have to pound corn, haul water, wash clothes, tend to the crops, or cook until you and your baby are stable. Now, let me get you some prenatal vitamins." Asante opened a cabinet holding recently acquired plastic bottles of pills, vitamins, and tubes of ointment. "Such an abundance of riches." She counted a month's supply of vitamins and handed them over. "You will come to see me again when these pills run out. Remember, one a day." Holding a baggie of prenatal vitamins and her chart, the patient ducked out, and immediately, another pregnant woman took her place.

Strapped to the expectant mother's back with a wide cloth tied over her breasts was a six-month-old infant, who was fast asleep. His head lolled at an impossible angle. And in the woman's arms was a toddler whose eyes protruded from their sockets. The child was listless, her scalp almost bare. Asante quickly assessed the girl and then, murmuring sounds of comfort, inserted an IV into her arm. Grace had taught her how to start intravenous lines when she first arrived. Now Asante was doing it like a pro.

"They finished building this medical center a week ago, and before that, we didn't have the supplies to start an IV or give fluids. This little one has a fighting chance because of the World Health Organization, WAGER, and volunteers like you and Lee." Asante spoke to Grace, then translated in Chichewa for the young mother, who nodded.

How had Asante been doing this? Save for the medical assistant Lee was training, she didn't have help. She didn't have a safety net of paramedics, ambulances, or emergency rooms. And she had been performing these services without electricity or running water. Fingers crossed, that would change soon.

"Show time, everyone!" said a swarthy electrical

engineer from Sweden who had been working tirelessly to connect the medical clinic to Gizmo's substation. Dyman, the Malawian villager he'd been training to run things after he left, sauntered to the single bulb dangling from the ceiling. "This is for you, Asante." His face shone with affection. "This is what my love can do for you." Asante blushed.

Dyman pulled a long chain. The dark interior sprung to life with light.

Camila, a volunteer from Spain, grabbed two fans and plugged them into the electrical sockets. As the heavy air oscillated, Asante began to clap in delight. Light and wind in an interior without windows, what wonders. Her awe was a contagion; the clapping moved along the line of waiting people into the village. And to this rhythm, the children, some clutching their bottles of urine, some hanging onto their mother's thighs, began to dance. Though living in a world fraught with challenges, where everyday existence was a monumental task, the youth moved with ease and wonder.

****

Grace dressed quickly. She and Lee were on breakfast duty, and she wanted to be there first. She pulled on her work clothes and, in the process, bumped into the wooden crate that served as her cot's bedside table, knocking off the picture of her family. She studied the images, running her fingers over their faces, then placed the photo in her day bag before slipping out of the tent and heading to the kitchen.

Deeply tanned by the warm heart of Africa, Lee handed Grace a bowl of thick corn porridge.

Grace smiled. "The Nsima looks particularly

delicious this morning."

He laughed. "I made it myself."

He wasn't kidding.

Grace sat on one of the logs surrounding an open campfire in the middle of the International Campsite. Soon, the rest of the volunteers would join them, but for a moment, they were alone. She leaned over, giving him a long, good morning kiss.

Dawn's rays languidly lengthened across the open grasslands, stretching, but not quite reaching, the base of Mount Mulanje, which rose sharply from the surrounding plains, silent in a plumb haze of sleep.

Before coming to Malawi, Grace and Lee studied WAGER'S website, examining all the areas where they might volunteer. They chose one of the poorest countries on earth. With only four percent of the rural population having electricity, the independent country, riddled with extreme poverty and food insecurity, also had one of the highest infant and maternal mortality rates. In preparation for their trip, Grace and Lee took intensive online courses, learning the language and culture. Their five-day immersive orientation in Lilongwe, Malawi's capital, solidified everything. Now, thanks to the Gizmo prototype seeded deep in the earth, this impoverished community was taking steps toward sustainability.

"I can't believe we only have two days left. How are we going to leave?" Grace's question was rhetorical, but Lee understood her meaning.

Lee hoisted their day pack onto his back and slung an arm around Grace. "Ready for another day of challenges?"

They navigated the rugged kilometer trail from

their campsite to the family clinic on the edge of the Malawi village. Grace's stride matched Lee's.

As they grew closer, lights blinked, fledgling stars of a new dawn, just finding their strength.

****

Grace and Asante had been awake all night, tending to a difficult delivery. They barely had enough time to splash their faces and share an energy bar before welcoming the first patient into the clinic.

Each day, the clinic's lines grew longer as word spread throughout the region. People who had delayed seeking treatment for ailments and accidents were coming. With the village well hooked up to the power grid and a new filtration system installed, the number of women waiting for clean water also increased.

When their last day was done, they were spent but energized.

"Did you bring me a picture of your family, like you promised?" Asante asked as she finished wiping down the treatment room mats.

Grace pulled out the New Year's Day photo. "According to my sister," Grace said, laughing, "this picture is an epic fail."

"I don't understand," Asante replied, peering closely at the images.

"Dallas insisted we all wear blush and teal color-coordinated outfits. But, as you can see, I forgot to tell Lee about the dress code. He's wearing a bright orange cable-knit sweater. Another thing is, we're all supposed to look happy, you know, like a perfect family. But Mikey is in his terrible twos and was pitching a fit." Grace pointed to the toddler, red-faced and wailing in his mother's arms. Dallas was looking at Bryce with a what-do-we do-now expression.

"My daughters were fighting over who got to hold the cat." In huffing pouts of dissatisfaction, Ally, Amanda and Ora each held a limb of the ever tolerant outstretched kitty. "And my mom, in her screw-the-dress-code red plaid shirt and jeans, who can tell what that smirk means."

An epic failure? Grace didn't see it this way. This photo was perfect—a snapshot encapsulating the life force of the people she loved most.

Asante reverently ran her fingers over the faces. "Your family is beautiful. I see you in each of your daughters. Are you sure you don't mind me keeping this?"

"It would be my honor. There are plenty more outlandish versions at home."

"And speaking of honors, it would be mine if you wore this tonight." Asante rummaged through her birthing bag. "Party time," she said, pulling out a vibrantly patterned turquoise, yellow, and black pagne made of chitenge cloth, with a matching shirt and scarf. "Each design holds meaning and tells a story of our heritage. This is for you, Grace. My father made it with a foot-powered sewing machine as a gift for all you have done."

Grace accepted the offering, a catch in her throat. How could it be that this was their last evening in Malawi? After sundown, the villagers and volunteers would celebrate their accomplishments. Grace would miss the friendships formed, the good-natured, compassionate, and gregarious nature of the village residents, and the dedicated enthusiasm of the international volunteers. But primarily, she would miss

Asante.

"Let me show you how to put the outfit together. Tonight, we dance."

"Asante, I don't dance. You know this. Even my daughters laugh when I try. Being on the sidelines is enough for me."

"No, Grace, that is not enough. Not for you."

Asante's fingers flew as they tucked, tugged, pulled, and adjusted, wrapping a riot of color around her. "Oh, sister, that man of yours isn't going to be able to take his eyes off you."

****

"Camilla, Lee, Grace, over here." The volunteers' names rose into the night air, rippling through the crowd as the villagers opened the celebration sphere, making space for them.

"Move back, move back," a dapper Dyman called as he swaggered around the circle's periphery, pushing the throng away from the center. "Dancers need space." He winked and flashed a wide, cheeky grin in Asante's direction, then leapt toward the stars as a steady drum beat pulled him down. From the gathering, a line of school-aged girls appeared in the performance space, facing a line of boys. The girls swayed and, with intricate footwork, danced upon the earth with their hands raised to the heavens while the boys squatted, twisting and turning their bodies to the rhythm. A big drum and two smaller ones accompanied them. The music tracked the dancers, rippling and conforming to their movements. Sometimes, the dancers adjusted their swaying to the drummers' tempo shift–a seamless interplay of music and motion. Within minutes, others from the sidelines joined the festivity.

From the periphery, the circle of people appeared too small to contain such energy. With another wave of volunteers to follow and promises that she and Lee would return in two years, this celebration made leaving feel more like the arc of a developing circle than the end of a line. Grace was humbled, to know this place and the people. She took Lee's hand.

Asante began to dance. Her feet were quick and light, like a butterfly's wings, sending a soft cloud of dirt around her bare ankles. The crowd accommodated, forming an additional space around her. She moved and grooved, the lower half of her body undulating, her shoulders nimbly following. Asante reached into the sidelines and grabbed Grace by the arm.

Grace, mortified, dug her feet into the soil. "I don't dance, Asante. Remember?"

"You do now, my sister." Asante pulled her into the revelry.

Grace looked at Lee, who grinned. "You're on your own."

The crowd whooped as she tried to escape, but laughter grounded her. She looked at the villagers and the volunteers, a community creating something no individual could do on their own, and she thought of her daughters, who were thousands of miles away but still connected to this earth. Then, she willed her appendages to move.

And they did. Grace rose on the balls of her feet and pivoted, following Asante's lead. Though her lower extremities trampled the ground wildly like the hooves of a panicked animal, she gave in to the surrounding jubilation, absorbing the vibrations. A microcosm of the universe, she moved with the pulse of humanity, grateful for her journey, her life. The miracle of it all. Under a star sequined sky, Grace danced.

A word about the author…

H.G. Hedger, an avid reader and a lover of nature and animals, is a nurse who grew up in Oklahoma. She currently resides in Michigan with her husband and rescue dog, where they raised three sons. She attended the University of Michigan (double majoring in Psychology and Literature & Creative Writing), where she was a Hopwood Undergraduate Award Winner. Her first novel, The Circle of Willis, was published in February 2024.

hghedger.com

Thank you for purchasing
this publication of The Wild Rose Press, Inc.

For questions or more information
contact us at
info@thewildrosepress.com.

The Wild Rose Press, Inc.
www.thewildrosepress.com